Sven's Promise

Virginie Marconato

All rights reserved.

No part of this publication may be sold, copied, distributed, reproduced or transmitted in any form or by any means, mechanical or digital, including photocopying and recording or by any information storage and retrieval system without the prior written permission of both the publisher, Oliver Heber Books and the author, Virginie Marconato, except in the case of brief quotations embodied in critical articles and reviews.

NO AI TRAINING: Without in any way limiting the author's [and publisher's] exclusive rights under copyright, any use of this publication to "train" generative artificial intelligence (AI) technologies and/or large language models to generate text, or any other medium, is expressly prohibited. The author reserves all rights to license uses of this work for the training and development of any generative AI and/or large language models.

PUBLISHER'S NOTE: This is a work of fiction. Names, characters, places, and incidents either are the product of the author's imagination or are used fictitiously. Any resemblance to actual persons, living or dead, business establishments, events, or locales is entirely coincidental.

Sven's Promise Copyright 2026 © Virginie Marconato

Cover art by Dar Albert at Wicked Smart Designs

Published by Oliver-Heber Books

0 9 8 7 6 5 4 3 2 1

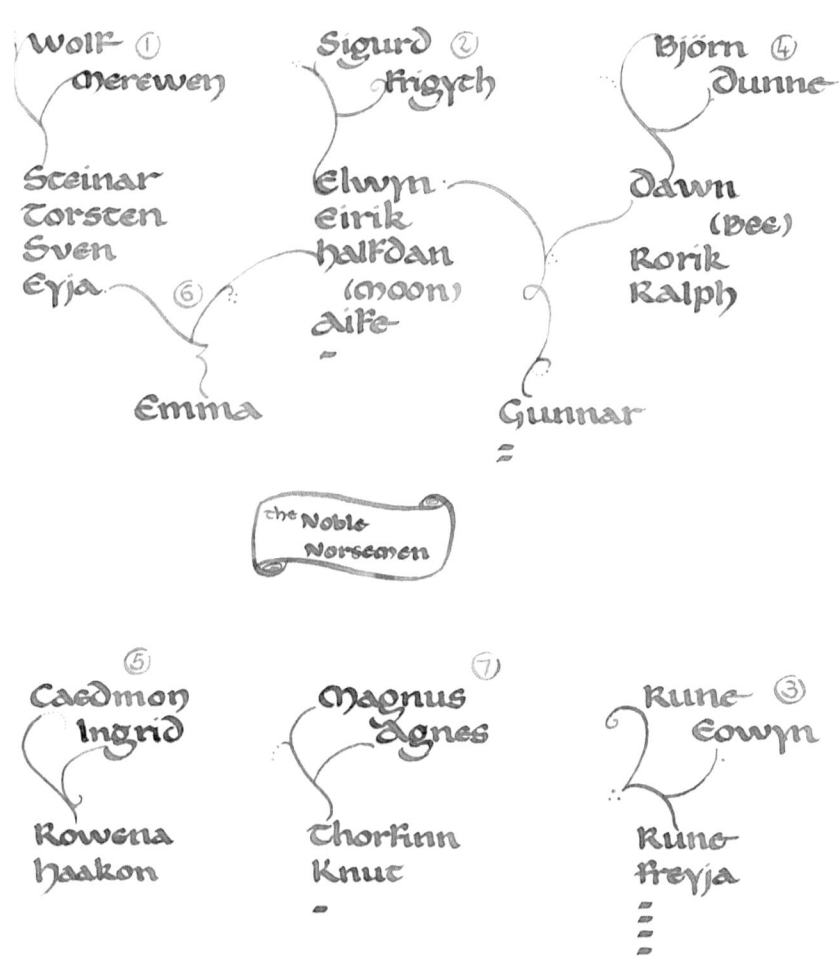

PROLOGUE

"Oh, God, Sven! Harder. Yes! Just like that. Ah, yeeeessss..."

Sven grunted his approval at the woman's unfettered and very vocal enthusiasm. How often had he heard those words over the years? Dozens of times. And yet today...today they sounded different. From the heart. The woman under him, so soft and luscious, felt different, which was no wonder.

Because everything *was* different.

Though he was by no means an untried lad, and he'd had his share of women, Sven had never taken a woman to his bed without getting to know her beforehand, without even knowing her name. And yet here he was, buried deep into this unknown woman's heat and marveling at everything she did. She was wholly unrestrained, telling him what she liked, expressing her pleasure and her needs in the most honest way.

He'd not been able to resist the admiration in the Saxon's black eyes when he'd caught her staring at him earlier. He'd been exiting the hut, ready to go into the forest, and she had happened to be walking past at that exact moment. The naked desire he'd seen on her face had singed each and every one of his nerve endings. The connection between them had been palpable, almost visible. Sven could no more have resisted it than he could have stopped himself from hurting if someone had shot an arrow through his chest. He'd held out his hand to her, and after the briefest of hesitations, she had taken it.

He'd closed the door and told her his name was Sven. The only reason he'd only told her was because he'd hoped she would scream it when pleasure overcame her. When he'd sat her on the table she had let out a sigh so filled with lust that he'd feared for a moment he would unman himself. His head had disappeared underneath her skirt before she could say anything else.

A moment later, he'd heard what he wanted to hear. His name, uttered on a long, raspy moan.

By the gods, every moment from then on had been spectacular. He'd made her erupt more times than he could remember. And now, at last, it was time for him to let go. He reared up and brought both her legs up onto his left shoulder. If she wanted it harder, he would give her harder; if she wanted more, he would give her more. Because he, too, needed more, needed to be deeper, needed to become a part of her, like she was already part of him.

Knowing this wouldn't be the last time he reached his release that day, he withdrew before his seed shot out of him in a series of uncontrollable spurts. For a long moment, the Saxon remained there, limp, her stomach drenched with the pearly substance. Marked as his in a primal, indisputable way. The male in him roared his satisfaction.

She was his. There would be no going back after this. Deep down, Sven knew it. She was his.

"What have you done to me, woman?" he mumbled in

Norse, knowing she wouldn't understand him. They would talk tomorrow once he'd gotten his sanity back. For now, he was too bewildered. "What the hell have you done?"

1

EAST ANGLIA, SUMMER 1073

"Are you all right, my dear? You sound tired."

Eahlswith gave the old man's hand a reassuring squeeze. Trust him to know how she was feeling, even if he could barely see. And in truth she was tired, not that she could tell Osbert the reason why. She had spent the night being thoroughly debauched by a big, hulking Norseman called Sven.

Sven.

She only knew his name because he'd told her before burying his face between her thighs with the obvious intent of making her scream it out loud—which she had, only a moment later, when his scandalous tongue had catapulted her into a place she wasn't sure was altogether of this realm.

He'd been without a doubt the most wicked, the most generous and the most insatiable lover she had ever had but other than that, and that he looked indecently handsome, she didn't know anything about him.

Their meeting had been completely fortuitous and what had followed, little more than folly, an indulgence she had allowed herself in a moment of madness. As she was exiting her friend

Cwenthryth's hut after her visit to her newborn daughter and getting ready to walk back home into town, she had turned her head in time to see a man coming out of his house bare-chested.

Not just a man, but surely the human equivalent of a Norse god.

Grinding to a halt, she had stared at the most perfect example of masculine beauty she had ever seen—or was ever likely to see again. Everything that made other men appealing had somehow been enhanced in him. His hair was long and clean, of a stunning golden color and braided around the temples. His eyes were of a blue as cool as the fire in them burned hot. His chest, his arms, his hands even, every inch of him was utter perfection.

All the female parts within her had surged at the same time.

Her nipples had gone hard, her core had burst into flames, her tongue had darted out of her mouth to come lick at her suddenly too dry lips. After a long, tension-filled moment during which their gazes had locked, he'd held out his hand to her and it had seemed the natural thing to take it, even knowing what it entailed. She'd followed him into the hut. Doing anything else would have been unthinkable. As soon as he had closed the door, he had taken her into his arms and whispered that his name was Sven. Before she could reply, he'd sat her on the table and proceeded to lick her until she'd screamed the name he'd just given her in a series of shocking cries.

After that, he had not let her go until he'd finally collapsed by her side late into the night, as spent as she was.

Never had she been so well pleasured, nor for so long. The handful of lovers she'd had in the last five years had not been as determined to ensure her total and complete satisfaction as the Norseman. One release had not been enough for him, or even three. Even with Edwin, she had not reached such dizzying heights. No, she had not, and that was precisely the problem. Precisely why she felt so wretched.

A new wave of guilt sliced through her.

She did not regret giving in to her impulse, after all it was not the first time she had allowed herself to act on her desire for a man, even if, admittedly, she usually got to know them before she allowed them to take her to bed. But she had not anticipated that this wild lovemaking would open something inside her. How could a complete stranger threaten to force his way into her soul when the other men she had taken to her bed since Edwin's death had not even scratched its surface? It was frightening, and the reason why she had left the hut in the middle of the night, before Sven could stop her.

She had fled as soon as she'd been certain he was asleep, unable to deal with whatever unexpected wave of emotion had submerged her, ashamed at the sacrilegious thoughts fluttering in her mind.

"I'll be fine after a good night's sleep, don't worry," she told Osbert, forcing joviality into her voice.

How could she face Edwin's father after what she had allowed another man to do to her? Not that he did not suspect she'd had other lovers since her beloved's death. But he also knew those men had meant little.

"What about you, Osbert? How are you?"

He didn't look too well, and she berated herself for not having visited him in the last month. She'd been busy, but everyone was always busy. It was no excuse. She should have made more of an effort. Edwin's father was as dear to her as her own had been, the closest thing she had to a family now.

He patted her hand. "I'll be fine, even though a good night's sleep is sadly a thing of the past for me. Come, there's something I wanted to show you."

Smiling, Eahlswith followed him into the busy street.

As soon as Sven woke up he knew that something was not as it should be. Or rather, that everything was exactly as it always was, which, on any other morning, would have been fine. But today was different... Today there should have been someone in bed next to him.

A dark-haired, wicked Saxon with curves to make a man lose his mind with lust and a smile to make him forget he'd ever found someone else attractive.

Had he dreamed her up? He reached up to his left bicep and felt the scratches she had left there when he'd pumped into her with all the determination he was capable of. No, she'd been all too real; these proved how wild their night had been. So where was she? It was still early, and given the intensity of their lovemaking, she should be asleep, curled up against him, dead to the world.

What made her absence even more galling was that he never let the women he bedded stay the night. He preferred going to their place or dallying with them during the day, in the forest, at the back of the forge, or the watermill, by the smoke house or wherever else desire struck. On the rare occasions when he'd brought a woman home at night, he'd always made the effort to walk her back home afterward.

Not last night.

Last night he had been too exhausted to do more than roll off her and gather her into his arms before succumbing to a deep, deep sleep. He couldn't have walked her home as she didn't live in the village, and anyway, he wouldn't have had the strength to leave the pallet even if she'd lived in the next hut.

He frowned. Where was she? Had she slipped outside a moment to see to her needs or had she left the village already? The pallet next to him was cold, which did not bode well. She might very well have left without saying goodbye. Shrugging on his braies and shirt, he peered outside the door.

No one. And no trace of her.

Damn. How would he find her now? He didn't even know her name and he had no idea why she had come to the village.

His best bet was his father, Wolf the Icelander. Since the woman had been a Saxon, it made sense to think that she had come to see him about some problem or other. Yes, but that notion caused his chest to squeeze in fear. Men came to him with a variety of complaints but usually women came to him for one specific reason. They had been raped and they wanted their attackers to be punished. They had heard that the formidable Norseman would champion their cause, no matter that they did not belong to his community.

So, had the Saxon been raped?

He wanted to believe she hadn't. Certainly, her response to his touch had not raised his suspicion. She had behaved like a woman overwhelmed by pleasure, not dread. Having once held in his arms a lover who'd suffered at the hands of men in the past, he thought he would have seen the difference.

Well, there was only one way to know.

Hoping to have some answers, Sven went over to his parents' hut. He found his father outside, whitling the end of a long piece of wood, sharpening it to a deadly point. Was he making a spear? It was possible. The man hated to stay idle, a trait of personality all his children had inherited.

"Good morning, son."

"Good morning."

Suddenly at a loss as to how to broach the topic of the Saxon woman, Sven sat down next to him and took some of the wood shavings piled at his feet in his hand.

"These would make good kindling for the fire," he said,

observing how the wood had curled into all sorts of graceful shapes. "They would catch on fire in no time."

The image brought him back to the night before. The passion between him and the beautiful temptress had burned bright from the start.

"You came here to tell me things I already knew? I'd already planned to use them for that exact purpose."

His father threw him a sideway glance and scoffed. Sven shook his head. He should have known he wouldn't be able to pretend nothing was weighing on his mind. What was he doing, talking about chips of wood when he'd come with a purpose in mind?

"There was a Saxon woman yesterday in the village," he started, clenching his fist repeatedly. Although he was close to his father and they didn't have any secrets from each other, he rarely talked to him about his conquests. It had always seemed rather indelicate. "Taller than most, dark-haired, with eyes as dark as mother's. I was wondering if she'd come to see you?"

His father didn't even seem to hesitate. Evidently, the description didn't correspond to anyone he knew. "No, I'm sorry. The last Saxon who came to see me at the village was a man and that was more than a month ago."

There it was. His only hope, gone up in smoke.

"What did you want with her?"

More dejected than ever, Sven threw the wood shavings, which had been reduced to dust, back into the pile. "Nothing."

There was no point answering the question because it would seem he'd had all he would ever have from the mysterious Saxon.

2

FIVE MONTHS LATER

It was her. The woman. Alva, as he'd started to call her in his mind.

Sven could not believe what he was seeing.

The woman who'd just slipped inside his brother's hut was none other than the mysterious Saxon woman he had lost hope of ever finding again. The cloak covering her body was hiding all the luscious curves he remembered, but the riot of midnight curls that made her so distinctive and the reaction in his body at the sight of her could not be mistaken.

It *was* her.

What was she doing here, in Steinar's hut of all places? Only the fact that his brother was besotted with his wife and the epitome of the faithful husband prevented jealousy from ripping at Sven's guts. She wasn't there because she was having an affair with him, that was for sure. What, then?

Determined not to let her slip away a second time, he placed himself by the fence surrounding the geese pen. As soon as she passed through the door on her way out, she would see him. If she had gone in, he reasoned, she would come out again eventually, and the hut only had one opening.

Finally, after what felt like an eternity of waiting, she emerged from the hut.

"Good afternoon." The words left his lips in a growl that bore little resemblance to his normal voice.

He had the satisfaction of seeing her jump—and look guilty. So, she had recognized him and was aware that she had behaved inconsiderately toward him back in the summer, leaving his bed without a word while he slept on, oblivious to the fact.

"What are you doing here?" he asked when it became obvious he was going to have to start the conversation himself.

"I came to see Cwenthryth to congratulate her on the birth of her new daughter," she said, glancing back to the hut she'd just left. "She's my closest friend."

Her friend!

Sven recoiled. unable to believe how stupid he'd been. Of course, if she'd not come to see his father, she would have come to visit one of the Saxons living in the village, and there weren't many, much less the same age as her. He should have asked Cwenthryth if she knew the dark-haired Saxon. If he had, he would have known who the woman was, and where to find her.

He wouldn't have spent the last five months feeling like something was missing from his life. He'd lost some of his usual gaiety, and he didn't like it, nor the comments that came with it.

"And how do you know Cwenthryth?" Alva asked, making a polite attempt at conversation even if he could tell she wished herself miles away from here. Her attitude today was completely different to what it had been back in the summer. If he didn't know better, he would think her a shy woman unused to male attention.

But he did know better. She was anything but shy, in bed at least.

"Cwenthryth is my sister-in-law," he said, doing his best not to let the memory of their wild night rankle him. The last thing he needed now was to think with his cock. "She's married to my eldest brother."

And she'd just given birth to their second daughter, which was apparently the reason for the Saxon's visit. Sven made a mental note to kiss little Liv the next time he saw her. Thanks to her, he had been reunited with the woman he had spent five months obsessing about.

At first, refusing to be defeated, he'd gone into the surrounding villages and even into town a few times, to enquire about a tall, curvy, dark-haired woman. Unfortunately, his description could apply to dozens of women and without a name to offer, he'd not been able to get any useful leads. There had been no need to bestir himself thus.

It seemed that all he'd had to do was wait, and she would come to him.

How amusing.

"So, your best friend is my brother's wife. Well, if that isn't lucky," he told her, his lips stretching into a grin.

Lucky?

In truth, Eahlswith couldn't believe how *unlucky* she'd been. Of course, she had guessed that Sven would still be in the village, but now she was told he was none other than the brother of the only Norseman she knew. Although, now that she thought about it, she wondered how she had not seen the similarities before. The two men looked so alike they could have been twins, but for the expression on their faces. Steinar always seemed rather serious, whereas Sven appeared carefree and full of mischief. Which, of course, he was, mischief and wickedness personified. She knew from experience.

Would she have come today had she known there was a good chance she would walk into him? She wasn't sure.

She had not wanted her moment of folly to get in the way of

seeing her friend and her new baby, but she had hoped to slip in and out of the village without being seen.

No such luck.

She had spent five months trying to forget the scandalous Norseman. In vain. And now that he was in front of her, she understood why. It was not the crystal blue eyes, striking as they may be, that drew her to him. Nor was it the intricately braided hair falling over his shoulders, even if she had never seen anything like it before she'd set foot in the village where her friend now lived. Or even his impressive height and body, though she certainly remembered the advantages his strength could offer. It was the gleam in his eyes, the mirth lurking under the surface, the smile always ready to burst out.

Sven was someone anyone would have been drawn to, a man any lone soul would have found attractive, a lover any woman would dream of having.

"Alva, now that you're—"

"What did you just say?" Eahlswith interrupted. Had he insulted her in Norse?

"I called you Alva."

"That is not my name."

Sven gave her what she imagined was his naughtiest smile. "I know it's not, but since you never told me your actual name, I had to make one up for you."

Why? Why had he needed to give her a name in his mind? Her heart fluttered in what felt suspiciously like pleasure. If he'd thought never to see her again and hadn't minded, then he wouldn't have bothered. He would simply have forgotten her. But, far from that, he had jumped on her at the first opportunity to speak to her. It looked like he most decidedly had not forgotten her.

He crossed his arms over his chest and leaned a hip again the fence. Did he have any idea how that move made him appear? Both lethal and approachable. Both intense and mischievous. Such a combination should not exist, should not make sense. And yet it did.

Just like her feelings for him. They should not exist, yet they were burning a hole in her chest.

"What is your real name then?" he asked. The naughty smile had still not completely disappeared.

"Eahlswith."

Telling him felt so absurdly intimate.

"Eahlswith. It's beautiful. I've never met anyone by this name before."

Why did it feel as if he'd told her something of significance? She had no idea, but it was clear that she could not behave naturally in front of this man. Perhaps it was little wonder, given the way he looked, the heat in his gaze when he looked at her—and the memory of their fiery encounter playing on her mind.

"It's cold. Will you come inside, have a drink with me?"

"I..." Could she accept? Of course, she was free to do what she liked. Should she?

No.

"Yes."

The word shot out of her mouth, and she forced herself not to change her mind. After all, she was thirsty. Well, not really, but she might be in a moment, and it was better to have a drink before setting off for town. Yes, probably. One could never be too prudent.

"This way."

She followed, though she already knew the way to his hut, which only increased her uneasiness. How many women had he taken home with the intention of tumbling them into his bed? It was better not to wonder.

As soon as Sven had closed the door behind her, Eahlswith was transported back to the night they had shared in the summer. Her gaze landed on the table where he had sat her while he knelt on the floor and burrowed under her skirt. Her spasms of pleasure had been so fierce that she'd thought never to get up again. As if he'd sensed it, he had picked her up and pinned her against the wall. Keeping her trapped between the smooth stone and his equally hard body, he'd buried himself inside her and forced her into a second, even more shocking release. Then instead of following her into the abyss, he had brought her down to the pallet and thrust into her with astounding skill and determination.

Her world had exploded and she wasn't sure the pieces had all come back into place just yet. Wasn't sure they ever would.

"What would you like?" His deep voice cut through her thoughts.

Another night with you.

Could she tell him as much? Could she admit it to herself?

"I have ale or milk. Or I could go get some mead from my neighbor."

Eahlswith blinked at him. He wanted to know what she wanted to drink, of course. That was why she was here, not to be stroked with tender care, licked with wicked intent or fucked until she dissolved in ecstasy.

She blinked again in disbelief. Fucked? Since when did she think such crude words? But that was the only way to describe what Sven had done to her. It had been too intense to be anything else, and anyway, she refused to think that it had been more significant than that.

"Ale will be fine, thank you," she answered. Anything would be fine at this point, for she was suddenly parched.

He handed her a cup filled with the sweetest smelling, frothiest ale she had ever drunk. Once she'd downed half the cup, she noticed the unusual shape of the earthenware vessel. It was wide and smooth, almost like a bowl and the rim was very thin.

"Did you make this?" Without knowing why, the idea of a man like Sven creating such a delicate object set her nerves aflutter.

"No. My friend Eirik, the one who makes the mead, did. This one was an experiment and, in truth, it is too delicate for me. I never use it, as I'm too afraid of breaking it."

"I'll be careful."

"I know. I've seen how you handle delicate objects before. And based on what I saw, I would trust you with anything of mine."

He winked. The impossible man actually winked at her and, to her utter mortification, Eahlswith did what he had no doubt meant for her to do. She stole a glance at his groin.

He was hard.

What was left of the ale was gone in two gulps and Eahlswith decided to treat herself to another drink. It would help with the furnace burning in her body, would it not?

It did not, because apparently she was in no state to attempt even the simplest of tasks. She was flustered, and the cask was not full, as she'd imagined, but almost empty, and therefore lighter than she'd expected. It happened in the blink of an eye. One moment she was reaching for the tap, the next the cask had toppled off the shelf where it stood, landing straight on her right foot. Somehow, despite the explosion of pain, she managed not to shout. But she did cry out when she saw the beautiful cup on the earthen floor, broken in two. In her distress she had dropped it.

"Oh, no, I'm so sorry," she cried out, making to reach for the biggest half.

"Don't worry about the cup," Sven said, stopping her before she could bend down. "I told you I never used it. But your foot is—"

"I'll be fine."

Yes. Eventually. For now, though, it hurt something fierce.

"But you're not fine now. Sit down."

There was a stool to his right. He grabbed it and made her sit on it. Her foot was throbbing so severely that she didn't protest. How stupid of her. She was not usually clumsy, but neither was she used to dealing with impossibly forbidding men who knew the taste of her most intimate parts.

"Let me see," Sven said gently, kneeling in front of her.

See? Did he really think she would agree to have him lift her skirt, remove her stocking, take her naked foot into his hands and feel for an injury? With any other man it would have been embarrassing, with him it would be...impossible. Pain or no pain, having his fingers on her would make her want to feel his hand creep higher, until it reached—

"You don't need to do that. I'll go and see Cwenthryth," she declared, squirming on the stool. "She will know what to do."

For a moment it looked as if Sven would protest but then he nodded. "Yes, perhaps it is for the best if she deals with it. Come."

He straightened back up and held out his hand to her. Assuming he wanted to help her get up off the stool, she refused to take it. "I can stand on my own, thank you," she said, doing just that. "It is not a serious injury, nothing is broken, it's just a bit painful, that's all."

"Yes, I know that, but you cannot walk all the way to Steinar's hut so I'll carry you."

His hand was still extended, he was still waiting for her to take it.

He wanted to carry her. Eahlswith gulped and looked down at herself. She was a grown woman, taller than most, and with curves to match. She would be heavy. "You cannot carry me all the way there. I'm...too heavy."

He didn't even blink. Instead, he leaned in toward her. "And

I'm no weakling, as you know. Or have you forgotten the way I held you up against the wall while I pounded into you?" he purred into her ear. "I don't recall hearing any protests then."

Of course she had not protested, she had been far too aroused for that, and it had felt too good. Still.

"It's hardly the same," she said weakly.

"Yes, unfortunately."

Oh. Her legs suddenly felt too weak to support her, and she knew Sven was going to have to carry her. "I should be able to at least try to—"

"Alva. Make no mistake about it. I *will* carry you to Cwenthryth's hut. Whether I do so over my shoulder because you fight me or in my arms because you agree it is for the best is up to you. So, which do you prefer?"

There would be no convincing him. And if she were honest, she was dying to be held against his chest. This was as good a reason as any. The other option was to allow him to kiss her and that, she definitely could not allow.

"In your arms." That was the least mortifying option, not to mention the most comfortable.

He nodded, before sweeping her up carefully, making sure not to jolt her. "Good girl. I knew I could trust you to be sensible."

His eyes bore into hers, and she noticed that the blue was slightly tinged with gold in the middle of the irises. That explained why they could seem more luminous when his pupils closed in the sunlight. How fascinating.

They were now within kissing distance, and she could tell they both wanted to kiss. The difference was, she knew it would be wrong whereas he didn't seem to care about the consequences. Perhaps he didn't, because he knew this was not serious. But Eahlswith didn't have that luxury. Unfortunately, for her, it could all too easily become serious.

"Please, I'm ready. Let's go."

"Eahlswith, what on earth happened? I thought you'd left the village. Are you all right?"

"I'm fine."

Sven entered the hut and walked straight past Cwenthryth. He deposited Eahlswith into a chair and took a few steps back. He would let her explain to her friend what had happened.

"A stupid accident." She winced. Whether it was in pain or in mortification, Sven wasn't sure. Probably both. "I had already left, as you said," she continued, "and I was in the forest on my way back home, when I thought I saw something glimmer under a rock. I picked it up to check but it was too heavy and I dropped it on my foot... Your friend, who had gone to collect wood, saw me and kindly brought me back to the village."

She looked at him meaningfully, indicating that he should go along with this version of the story. Apparently she didn't want Cwenthryth to know she had been in his hut, or that they knew one another. "Your friend" she'd called him, as if he didn't have anything to do with her, as if she didn't even know his name, as if she had not moaned it, screamed it time and time again while he made love to her in every position imaginable last summer.

All that told him she had not mentioned their night of passion to her friend but, of course, he'd guessed that already. If Eahlswith had told Cwenthryth she'd slept with her husband's brother, the Saxon would have said something in the five months since the encounter. The two of them got on well. A special bond had been created between them when he had ensured her protection shortly after her meeting with Steinar.

And yet she had no idea that he knew intimately the woman who claimed to be her best friend.

"Thank you for bringing her back to me, Sven," Cwenthryth told him. It was clear she was not suspicious in the least. But why should she be when Eahlswith was acting so coldly toward him? "If you could go get Helga so she can have a look at Eahlswith's foot?"

Sven bunched his fingers into fists. He was being dismissed, when he wanted to stay and check that Eahlswith was all right. He was going to have to let someone see to her injury when he wanted to do it himself. He was having to be silent when his lips were burning with words straining to get out.

It was not a rock that fell on her foot. It was the cask of ale in my hut. Eahlswith was with me in my hut, where I fucked her for hours on end last summer and felt my life being irremediably changed in the process.

Of course, he couldn't say any of that, not when it was both crude and felt impossibly intimate, not when Eahlswith was looking at him with big, imploring eyes. There was no mistaking the meaning behind that look. She didn't want anyone to know about them.

"Yes, I'll get Helga for you," he said curtly.

"Thank you."

He'd barely taken ten steps out of the hut when he walked into Steinar, who was heading back home, an axe swung over his shoulder. He, together with their friend, Elwyn, had gone to fell some trees in the back of their parents' hut.

"Sven. Have you come to see Liv?" A smile bloomed on his lips at the mention of his newborn daughter.

"No. I just brought in a friend of your wife's." He, too, could pretend he had no idea who she was, he thought savagely. "A tall Saxon woman with black hair."

That description felt sorely lacking. Because she also had

maddening curves, a bewitching smile, amazing breasts, mysterious eyes and the most infuriating determination to keep him at arms' length.

"Eahlswith?" Steinar wiped his brow with the back of his hand. "I thought she'd left earlier this afternoon?"

"She had." But then he had stopped her, because he was damned if he was going to let her slip through his fingers a second time. "But she hurt her foot as she was leaving and cannot walk home. Cwenthryth is seeing to her as we speak."

"Is she all right?"

His brother sounded unusually worried, as if he cared for her. This made Sven wonder if Eahlswith was the friend who had helped Cwenthryth a few years ago, when she had lost her unborn child. Steinar had told him the tale shortly after his wedding to the Saxon and it was a sordid one to say the least.

The poor babe had been fathered by a man who'd posed as her half-brother in order to take advantage of her and her ailing father. The ordeal had gone on for months, until Steinar had killed the bastard the day he had walked in on him assaulting the woman he had come to love.

Sven gritted his teeth. If only he had asked her name that night he had pounded into her, he might have realized that the woman he was looking for was none other than his sister-in-law's best friend. Well, it mattered not. He had found her now.

"I'm sure she will be fine but let me go get Helga to be sure."

Steinar nodded. "Thank you."

"I'm sorry to cause you all this trouble," Eahlswith said, looking at her bandaged foot.

Helga, the village healer had applied a poultice earlier on and declared that everything would be all right if she just took it easy for a day or two. Nothing had been broken, at least, which was a relief. She already felt silly enough.

"Nonsense," Cwenthryth replied. "You're hurt and night will fall soon. Of course you cannot go back home now. And it is no trouble. You're welcome here."

From his place at the table, Steinar grunted his agreement and started to slice some mushrooms. It surprised Eahlswith to see a man such as him do a task she had only ever seen women do, but it was obvious he knew what he was doing. The onions frying in the pan attested to that. She could already tell the omelette would be delicious. Really, the men in this village were full of surprises. Virile, but caring. Masculine, but willing to help. Formidable, but loving.

An image of Sven flashed in her mind. Yes, he was all that and more.

"You will stay for as long as you need," Cwenthryth said, placing a cup of ale in her hand. The cup was sturdy and made of wood, nothing like the delicate one she had broken in Sven's hut.

Guilt sliced through Eahlswith. She had broken the precious object. And then, as if that were not enough, she had pretended not to know Sven. It had hurt him to be dismissed thus. She had not missed the flash of pain in his eyes when she had called him Cwenthryth's friend. She could tell he would have no problem telling the truth. And yet he had respected her wishes, he had not exposed her lies, or told her friend or his own brother that they knew one another already. That they had spent an explosive night together.

Which begged the question. Why was *she* so determined to keep their night of passion a secret? Was it because he was her friend's brother-in-law?

No, as she hadn't known about that when she had decided not to mention it.

Was it because she was ashamed to have gone to a man who was not her husband?

No. Cwenthryth was her friend, she knew she was not a virgin, and she would not judge her for allowing herself a harmless night of passion, like she did occasionally. But that was precisely it. The night had not been harmless. The other men she'd welcomed in her bed hadn't meant a thing. Sven did. Or would, if she let him. And she didn't want to.

"Tell me all about our friends in town."

Understandably, Cwenthryth was curious. She had vowed to never again set foot in town after the man posing as her half-brother had been killed by Steinar for assaulting her. She had kept her word, only going back once in order to save the man who was now her husband from a false accusation of murder.

"Wassa's daughter has finally made her choice. She is going to marry the tanner. Poor William is heartbroken over her decision, as you can imagine. Leofric broke his leg last week, falling from a ladder, probably because of the ice covering the rungs. Godgifu's father has recovered from his illness and Osbert's house is falling apart," Eahlswith said, glad to have something else than the brawny Norseman who had carried her across half the village to think about. "The roof is in bad need of repair."

Cwenthryth sighed. "Good and bad news then, as could be expected."

"Yes."

Exactly. Wasn't that what life was about? Happy one moment and then heartbroken the next.

"My love, can you pass me the garlic from over there?" Steinar asked, as he transferred the mushrooms into the pan.

Eahlswith had never thought envy was a sin she would ever be guilty of. But now she was wondering if she knew herself as well as she thought because as she watched Cwenthryth hand over a head of garlic to her husband, who rewarded her with a tender kiss, she realized that she was jealous. Her friend was married to a man who fried omelettes without being asked, who welcomed her friend under his roof without question and who had just given her another adorable little baby.

Who loved her for who she was.

Later, as she lay on the pallet Steinar had prepared for her, she fought hard against the feeling of dejection. It was not new, but tonight it was especially strong. Five years ago she'd had what Cwenthryth had. And yet now she was all alone.

Eventually, after a long time spent tossing and turning, she fell asleep.

In the morning, though she was limping, Eahlswith found that she could place her foot on the ground. Her injury was indeed not severe. Pretending she had someone important to see in town, she asked Steinar if he could take her back home. Fortunately, he agreed without comment.

The hug she gave Cwenthryth when they said their goodbyes was particularly poignant. Her friend refused to go into town and Eahlswith had decided she would have to avoid the village—or rather a particular Norseman living in it—for the time being. This meant she wasn't sure when or how they would next meet.

"Take care of yourself," she told Cwenthryth, feeling bad for not even hinting that this might be her last visit for a while.

Eventually, she would return. Her obsession with Sven would not last, and he surely would forget about her. An uneasy feeling invaded her. It had been almost six months since their night of passion, and she had thought about it constantly. What was there to say that another half a year would be enough to root him out of her mind?

As for him, he had pounced on the first opportunity to renew his acquaintance with "Alva" and he now knew where to find her, or rather he knew who to ask if he wanted to find her, which she felt sure he would when he saw that, once again, she had left without saying goodbye.

"Take care, as well," Cwenthryth replied.

After one last hug, Eahlswith climbed onto Steinar's horse, Fáfnir. He had decided, upon being told that she wasn't confident on horseback at the best of time, to walk next to the beautiful stallion.

"Even if you could ride another horse next to me, it's better if you don't, with your foot injured as it is," he'd declared.

She had been too relieved to agree. Having never had any real opportunity to ride, she would have been nervous managing her own mount.

As they left the village, she couldn't help but steal one last glance behind her. Nestled in the middle of a neatly-kept vegetable patch was Sven's hut. What was she doing, leaving him without a word again? Would he come after her when Cwenthryth told him she had already left?

Only time would tell.

She turned her head and looked resolutely onward.

3

"We're going to have to do something about the hole in the roof. 'Tis past time."

Eahlswith looked at the corner of the room with concern. Moments after she had walked through the door, bringing bread and cheese for Osbert's lunch, another plank had come crashing down. They could not ignore it any longer, his house was falling to pieces. It had been bad enough in the summer but now that winter was here, it meant that wind, rain and snow, when it eventually came, would get in. Not only that, but one day a plank could fall on his head and injure, if not kill him.

Of course, the old man could have come to live with her. It was the obvious solution, but he'd refused her offer every time she'd made it, arguing that a young woman needed her freedom. No matter how many times she'd assured him she rarely received any guests, he stubbornly refused. She had the impression he wanted to leave her the possibility to welcome a man in her life if she ever decided it was time to put the past behind and settle. Like the coward she was, she had not insisted.

That discussion was not one she was ready to have, least of all with him.

"I know we need to see to this roof," he told her with a sigh. "But as you know..."

Yes, she did know.

Finding someone ready to take on such a momentous task for no monetary reward had proven impossible. The people willing to help were either too busy or incompetent to do what needed to be done.

"I suppose I could try to—"

"You are not to go up on the roof in this icy weather, or do anything else equally dangerous, young lady. I will not have your injury on my conscience."

"I thank you for the faith you put in my ability," she mumbled, though in truth she was relieved he'd not agreed to her suggestion. She didn't know the first thing about carpentry and she dreaded the idea of being up so high. Only the other day, her friend Leofric had fallen off his ladder and broken his leg. If he, who knew what he was doing, could lose his footing, what would happen to her?

"It's not a question of faith, but I—"

A knock cut Osbert mid-sentence. Glad of the interruption, Eahlswith went to open the door—and froze.

A man was standing in front of her. And not just any man. A tall, forbidding Norseman. More than ever, she felt sure he had to be the human equivalent of a Norse god. Her insides quivered. What was Sven doing here, in front of Osbert's house? Then she noticed a bag was slung over his shoulder. Planks of wood were sticking out of it and the way it sagged indicated that it was loaded with heavy tools.

Was he really— Had he really come to—

She had fully expected to see him again, but she had imagined he would come to her door, demanding explanations for her sudden departure, not that he would visit her old friend.

Before she could say anything he pointed at himself and then to the hole in the roof. Then he said something in Norse. She stared in fascination as guttural, incomprehensible words flowed from his mouth. Dear Lord, but he was a completely different man to the one she had bedded back in the summer, or even seen in the village three days ago. Gone were the gleam in his eye, the suggestive grin, the relaxed attitude. Today he was a man made of stone, and he would not be deterred.

Everything within her quivered.

"Who is that?" Osbert asked, coming to stand next to her. "I thought I heard— Heavens!" he exclaimed, taking in the formidable sight. He might not see as well as she could but he would not have failed to notice their visitor's unusual size and bulk. "A Norseman!"

Sven nodded and uttered another comment in Norse. He evidently meant to pretend he could not speak or even understand their language, though why that might be, Eahlswith couldn't fathom. Her mind was too addled by his sudden appearance to allow her to think straight.

"What on earth is this, Eahlswith? Do you know this man?"

"I do. And I think he's come to repair the roof," she said, torn between gratitude and irritation.

"Has he? But how does he even know about it?"

That was a good question. She'd been wondering the same thing. "You know my friend, Cwenthryth, is now married to a Norseman? Well, this man is her husband's brother. He will have heard me tell her about it on my last visit to her village."

Except he hadn't been anywhere near when she and Cwenthryth had discussed their friends in town. No, but Steinar had been there, cooking... Suddenly she saw what had happened.

The day she'd left, Sven had come to speak to her, see how her foot was. Upon finding her gone, he'd flown into a rage and decided to pursue her. His pride would not allow him to let her get away with fleeing him a second time. When Steinar had come back from town, he'd made him tell all he knew about her life. Cwenthryth's husband, who'd overheard the conversation about their friends, would have mentioned the roof in need of repair.

The determined, devious man had guessed that if he simply showed at her door she would avoid him again. So he had found a way to be with her that she couldn't refuse. This was not about what she wanted but about what Osbert needed. She would not send away the only person who had volunteered to do what needed doing.

"But how could he have understood what you were saying about my roof or indeed anything else if he doesn't speak our language?" Osbert insisted. Though he thought Sven could not understand them, he still whispered the question.

"I mean that his brother, Steinar, heard us talk. He was in the hut and he does speak our language. He must have told him later."

Unsurprisingly, this explanation didn't quite satisfy him. "But why? What is it to either of them?"

Eahlswith did her best not to let her irritation show. "I know not. Perhaps this man is a carpenter and Steinar asked him to come, as a favor to his wife's friend. He's madly in love with her and would do anything to please her."

"Mm. Yes." This seemed to placate Osbert. He was so generous this was the sort of thing he would do himself so he didn't see anything odd in Steinar sending his brother to help a stranger." "He looks very fierce, though. Are you sure we can trust him?"

"Yes." This, at least, made no doubt.

As if he'd decided he'd given her enough time to reassure the old man, Sven made to walk past them. Eahlswith had no choice but to let him through.

She and Osbert watched him put his bag on the table and extract from it a dozen tools and planks of various sizes. Heavens, how heavy must the bag have been? Then he pointed to the roof and pretended to climb up.

"Do you know anyone who could lend us a ladder?" she asked Osbert, understanding what he was trying to ask. He'd come with tools and even wood, but, understandably, he had not brought a ladder with him. "One long enough to reach the roof? And possibly a few extra pieces of wood?"

"I know Godric, at the end of the street, has a ladder."

"I'll go get it now."

As reluctant as his neighbors had been to repair the hole themselves, they would not begrudge the old man the loan of a ladder. Now that she had someone ready to do what had to be done, she would make sure to give Sven what he needed. Finally the hole that had been the bane of her life for months would be repaired.

Filled with a new sense of purpose, Eahlswith set off in the direction of Godric's house. As she'd expected, the man was all too willing to help, now that someone else was doing the actual job. She thanked him and a moment later, was back with the ladder and a bag full of planks. They were smaller and lighter than the ones Sven had brought but she hoped they would serve. Opening the door, she gestured at Sven to come outside so she could show him what she'd found. He nodded his approval when he saw the wood and took the ladder from her to position it against the wall.

"My thanks, Alva," he purred into her ear, leaning close enough for her to feel the brush of his lips against her hair.

Lord.

Her knees almost buckled out from under her, but she managed to take a hasty step back. A mistake. Feeling her against him had set her nerves aflutter but seeing him was not much better. During her visit to Godric he had attached the tools to the belt hanging low on his hips. As a result, he looked almost like a warrior armed for battle.

"Eahlswith, is the ladder all right?" Osbert called from inside the house.

"Yes, it will do," she answered, her voice surprisingly steady. "Please be careful," she added under her breath, addressing herself to Sven. The last thing she wanted was for him to break his leg or worse. "In this weather, it—"

"I'll be careful." His blue eyes flashed, as if he were pleased to see her worry herself over him.

She hurried back into the house, certain she would betray her inner turmoil if she stayed any longer in his presence.

"Well, this was certainly unexpected, but highly welcome." Osbert rubbed his hands in a familiar gesture of delight. "You will have to thank your friend's husband for me next time you see him."

"Yes."

They fell silent when Sven re-entered the house to grab the two biggest planks he'd brought. Giving them a curt nod, he exited again. A moment later there was a hammering noise above their heads. Eahlswith looked up just as Sven's face appeared through the hole. He saw her watching him and, without missing a beat, he winked at her.

She felt herself go red from the roots of her hair to the tip of her toes, something she wouldn't have believed possible until now. But this man made her feel all sorts of things she had never thought possible.

"If you'll excuse me, my dear, I think I will try to have my nap despite the noise," she heard Osbert say from behind her. "I didn't sleep too well last night. Not that I ever do, mind you."

"Of course."

She didn't mind, far from it. She knew he always took a nap after his midday meal and anyway, she needed time to compose herself and make sense of Sven's behavior. What was he doing here, in Osbert's house? That he would want to see her again did not surprise her. She had been bracing herself for his visit for three days. That he should choose to repair her friend's roof, however, had come as a surprise. She had been expecting—dreading was perhaps a better word for it, for she knew she would have found it a challenge to resist his allure—to see him barge into her house and sweep her off her feet like he had done that summer.

For want of anything better to do, Eahlswith started to cut vegetables for the soup. It was not long before Sven was back inside for another couple of planks.

"Can you tell me just what you think you're doing?" she whispered, though she was sure Osbert would not be able to hear. He had fallen asleep as fast as usual.

Sven looked at the pieces of wood in his hand and the hammer at his belt. "I'm about to nail these two planks next to the ones I already—"

"Not that! You know very well what I mean."

He tilted his head and she could see that he was fighting a smile. "No, I don't know what you mean. I would have thought it obvious I was repairing the roof, yet you seem confused."

"I'm not...confused!" she hissed. How could he play with her thus? "I know you're repairing the roof. But *why* you are doing it, when you don't even know Osbert and he hasn't asked you to do anything, is what I don't understand. And why are you pretending you cannot speak our language?"

He sighed and placed the planks back down on the table. "Alva. I'm repairing this roof because it needs to be repaired and no one else is doing it. I may not know Osbert, but you do, and you care about him." The expression on his face was one she had never seen before. One she would not have thought possible to see on a man such as him. He was no longer teasing her. He seemed…dejected, as if he'd hoped better from her. "As to me not speaking your language, I thought it the best way to avoid a conversation in which you both tried to dissuade me and convince me it was not my responsibility to see to the roof."

"But it's not your responsibility to do that," she said feebly, utterly undone by his generosity. She didn't know much about the Norseman, true, but what little she did know, pointed to a good man. Damnation, this wouldn't help keep her fascination for him at bay, quite the contrary.

"It might not be my responsibility, but it's my pleasure." He shrugged. "Cwenthryth told me you were looking for someone to see to the roof because you cannot do it yourself. Well, *I* can. Why would I not want to help a poor old man you care about stay warm and safe for the winter when it costs me nothing? What else was I going to do today? Feed the pig? Gather wood for the fire? I already did that before leaving."

Put like that, it sounded very reasonable. "But we have nothing to give you in ex—"

"I want nothing. Except perhaps…"

Eahlswith's breath caught in her throat when Sven arched a brow. Was he really about to ask what she thought he was going to ask? How would it make her feel to know she had paid for his help with her body? How would Osbert react if he ever heard that she had sold her favors in exchange for his well-being? He would be horrified at best, shun her at worst. It would be unbearable.

Before panic overwhelmed her, Sven finished his sentence.

"A smile?"

All the tension left Eahlswith's body at the two words. Was that all he wanted? He wasn't about to blackmail her into surrendering. She was so relieved the smile he was after instantly bloomed on her lips. "I can do a smile," she murmured.

"Good," he said, smiling right back. "I prefer it that way. You've done nothing but scowl at me since I arrived."

Had she? She hadn't been aware she was doing it. "I'm sorry. I was surprised, that's all."

"Fret not, I could tell you were." He glanced at her feet, and his smile disappeared. "How is your foot by the way? I meant to ask you."

"It's fine. I told you, it was never a serious injury."

He nodded. They both knew he should go back to his task and she should finish what she was doing but neither seemed willing to move and put an end to the conversation.

"Can the old man see?" Sven surprised her by asking next.

"Not well at all. Neither can he hear as well as he used to." It was sad to see him reduced to a shadow of what he had been a mere five years ago. No doubt grief was contributing to his decline.

"You're truly fond of him, are you not?"

"Yes. He's like a father to me." He had almost been her father-in-law, so it was no wonder.

"Now, if you'll excuse me," Sven said, picking up the two planks again, "I'd like to make sure the hole is covered before nightfall, in case it starts snowing. I don't trust that heavy sky."

Yes, that was the whole point of his intervention, what she had told Cwenthryth she needed to do, so why was she questioning him instead of letting him work?

Once Sven had exited the door, Eahlswith turned her attention back to the onions waiting for her on the table. She was certain their smell was not responsible for the tears stinging her eyes when she started to chop, but something altogether more worrying.

A moment later, Osbert awoke.

"What is that wonderful smell?"

"I've started to cook soup for tonight," Eahlswith answered, stirring the pot. "It's leek, your favorite."

"Perfect."

"I will go home for a moment. I have a piece of salted pork I can add to the soup, seeing as there are three of us eating. I will also buy bread to go with it." She wiped her hands on a piece of cloth. "I won't be long. Don't worry about Sven, he knows what he's doing."

"You do know his name then?"

Know it? She had whispered it, moaned it, shouted it over and over again when pleasure had overcome her. Eahlswith made sure to keep her back turned because she guessed she had gone crimson. It seemed she had done little more than blush today.

"Yes. I remember Cwenthryth telling me."

She ran past him and out of the door, ignoring the slight pain lingering in her foot. She had not lied when she had told Sven it had not been serious but she still had a mighty bruise to remind her of her clumsiness.

Once in her own house she sat on her chair, trying to contain the wild beating of her heart. For three days she'd thought of little else than the moment she would see Sven again and what she would do when she did but nothing had happened like she had imagined. She had feared an attack on her senses, anticipated a battle with her reason, but she had not thought to prepare for a direct hit to her heart. He had not tried to seduce her, he had not demanded anything. It had been much, much worse. He had gifted her and Osbert with his skill and time—and utterly stolen her heart in the process.

She placed the piece of pork and some spices she had been lucky to buy at a good price the week before in a basket. If ever there was a moment to use them, this was it.

Eventually she had no choice but to go back to Osbert—and Sven.

4

The smell of salted pork simmering with leeks and onions had been torturing Sven for hours, or so it seemed. Well, it wouldn't be long before he could stop and taste what Eahlswith had prepared. The repair could have been finished by now, but he had made sure to work slowly so as to have an excuse to remain in town for another day. Now that he was here, he would make the most of it.

He had been so very vexed to be told Eahlswith had already left for town when he'd come to visit her the morning after he'd brought her to Steinar's hut... For a moment, anger had clouded his judgment, made him fantasize about punishment. He would make her pay for another disillusion. Why was she so determined to not be part of his life? What had he done wrong? Give her pleasure such as two people rarely experience? Offer her a drink of good ale? Carry her to her friend's house when she couldn't walk? None of these actions could explain, much less justify, her attitude.

She would pay.

Then once he had calmed down, he had seen that he was losing his mind. Aggression had never been his weapon of choice and would not be the way forward with Eahlswith. He didn't want to frighten her away, rather the other way around. And barging in would achieve nothing but to make her turn from him for good.

He needed to understand what motivated her actions.

She had disappeared, just like she had in the summer, but the difference was, this time, he knew where to find her. This time, there would be no escaping him; he was now more determined than ever to find her. When he'd heard Cwenthryth tell Steinar an old man Eahlswith cared about needed his roof repaired, he'd known it was his chance. Out of his brother's hearing, he'd asked her where he could find this Osbert's house. And the following day, he'd been there, ready to do what needed to be done.

The shock on her face when she'd seen him had been worth the effort, as had the result. A whole afternoon with her and if his luck held, a second day tomorrow. Had he gone to find her at any other time, she might have found a way to avoid him, but as the old man indeed needed his roof repaired, she had been unable to do what she'd been itching to do and send him on his way. His idea of pretending not to be able to talk to her had been a stroke of genius. It had prevented any arguments, at least while they were in the house. And now the hole was covered, which ensured the old man would survive the winter.

Yes, all in all, the day had been a success.

He climbed down from the roof, remembering Eahlswith's urging to be careful. Say what she might, she cared, a least a little. And that smile she had given him as a reward for his work had been... Stunning.

Night had already fallen when he finally pushed the door of the house open.

"Thank you, young man," Osbert told him, taking his hand in a surprisingly strong grip.

Sven shook his head and gestured at his bag, then at the roof. He waved his wrist in the air a few times. The man just stared at him in incomprehension.

"I think he's trying to tell us that he's not quite finished yet and will have to come back tomorrow," he heard Eahlswith say. Sven barely repressed a smile. They were very good at understanding one another, even without words, in whatever circumstances.

"But we couldn't put him out thus. Look, the roof has been patched up. What else could the man do?"

She made a helpless gesture. "I am no carpenter but there is probably some consolidating to do."

There was. Sven had made sure the planks were in place so as to protect the interior in case it started to snow in the night, but he'd left some work for tomorrow, just enough to ensure another day in Eahlswith's company.

When he turned to her he could see the urge to scowl at him again swirling in her eyes. The effect was most fetching. He almost smiled.

"Well, if he means to come back tomorrow, I'll have to offer him a place for the night," the old man started, looking slightly flustered at the idea. "He cannot go all the way back to his village only to come back again in the morning. But I'm afraid I can't play the host tonight. I told Wassa I would—"

"Worry not. Sven can sleep with me."

Sleep with her? That sounded promising. Sven arched a wicked brow at her, confident Osbert could not see him, placed where he was. Eahlswith couldn't stop the most delightful color from spreading to her cheeks. His cock twitched.

"I mean... There is room in my house," she amended, for his benefit rather than Osbert's. She didn't want him to get the wrong idea. Too late. He was already imagining the two of them in bed together. Moving as unobtrusively as he could, he placed his clasped hands in front of his groin. If Eahlswith carried on talking about welcoming him in her bed it would not be long before the tingling he was feeling grew into a full erection.

"Are you sure, my dear?" Osbert didn't seem to suspect anything.

"Yes, I told you he is Cwenthryth's husband's brother. I trust him," Eahlswith breathed. "He will not dare do anything to inconvenience me."

Sven could only agree. Inconvenience her was the last thing he wanted to do. Nevertheless, as he was supposed not to understand a word of the conversation, he remained impassive.

"Let's eat then," the old man decided, gesturing at the table. "I daresay the Norseman will be famished after all he's done."

Sven sat down gratefully. Not only was he relieved to hide his lap under the table but he was indeed famished. His bowl was filled up first and he plunged his spoon in it as soon as everyone was served. Mm. The soup was just as tasty as the smell had promised, and the bread crusty and fresh. Sven did not even pretend to refuse when Eahlswith filled his bowl again moments later. He was too ravenous and the soup too delicious for that.

"Dear me. The man eats for three!" Osbert exclaimed. His own bowl was still half full. "Oh, what it is to be young and healthy. Mind you, I was never as strong as that man, far from it." He chuckled. "But I never got any complaints, if you know what I mean. Some women like a gentler touch. My late wife, God rest her soul, was like that. There was nothing she liked better than being licked and that is something even the puniest of men can do. She would beg me to—"

"Osbert, please stop!" Eahlswith chided, going red to the roots of her hair. She had stilled at the word "licked", as if she couldn't believe what she was hearing. In truth, Sven himself had flinched. It was not often you heard such talk at the dinner table. "Really, you shouldn't be telling me this."

Sven worked hard at pretending he could not understand what was being said and busied himself pouring more ale to everyone. He liked the old man, who reminded him of some of his father's friends. And indeed, he agreed with him. Some women liked a gentler touch. But most liked their lovers to be tender at times and assertive at others, and he was glad to be able to provide both options, as well as a few others.

"Come, my dear. I know you agree with me considering that Edwin—"

"Oh no!"

Eahlswith stood up abruptly and stared at the soup stain on her dress. Had she dropped her spoon on purpose, so as to interrupt a conversation that was making her uncomfortable? Sven couldn't help but wonder. The gesture had seemed particularly clumsy on her part. But perhaps she was prone to such mishaps. After all, she had dropped the cask of ale on her foot the other day.

"I'll have to wash that now," she lamented, staring at her bodice.

"You will find fresh water in the bucket over there," Osbert offered.

"No, thank you," she answered, gesturing that they should leave. This was his cue, seeing as he was not supposed to understand what she was saying. "I think I might as well do that at home now. It's almost time to go to bed anyway."

Under the table Sven's groin manifested its approval.

Yes.

Time to go to bed.

THE FIRE WAS REDUCED to embers by the time they reached her house. Muttering to herself for her carelessness, Eahlswith she set about rekindling the flames. It would not be too difficult, as she had all she needed, but having had no lively fire for a whole afternoon meant that the house was far colder than she would have liked. In this season it was not a good idea to let the fire die out. Why had she not seen to it when she had come to get the salted pork earlier? Because she'd been distracted by the appearance of Sven, that was why. Well, she would have to regain her composure, and fast.

She was about to spend a night alone in the same room as Sven. She would need all her faculties to ensure it did not end in disaster. In the summer she had surrendered to the violent desire he had provoked in her because she'd imagined it was safe, because she would never see him again. Since then she had discovered he was her best friend's brother-in-law. If she wasn't careful, this could end badly.

Once she had a satisfactory fire going, she went back outside in search for food to give to Sven's horse. Godgifu at the end of the street had an old nag and might give her a bucketful of oats in exchange for the remainder of the spices she had bought the other day. Indeed, her friend was all too happy to swap the oats for the precious commodity.

"Here," Eahlswith told Sven a short time later, as he was making his stallion comfortable for the night. He'd already filled a bucket with water. "Some food for him."

"Thank you." The smile he gave her could easily have beguiled her, if she'd let it. She didn't. Instead, she gave the mighty beast a stroke on the neck. For years she'd wished she could have a horse. But they cost money to buy and to feed, money she didn't have. Besides, she rarely left town. Why would she need a horse?

"He's beautiful," she whispered, knowing she would have chosen one just like him if she had been able to. "What's his name?"

"Gulltoppr."

She arched a brow, having expected something far more obvious like Ghost or Snow, given his pristine white coat. Gulltoppr. Though the name was unusual, she was sure she had heard it somewhere before. Where? It was obviously Norse, so it had to be one of the deities or creatures Cwenthryth had told her about.

"It means Golden Mane," Sven explained, ruffling the shiny mane. "Gulltoppr is a horse belonging to one of our gods so it seemed appropriate. At the village, all the horses are descended from Demon, the stallion my father bought upon his arrival from Iceland, so they bear the name of a dark creature. Demon, Imp, Grendel, Satan to name a few. We are getting short of ideas, to be honest, and might have to start reusing the same ones."

"Perhaps from now on you should start giving them names of other animals. They can be quite fearsome too. Hawk, Bull, that type of name."

"Mm, yes," he said, detaching a bag from the horse's saddle. "That's a thought."

After one last pat to Gulltoppr, he followed her into the house.

"Thank you for welcoming me here tonight."

Eahlswith crossed her arms over her chest, half amused, half annoyed at his pretense at gratitude. As if she hadn't realized it had been planned... "You didn't leave me much choice, did you?"

"No. Can you blame me? After the night we shared back in the summer?"

And just like that the tension between them escalated again. They had enjoyed a respite outside, talking about his horse, but now that they were back behind closed doors, desire flared anew.

"I thank you for repairing Osbert's roof. It was very kind of you," she said instead of answering.

He shrugged, as if that were normal. "I already told you. It didn't cost me much. A day's work. Well, two, as it turns out." He winked, confirming her suspicions.

"So you could have done it in one day?" She had thought he could have gone much faster.

"Of course. Mayhap even half a day."

Should she remonstrate? What would be the point? The man would not be made to feel guilt.

"Now, let me wash the soup stain before it dries," she said, reaching out for a piece of cloth.

"Do you want me to do that?"

She shook her head in disbelief. Was he really offering to wash her dress? "I'm not washing everything in this weather, as it would take forever to dry. I only mean to rub the stain away for now."

"Yes. I had guessed as much. And I'm saying I can do that for you." His eyes darkened as his gaze settled on her bodice. The stain, she now realized, was exactly where her left nipple was. Really, why did she have to be so unlucky? Her mouth went dry because now she was imagining Sven rubbing at her breast with sensual intent.

She'd done the first thing that had come to her mind to interrupt Osbert before he could mention Edwin, but she was now regretting it. Because it was giving Sven wicked ideas. Not that he'd not had them before, she imagined. Or that she had not spent the whole day trying to suppress the same wicked, licentious ideas herself.

To hide the effect his words and heated gaze were having on her, she tried sarcasm. "Carpenter, now washerwoman. Is there anything you can't do?"

"I don't know. You tell me."

Oh, no. She wasn't falling into that trap.

"I couldn't possibly. I don't know you well enough."

With those words she turned around and dipped the piece of cloth into the basin on her table. Keeping her back turned to Sven, she started rubbing at the stain as unobtrusively as she could. To her relief, he didn't snatch the cloth from her hand and take over. Her nipple, however, didn't seem to have realized nothing wicked was going to happen. It seemed to be on fire, demanding attention. She ruthlessly ignored it.

"Here," Sven said once she finally turned back to him. "I brought some nuts and dried beef with me, not knowing what the old man would have to offer. Do you want some? Perhaps you're still hungry, considering we left his house rather precipitously?"

He produced a basket from his saddle bag, a very small, finely-made pot complete with lid. She stared at the object in amazement. It was like the cup he'd given her in his hut the other day, impossibly delicate. Even better, she was at no risk of breaking it.

"Did you make that?"

"No. He gave a wry smile, as if he wished he could say he had. "My brother-in-law, Moon, did. He's even more talented than his father, who taught him. I, for one, could never master the skill."

"No, me neither," she said, helping herself to a piece of dried meat. It was delicious but she didn't dare ask if he had prepared it himself, in case he had not.

They each finished their piece in silence, then Eahlswith knew she could not stall any longer, and in truth, she was tired. The last few nights, she had been too busy worrying about what she would do when Sven visited to sleep as well she could have. Now that he was actually here, it was as if her body were allowing itself the rest it needed.

"Time to go to bed." She eyed the corner of the room pensively. What would be the best way to proceed? "Perhaps I could put some furs for you in the—"

"Don't even try to pretend we are not going to sleep together," Sven growled, cutting the air with the flat of his hand.

"We are not," she replied, ignoring the heat flaring between her legs at his comment—and the gruffness in his voice. My, but the man was temptation personified.

"I meant in the same pallet." He nodded at the straw mattress she used. "'Tis big enough for two and the only comfortable place in the house."

It was, especially in a cold house. After what he'd done today and what he would do tomorrow, he needed a comfortable place to rest.

"Very well. But you will keep your hands to yourself," she warned. "Or else you will find yourself out in the snowy streets."

"Why?"

"What do you mean, why?"

"Why deny ourselves the pleasure we've already shared?" He took a step toward her, eyes ablaze. Heat burst inside her. Again. And she had to admit that in that moment she wasn't sure why she was resisting his allure. "I thought you'd enjoyed yourself?"

She had. Far too much, which was the problem. The last time the intensity of her feelings had frightened her. She didn't want this to happen again. She wanted to be in charge of her own destiny, didn't want her senses to take control of her life.

Instead of answering, Eahlswith took a step backward.

Sven saw her reaction and mistook it for fear. He raised his palms and took a step back himself. "You have nothing to fear from me, Alva. I want you, it is true. But I will not force you to have me if you don't want me." He tilted his head, nostrils flaring. "I swear I will, as you say, keep my hands to myself, until you beg me to put them on you. Then I will most certainly use them to give you what you need."

Oh, Lord.

As reassurances went, this one was a dangerous one. He wouldn't touch her, unless she asked for it. And right now she wasn't sure she wouldn't beg.

Moments later they were both lying side by side on her pallet, still in their clothes.

Eahlswith screwed her eyes shut and turned her back to the wall, determined to ignore the big, warm, strong body next to her. Then she felt Sven's arm close around her and his chest come flush against her back.

"Sven. You promised," she reminded him weakly. Too weakly. Surely she should scream, push him away, hit him even?

"I promised to keep my hands to myself, not my body," was his curt reply. "You need warmth, so you're getting mine. I will not discuss this further. Go to sleep, Alva. I promise I won't do anything."

Go to sleep. When a massive arm was holding her. When a massive chest was pressed against her. When a massive rod was poking at her back. He was aroused, as hard as she was soft. And yet, as he'd promised, he didn't try to take advantage. The arm didn't tighten its hold, the chest didn't move, the rod gradually softened.

Moments later, Eahlswith was amazed to hear that Sven had fallen asleep.

Now she would just have to do the same.

5

Sven was woken up by a feminine moan.

The evocative sound caused need to bloom inside him and he let out a growl of anticipation before remembering where he was and who with. Eahlswith. He was in her house, in her bed, but not to give her pleasure, only to sleep. He opened his eyes, sanity prevailing once more. She was getting agitated. In the darkness he couldn't see much, and anyway, she had her back to him. Was she asleep or awake? In pain or in prey to a dream?

Suddenly she reached behind her and gasped when her hand landed on his arm, as if surprised to feel someone next to her.

"Oh, you're back!"

She turned and burrowed against his chest, holding him tight. He closed his eyes when happiness flooded him. Finally she was acknowledging that she'd missed him all these months, that she wanted him as much as he wanted her. He'd sensed it, which had been the only thing preventing him from succumbing to despair, and it was wonderful to have his feelings confirmed.

He cradled the back of her head in his palm, drawing her closer, showing her with his body what he'd been unable to make her see with his words or actions. "Yes, I'm back, I'm here. Calm yourself. It's all right."

Something like a sob answered him. "Edwin. You're here."

Edwin. Sven froze.

She didn't want him, she hadn't acknowledged anything. She was still asleep, dreaming, and she thought he was someone else.

Edwin. The name Osbert had said just before she had spilled soup on her bodice. He'd not been mistaken. She *had* wanted to interrupt the old man before he revealed who this Edwin was because she'd known he wouldn't like it. Well, she'd been right. He didn't like to hear that there was another man in her life.

"I'm sorry, Edwin, I'm so sorry. I never meant to..."

Never meant to what? Hurt him? Sleep with another man? His heart fell. Was that why she was refusing to accept what was between them, why she was keeping him at arms' length? Because she was already involved with someone else and she'd hoped that her moment of madness would never be discovered?

If that were the case, the situation was even more hopeless than he'd thought. Should he just give up and accept that a single night of passion was all they were going to have?

As soon as the question crossed his mind, his arms tightened around her, providing him with the answer. He was not ready to give up yet, not when he had not even tried. What could have been a call of the senses—Eahlswith was so luscious that he defied any man not to want her—had turned into so much more when he'd started to know her and seen the very real affection she had for the old man.

This woman was made to love someone. He wanted to be that someone. If this Edwin, whoever he was, had turned away from her because she'd erred, too bad. He would not make the same mistake.

"Hush, Alva, I'm here. Me, Sven, I'm here." He kissed the top of her hair and felt her relax into his arms. "Everything's all right. I'm here now. Sleep."

As for him, it was safe to say that his night was over.

"ALL FINISHED," Eahlswith translated when Sven pointed to the roof and nodded.

Indeed, the corner of the roof looked as solid as it had ever been.

"Thank you so much, young man," Osbert answered, emotion making his voice waver. "I wish I could do something to thank you."

"*Þökk*," Eahlswith translated next.

Sven arched a brow and gave a radiant smile. She reddened, not having expected that it would feel so intimate to use his language, or that he would be so delighted by her effort—or that heat would spread through her chest at the pleasure of pleasing him.

"You know how to speak their language?" Osbert was amazed, as well he might, because she did not.

"I don't. Only I heard Steinar use the word a few times with his friends and I thought...well, it makes sense to thank the man in his own language, don't you think? I mean, after all he did, it's—"

Thankfully, Sven cut her fumbled explanations short by bowing and throwing his bag over his shoulder. This was it. This time he was really going. Her chest inexplicably tightened. Waking up in a man's arms this morning had been wonderful. She had felt a sense of peace she had not felt since Edwin's death. As he often did, he'd visited her in her dreams, and she had begged for his forgiveness. And this time, he had granted it. Gratefulness, relief and hope spread through her chest. It was silly but when she had opened her eyes after her most restful night in years, it had felt as if something had changed. Yes, she had the impression Edwin had finally given her the forgiveness she'd needed. Now all that was left was for her to forgive herself.

"Goodbye," she heard Osbert tell Sven.

She wanted to add something, thank him again, but there was a sizeable lump in her throat. When he saw she was not going to say anything he nodded and walked through the door, stooping as he did.

And then he was gone.

Eahlswith remained a long time staring at the piece of wood. The relief, the joy, the comfort she'd felt this morning upon waking up in his warmth had well and truly vanished. She felt cold and alone once more. She should go after him, she should go tell him she—

Knock knock.

Eahlswith's heart leaped. Had Sven forgotten something? She rushed to open the door, only to find herself face to face with Godric.

"A huge Norseman has just put my ladder in front of my house," the old man said, peering inside the house with ill-concealed curiosity. Either he wanted to see more of the Norseman to check if he was as huge as he'd seemed to be or he wanted to inspect the repairs. Eahlswith couldn't help a pang of irritation. Couldn't he have come to help Sven, since he apparently had nothing to do? "I suppose that means he's finished with the roof?"

"Yes," Osbert answered in her stead. "He's gone."

The words were like a blow to the heart. He was gone. Just like Edwin.

Well, that was what she'd wanted, was it not? She had demanded he didn't touch her, she had certainly not tried to keep him just now, she had not even told him goodbye.

"I will leave you to it," she told the two men, who had already started to comment on the work Sven had done. "I have things to do at home."

"Of course," Osbert said, turning to face her. "And thank you again for your help these last two days."

"I didn't do anything," she mumbled. "Sven did."

"Yes, well. Thank you for the soup then."

She didn't comment.

Outside, the winter wind whipped at her clothes in the most unpleasant manner. Eahlswith lowered her hood over her face and hurried her steps as she could already feel the wet ground soak through the thin leather of her shoes. As Sven had predicted, it had snowed overnight and the street had been reduced to a mire. She shivered. Winter was decidedly her least favorite season.

As she finally turned into her own street, she skidded to a halt. A horse, his coat as white as the snow under his hooves, was tethered to the post Edwin had once planted outside her house. His owner was leaning against her door, his arms crossed over his chest, his legs crossed at the ankle, his posture relaxed. Her heart started to beat a fierce drum.

Sven. Of course.

How had she imagined he would leave without a proper goodbye? He'd simply left the house so they could say their goodbye away from Osbert's prying eyes and ears. A smile floating on his lips, he watched her walk the few remaining yards to get to him. Not knowing what to say she extended a tentative hand toward the horse's neck instead, intent on stroking him. At the last moment she stopped herself. Could she?

"You can stroke him, he doesn't bite." Sven's voice was little more than a purr, as if he wanted to coax her into petting the animal.

"He's rather impressive," she said, finally daring to touch the stallion's neck. So soft... Her lips stretched into a smile because now she knew where she had heard the name Gulltoppr before. It was the horse of Heimdallr, the god of war. She had thought about it all day and finally remembered what Cwenthryth had told her.

"He is rather impressive, but he's the gentlest horse you could ever meet."

Impressive, gentle and beautiful. Yes. Just like the man in front of her.

"'Tis too late to go back to the village now, I think," Sven said, looking to the skies. "Night will soon fall and it is snowing already."

Indeed a few flakes had started to flutter about while they talked, light as down feathers. "Yes. You should stay here for the night."

"I definitely should."

Her smile broadened. Would she have made the same offer if it had been the middle of summer? Would she have surrendered so easily? She preferred not to wonder because she had an awful suspicion that she would have.

"Come then. My feet are soaked."

After one last pat on Gulltoppr's rump, Sven followed her inside the house. As soon as she'd closed the door, he lifted the hem of her skirt. The gesture might have raised her heartbeat had there not been a frown on his face. Instead of looking at her exposed legs, or making lewd comments, he was peering at her shoes. This was definitely not a move destined to seduce her.

"No wonder your feet are soaked," he said, allowing the skirt to fall back down. "The leather of your boots is worn thin, it's not suitable at all for this weather."

He sounded as worried as if he'd actually seen an injury on her foot. Eahlswith knew he was right, the leather was so damaged that it had holes in, but she couldn't afford another pair of shoes at the moment, so there was nothing else to do than to endure it. Still, she wished she hadn't had her inadequacies exposed to him.

"I'll be fine," she said, hiding her hands behind her back before he could see that her gloves had holes in them as well.

"You will, once I have warmed your feet. Sit."

Though she should probably have protested at his high-handedness, she sat. The idea of having his hands wrapped around her frozen feet was far too irresistible. She was suddenly reminded of when she had dropped the cask of ale on her foot the other day. He had knelt at her feet and asked to see her foot. He was going to ask the same thing now. It had been unthinkable to accept then, it was impossible to consider refusing now. How quickly things changed.

"Lift your foot for me," Sven ordered, coming down on one knee in front of her. The voice was commanding, the look in his eyes fierce, but the position submissive, and he was waiting for her to agree.

Utterly under his spell, Eahlswith did as she was told and placed the tip of her foot on his muscular thigh. How was it that seeing him look after her, worrying about her well-being, was doing more to entice her than anything else he might have done? Not that she would have remained impassive if he had started to talk to her in that impossibly deep voice, and told her what he wanted to do to her, or kissed her with all the passion and skill she knew him capable of, but this...

She swallowed, watching as he untied her laces and removed her right shoe with careful gestures. It was so wet she already knew it would not dry overnight, even if she left it next to the fire. Then he reached under her skirt to find the ribbon holding her woolen stocking in place under the knee. Sven made a face when he felt that the garment was just as soaked as the shoe, at least on the part covering her foot. After sliding it off her leg, he placed it on top of her boot.

"Are you still pain?" he asked, taking her other foot into his hands. He'd remembered it was the bruised one. She was more touched than she could say. "Do I need to be extra careful?"

"No." He was being extra careful anyway.

By the time he'd rolled the second stocking down her leg, Eahlswith was breathless. Sven grunted when he saw the purple mark on the bridge of her foot but she was not worried about the bruise. As she'd told him twice now, it was nothing to worry about. Rather, she was waiting for the moment he would take her feet into his big, warm hands. Would he place them on his lap? Would he give her a massage?

Instead of doing what she had imagined he would, he stood back up and walked over to the pallet to take one of the blankets. Kneeling back in front of her, he wrapped her feet in the soft material and swiveled her so that her extended legs pointed toward the fire pit where the fire was still going, since she'd been careful to come back once in the morning to tend it.

She could not help a strangled noise from escaping her throat.

"What is it?" Sven asked, adding a few logs to the flames and stirring the fire back to a roaring furnace. He had already placed her stockings and boots next to it to dry, she noticed. So thoughtful... "Are you not comfortable like this?"

"I'm fine. Only I confess I thought you would take my feet into your h-hands to warm them," she stammered, too overcome by gratitude and desire to even think of lying.

The look he threw her was enough to burn her all the way to her frozen toes. Oh, what beast had she unleashed?

"Alva, believe me, you do not want that," he growled, coming closer to her, a predator on the prowl. A wolf, she realized, feeling her heartbeat pick up in what felt almost like alarm. "If I put my hands on you now it will not be to hold your feet. I will run my fingers all the way up your naked leg, and I will not stop until I have reached the sweet spot begging for my caresses. You will then have no choice but to open your legs wide and let me plunge my fingers inside you while I watch. And once you've drenched my hand with your release, it will be my turn. I will stand over you and watch you suck my cock until I flood your mouth."

Oh.

Lord.

Why had she told him what was on her mind? How had she forgotten about his propensity to talk dirty?

Eahlswith stayed where she was, stunned into silence. The place between her legs, the "sweet spot begging for his caresses" had gone liquid. Or swollen. Or hot. She didn't know which. Probably a combination of the three. And her mind was now the consistency of a puddle of melted snow.

"Are you still cold?" he asked, sounding just as affected as she was. Respectful of her wishes, he had not made a single move to take her into his arms, even if she could see from the look in his eyes and the bulge at the front of his braies that he was desperate to do what he'd just described.

"No, I'm not cold," she rasped, averting her gaze. "But I'm hungry. Let's make dinner."

Sven nodded his agreement slowly. It was better they stopped talking about what he wanted to do while his cock was still pulsing and his control was hanging by a thread. What had possessed him to tell Eahlswith what he wanted to do? He should have known it would only send him into a flurry of need.

Yes. Better to start cooking.

Before she could stand up he stopped her with a raised hand.

"Have you got another pair of stockings?" Her shoes were soaked, so she couldn't put them back on, but the floor would be cold on her bare feet. He couldn't allow it.

"No."

He'd suspected as much. Without a word, Sven sat on the stool and removed his own boots and socks. "Here, you can wear these until we go to bed," he said, handing her his woolen socks. They would be enormous on her but it was better than nothing.

"Thank you," she said, keeping her gaze averted.

While she put them on, he turned to the table and concentrated on breathing. How was he going to survive another evening without touching her? It would be bad enough until they went to bed but as soon as she lay down next to him he would be overcome by the need to plunge inside her soft heat. How would he control himself?

Eventually she joined him, looking rather flushed. He resisted looking at her feet, even if they were covered with her skirt. The idea that she was wearing something of his was very pleasing, intimate.

"Do you still have your nuts and dried meat?" she asked, finally looking at him.

"Yes."

"We can perhaps start with those while I make the soup."

He nodded, and extracted the small basket from his saddlebag. "Here. Help yourself. What can I do to help?" he asked, when she reached for the half cabbage lying in the middle of the table.

"Carpenter, washerwoman and now cook?" Her eyes glimmered at the pleasure of the jest they shared.

"You haven't seen the extent of my skills," he couldn't help but reply. As he could have predicted, his cock lengthened at the comment. Damnation, what was wrong with him? He'd only just about managed to coax it down.

"You can start by chopping this cabbage into strips while I go get the rest of the salted pork from the storeroom."

"How thin do you want the strips?"

She tilted her head, as if considering. It amused him to see her taking the question so seriously. "As thin as possible. Then we will see how talented you really are."

If she thought she could issue a challenge and not see him rise to it, she could think again. Having something to concentrate on would help keep his desire in check. Once the cabbage had been reduced to strips barely thicker than horse hair, he watched Eahlswith assemble everything together in a big iron pot. She had such assured gestures that he could have watched her cook all day. She clearly was a talented cook because it took her no time to prepare another hearty soup flavored with the fat from the pork and the surprising addition of thick cream. A good idea he would replicate at home.

"That was delicious, thank you. Do you want a piece of cheese to finish?" he asked, reaching into his bag for the cheese he'd bought after leaving Osbert's house.

"You bought food for us. That is conclusive proof that you intended to spend another night under my roof," she said, shaking her head. "Not that I doubted it."

"No. You remind me of my sister, you know," he said, as he chewed the cheese.

Her surprise at the comment was evident. Nevertheless she tried to hide her pleasure with an offhand response. "Oh? You try everything you can to fuck your sister then?"

Sven almost choked on his mouthful of cheese, so shocked was he by her use of the crude word. Really, the woman was fearless. And yet... In the firelight he couldn't be sure but he thought she'd gone the color of a newly unfurled wild dog rose. That was intriguing. She had just asked him the most provocative question she could have asked, she had behaved with complete abandon in his bed and yet she was capable of blushing like a young maiden. Which made her look lovelier than ever.

Was it any wonder he was so enthralled? No.

"This is what I mean. Eyja is bold as you please. A veritable imp." He had often wondered how his friend Moon could have married such a spirited woman, who was bound to turn his life inside out, but now he thought he had a fair idea. When the woman in question was not a younger sister he'd spent all his life with, he could see the appeal. Turning something inside out was not always bad, as it often offered a new perspective. It was not until you looked inside a shell that you saw the marvellous colors swirling about in its depths.

"Do you have many brothers and sisters?" Eahlswith asked, cutting herself a slice of cheese. He could tell she was regretting her rash question and was trying to steer the conversation away from the type of women he liked to fuck.

"Eyja is my only sister. I have two brothers, both older. Steinar, who you know already, and Torsten, who's just had a little girl."

"Does he also look like you? I mean, Steinar could be your twin."

He let out a snort, having heard that comment many times before. "Yes, I know he could. We both take after our Icelandic father, Ulf, who everyone calls Wolf. But Torsten looks like our Saxon mother, Merewen."

Eahlswith was so taken aback by his declaration that she dropped the piece of cheese she'd just picked up.

"Surely you're not half Saxon?"

"I am," he confirmed, amused by her reaction. "I was even born here. How do you think I speak your language so well.?"

She eyed him dubiously. "But I... You look all Norse to me."

"That's because, as I said, I look like my father. But my mother has eyes as dark as yours. You will see when you meet her."

It was as if he'd just issued a terrible threat. He watched as Eahlswith seemed to shrink to half her normal size.

"I have no intention of meeting any member of your family," she said in a whisper. "What would be the point?"

"The point," he said, doing his best to stay calm. Would it forever be one step forward, two steps back between them? Only a moment ago they had been sharing a moment and here she was, saying that she didn't see any future for them. "The point is that I like you and I might want you to meet them."

She didn't answer, but he saw in her eyes that if she had her way, that would never happen. Was it because of this mysterious Edwin? He would have to ask her who he was one day, or he would go mad.

"I think we should go to bed," she concluded, standing up.

Sven's heart stilled in his chest. What might have sounded like an invitation to sin sounded like a condemnation to the worst kind of death.

6

As soon as they settled in the pallet Eahlswith found herself snuggling next to Sven, placing herself in the same position they had adopted the previous night, with her back moulded to his front. It had seemed the natural thing to do then, but suddenly she wasn't so sure. Worry spiked through her while she waited for his reaction. Would he refuse to hold her now that she'd told him she didn't want to meet his family? Would he point out that they didn't need to be so close as the fire had been kept going all day?

To her relief, he didn't tense or pass comment on the fact that it wasn't cold tonight. Instead, he wrapped his arm around her waist, like he had the previous evening, before bending his legs behind hers to engulf her in his bulk. She loved how feminine he made her feel. How desirable. How *desired*, and not just for her body.

Eahlswith let out a slow exhale, trying to hang on to her control.

Though his talk of meeting his family had frightened her, she could not deny that her mind was in turmoil—and her body on fire. He had been perfect with her tonight, attentive, patient and kind.

Which was the whole problem. Had he been a real bastard, not caring that her feet were soaked, not offering to help with the food, not making her laugh and opening up about his family, she would not be here, nestled in his arms. She would have made sure to signify her displeasure and lack of interest by keeping as far as she could from him. But here she was, melting into his delicious embrace.

"So, you know how to thank me in my language," he purred in her ear. The sound caused the hairs at the back of her neck to stand on end, but she could tell that he wasn't trying to seduce her. It was just his normal way of talking. "I'm curious. What else do you know? Can you beg me also?"

"No." The word could barely escape her lips. No, definitely not cold tonight. More like scorching hot.

"Not a problem. You will never have to beg me anyway. For anything."

"Sven…" A sigh. Damn, damn, damn, why did he always know what to say to her?

Before she knew it, Eahlswith had snuggled up even closer to him, and she was grinding her buttocks against his loins. Predictably, he was as hard as the nails he'd used on Osbert's roof. And she was so desperate to welcome that strong length inside her that her body was weeping with need. This was dangerous territory, deep down she knew it, but she didn't seem able to stop herself. Her body started to undulate of its own accord, indicating its need to be filled, betraying a desire she had fought for two days. She had reached a snapping point and she didn't even care.

She needed this.

Their last night together had been motivated by lust and ended up freeing unsuspected feelings from a place locked deep within her soul. Slowly but irremediably these feelings had coalesced into a hot ball of desire that was burning her from the inside. There would be no stopping what was going to happen.

She didn't want to. All day they had been playing with fire. It was time to accept that fire burned.

She moaned.

"Alva." That simple name, pronounced in Sven's most gravelly voice, frayed each and every one of Eahlswith's nerve endings. "I said I would keep my hands to myself, and I kept my word. That was last night, when you just lay still in my arms and allowed me to go to sleep. Now, I am a man. A man who wants you, desperately. I told you as much earlier. And so I'm warning you. If you keep moaning like that, I cannot be answerable for my actions. And if you keep on grinding your delectable ass against my cock, I cannot promise not to bury it exactly where you want me to bury it."

The same sensations that had assaulted her body earlier, when he had told her all he wanted to do to her in the crudest of terms assaulted her again.

"Sven..." A whimper this time.

"Aye. Sven." His arm tightened around her middle, holding her flush against him, making her feel how ready he was. "Me. I'm here, in your bed, by your invitation. So ask me to give you what we both want. Please. Beg me to take you, and give you pleasure."

"Sven." A surrender.

He didn't need any more. Nudging at her shoulder, he rolled her to her front until she lay flat on her stomach. Her shift was quickly disposed of and a heartbeat later soft lips surrounded by soft hairs were creating a blazing trail along her spine. Mm. She did love his beard, and it felt amazing on her skin. Groaning all the while, Sven kissed and licked her all the way to the swell of her buttocks. Palming her, he used his knee to spread her legs open before positioning himself between her thighs.

Just when she was certain he was going to enter her, he paused.

"Tell me this first. Is there another man in your life?"

Shock caused her to still. She would have thought him lost to all reason by now, just like she was. But here he was, wondering if he had to the right to take her.

"No," she managed to say. Not in the way he meant, at least.

"You've had other lovers, though?"

"Yes. But no one special." That was no lie. None of these men had meant a thing, she saw that now.

The reward for her answer was a growl, in her ear. "Good. You're all mine then. Can you feel this?"

How could she not? He was sliding his length up and down her opening, making her mad with need. She could feel it getting coated in her juices, and little wonder. Never had she been so aroused. Every inch of her tingled, the place between her legs throbbed, demanding to be filled. Even her nipples ached.

This bore no resemblance to their wild night in his hut, when he'd showcased his strength and skill by taking her in every possible position, up against the wall, on her hands and knees, making her ride him and supporting her weight when she thought she would collapse. Tonight he was being impossibly tender—which had reduced her to a quivering, incoherent mass of need.

"Please, Sven, please, I can't take it anymore."

"Hush, I told you, you wouldn't have to beg. Where do you want it?"

Where did he think? "I don't unders—"

The word died on her lips when she felt him push at an opening she had never once considered using for lovemaking.

That was what he'd meant when he'd asked where she wanted it? She had not known such a possession was possible but everything within her sizzled at the shocking notion. Could he really do that?

Could she agree?

Her eyes closed again. He was giving her secret cleft the most scandalous massage and it felt amazing. Until she understood what he was really doing—and remembered the size of his shaft.

"Wait, I-I'm not sure..." Panic flooded her. What was she thinking, of course, they couldn't—

"Hush, lovely, don't worry. We can do that some other time," Sven purred, placing a reassuring kiss in the crook of her neck, followed by a playful nip. "For now let me just do this the way I know you like."

"Yes." She didn't even pretend to hesitate. She arched her back in invitation and a moment later she felt him slide inside her with an ease betraying the strength of her desire. Finally. This was what she needed.

"Mm. Feel that? Your little cunt is soaked, ready for me. I like that I have that effect on you because you make me harder than nails."

Damnation, why did he have to have such a dirty mouth? She'd been shocked that first night in the summer when he'd used crude words with her, until she'd realized that it aroused her like nothing else.

Once he was buried to the root, he stilled and she almost screamed her frustration. Now was not the time to stop! She turned her head to look over her left shoulder. He was poised over her, his eyes gleaming in the firelight, the fiercest warrior she could imagine.

"Sven. Please." She tried to move and found that she could not.

"Yes. Ask me to fuck you."

Oh, the wretched man. Was he really going to stop now if she didn't say the words?

"You said you wouldn't make me beg," she rasped.

He lowered his head to come and speak with his mouth at her temple. "I don't want you to beg me to fuck you. I want you to *order* me to do it, because you can't bear another moment of not feeling me moving inside you. I want you to make sure I give you exactly what you need, and how you need it. I want you to use me, I want you to—"

"Fuck me, damn you! Now. I need—"

The first thrust interrupted her. The second made her eyes roll to the back of her head. the third one catapulted her into glorious release. He'd teased, stroked and prepared her so well that it only took three strokes for her to erupt in pleasure, something she wouldn't have thought possible.

Her face buried into the furs, Eahlswith convulsed around him, unable to stop the waves crashing through her. No! Too soon. She'd wanted this lovemaking to last hours, not mere moments. It had undoubtedly been folly to agree to another night with him, and she knew she would pay for it on the morrow. She'd at least wanted to enjoy it. Fortunately, Sven realized it. He never stopped moving, prolonging her ecstasy, showing her that it was not over yet.

"Worry not, lovely, we are far from done," he said once she had finally stopped spasming. "Do you want more?"

"Yes. More."

He chuckled at the relief in her voice and brought her to her hands and knees, raising her hips high into the air for him to plough. From then on his languid, sensual strokes became almost punishing, the rhythm frantic. Delirious with sensations, Eahlswith met him thrust for thrust. This was going to kill her. This was going to transform her. This was going to—

"I'm afraid I'm not going to last much longer than you," he said, his voice hoarse. "You feel too good around my cock. But we have all night. I'll make sure you never forget the feel of me inside you."

Oh, she already knew she would not.

SVEN HAD FULLY ANTICIPATED that Eahlswith would behave as if they hadn't indulged in the most decadent lovemaking of their lives as soon as she woke up. He was therefore not surprised when he found her already up and at the table, cutting cheese with her back to him. At least this time, because they were in her house, not his, she hadn't been able to flee.

"Good morning," he said, keeping the furs tight around his body. Not that he thought for a moment she would have forgotten he was naked. That was probably the reason why she was behaving as if she were alone in the room.

It hurt, undeniably.

After a night of delicious abandon, they had both fallen asleep, sated and content, in each other's arms. And yet here she was now, refusing to even meet his gaze. Was that why she had only allowed him to take her from behind last night? Because she couldn't bear to look at him? No, he was being silly. She had lain under him, then knelt in front of him and finally stretched on her side next to him because those positions had brought her immense pleasure. As it had him.

By the gods, he was already hard from waking up, he should not be thinking about how her sheath had welcomed him and squeezed him tighter than a fist every time she'd reached her peak. It would only make him do something he would regret.

"Are you hungry?" she asked, finally acknowledging his presence.

He was, but he thought it better to find some bread in town before he rode back to the village. She looked too ill at ease for him to enjoy this moment together.

"No. I have to go anyway, I know Torsten will be waiting for me," he said at random, reaching for his braies. No one was waiting for him and the last thing he wanted to do was leave but it was probably for the best.

She nodded, looking relieved, and didn't ask any questions, swapping the cheese for the loaf of bread instead. He'd been right; she couldn't wait to see him go. He got dressed in silence, seething with disillusion. She'd said there was no man to worry about, that she was free to bed him. Which meant she was also free to be with him if she wanted to.

And yet she wanted him gone.

Why? Was she like all the others, who only wanted him for a few hot nights? Like Freydis, who had left for Denmark mere days after allowing him in her bed? Like the women from his village who'd known him all his life and for whom he held no interest outside the bedroom? Was he good for nothing other than physical pleasure? Were his tongue and his cock the only parts of him worthy of interest? He was seriously starting to wonder.

He grunted, looking down at his groin. At least Eahlswith's coldness meant that his erection had vanished in a puff of smoke.

"When will I see you again?" he asked, fastening his belt. He hated sounding needy, but he had no choice. He could not bear the idea that it might be another six months before he saw her again and he could tell that was what would happen if he didn't contrive a meeting himself.

"I don't know." She cut another slice of bread. How many did she intend to cut? He'd just told her he wouldn't eat anything.

"Are you not planning on visiting the village soon?" he tried again a moment later. She had followed him outside, which surprised him. He had fully expected her to slam the door in his face as soon as he went to get Gulltoppr ready.

"I'm not sure. There is no reason to. Cwenthryth said she might—"

"Cwenthryth," he spat, unable to contain his bitterness any longer. Her friend was the only person she thought to come and see and she wasn't even trying to pretend it wasn't so. "There is another reason for you to come to the village, you know. Or have you forgotten I live there too?"

"No, but—"

"So what you are saying is that you couldn't possibly want to see me. That if I want to see you, I will have to ask my brother to father another child on his wife, because meeting the new babe is the only reason you want to come to the village?" he carried on, a bitter laugh escaping his lips. "It shouldn't be too difficult to convince Steinar. He and his wife can't seem to keep their hands off one another."

Just like the two of them. Eahlswith would be aware of the irresistible attraction between them by now. And yet she persisted in fighting it, for no reason that he could discern.

"I haven't bedded another woman since we spent the night together."

The air between them stilled, then a sudden shower of snowflakes came to blur his vision.

"Why are telling me this?" Eahlswith said in an agonized whisper.

He ran a hand through his hair, barely resisting the impulse to tug at it in helplessness. Why was he telling her exactly? Why did he feel the need to expose his vulnerability? To show her just how much he cared about whatever was between them, how much he wanted to see it grow? All this when it was clear she didn't care?

Why was he being such a fool?

"Because you need to know that no one but you interests me," he said through gritted teeth. "I cannot rid myself of the idea that we what we have is something special. And I think it's the same for you, even if you refuse to admit it. Tell me, Alva, that last night you didn't enjoy feeling me—"

"Stop calling me Alva!" she erupted.

"Why?" Why did she object to the name so much? It was hardly in insult. And why was *she* getting angry, exactly? She was not the one being discarded like so much dirt on the ground.

"Because it's not my name," she said lifting both hands to the milky skies. "How would you like it if I called you...Heimdallr?"

"*Heimdallr?*" Why on earth would she choose that name for him? How did she even know about the god of war? Saxons usually didn't know anything about the Norse gods, preferring a single deity with no power he could discern and who didn't even seem able or inclined to roam the human world.

He followed the direction of Eahlswith's gaze, which had landed on Gulltoppr, tethered just behind him. She knew that the golden-maned horse belonged to Heimdallr then. This was why she had thought of this name. The woman was full of surprises.

His bitterness vanished.

"How do you know so much about Norse gods, anyway?" he asked, both pleased and unaccountably aroused.

She shrugged, her own anger spent. "Cwenthryth is fascinated by them, and being married to Steinar, she's had the opportunity to learn. She's started teaching me what she knows. I have to admit, it is rather fascinating."

It would be, he supposed, for someone used to the single deity who didn't own a horse, a raven, a hammer or anything else of note.

"Well, to answer your question, I would love it if you called me Heimdallr," he growled, drawing her into his arms. They couldn't part like this, not without a kiss, at least. "It would make me feel like a god outside of bed as well."

She rolled her eyes at his answer calculated to exasperate her. But he was not jesting. This woman made him feel like no other had.

"Sven…"

Ah, his name in her mouth. He remembered how she had whispered it in surrender last night, before finally losing all restraint and ordering him to fuck her. It had been one of the most satisfying moments of his life. Unable to stop himself, he took her mouth in a kiss he'd intended to be fiery but which ended up being achingly tender. He put in it all he had not been able to tell her, and all he hoped to be able to tell her one day.

"This is what I mean," he breathed against her lips. "Don't tell me you don't feel like one of the goddesses right now?"

Without waiting for her answer, he vaulted onto Gulltoppr's back. Eahlswith was looking at him, her black eyes huge.

"This isn't over. Alva. Mark me, even if you don't want to come and see me, fate will ensure we do meet again."

7

No sooner had Sven ridden through the town gate than he was proven right.

A rider was cantering in the opposite direction, coming toward him on a familiar horse. Steinar, on Fáfnir. As soon as he saw him, his brother brought the stallion down to a walk and joined him by the side of the road.

"What are you doing here?"

His brother didn't know about his plans to repair Osbert's roof. No one knew, and he wasn't about to admit to it.

"I spent two days in town," Sven answered. He often did, so there was nothing suspicious in that. "What about you?"

"Cwenthryth sent me to get her friend Eahlswith. You know, the one who visited the other day, after Liv's birth?"

"Yes, I do know who you mean."

Indeed. He'd just said goodbye to her with the most amazing kiss. Only the night before he'd been buried deep inside her, making her moan in the most scandalous way. Mm, he really, really liked the way she moaned.

"Yes, of course, you brought her home after finding her in

the forest." Steinar nodded. "Well. I hope she's home. I wouldn't like to get back to the village too late. I meant to go to the harbor to meet a merchant called Gorm before he leaves for London and I—"

"Go to the harbor now," Sven suggested. "Let me take Eahlswith to the village. As you can see I was on my way home anyway."

"You wouldn't mind?" His brother sounded relieved. Trust him to put his wife's request before his own plans. "It's just that I'm not sure how long Gorm means to wait and I would hate to miss him."

"Of course I don't mind." Riding with Eahlswith's luscious body against his? He definitely didn't mind that. "Nothing wrong with Cwenthryth, I hope?" he asked, frowning. Why was she suddenly desperate to see her friend? He liked his sister-in-law and would hate to hear about a problem. "Or the babe?"

"No, no. Only, if Gorm has the news I hope he has, I might have to leave for a few days and Cwenthryth could do with her help. Little Liv is just as unsettled as Sanna was at her age and to tell you the truth, we are exhausted."

The shadows under Steinar's eyes made that clear, but the smile on his lips hinted that he didn't mind.

"Well, don't worry, I'll take her back to the village."

As he turned his horse around, Sven couldn't help the satisfaction swelling in his chest. Fate was indeed smiling on him. Eahlswith had refused to arrange another meeting between them, but she would have no choice but to spend another few days close to him.

"Thank you," Steinar said, nudging Fáfnir into a trot. "Come. I'll show you where she lives."

Even though he already knew where that was, Sven followed without comment.

Sven's Promise

SHE ALREADY MISSED HIM.

Eahlswith fell down on her chair in one heap. Dear God, how was that even possible? He'd only been gone a moment; she'd all but pushed him out of the door in her haste to see him gone and yet here she was, sitting on her only chair, staring at the pallet, reliving what the two of them had done the night before. How many times had he made her erupt in pleasure? She had quickly lost count and just let him do what he did best —make her lose her mind.

Afterward, he had cradled her against his amazing body and she had fallen asleep in the blink of an eye.

It had been perfect.

Until she'd woken up in his arms and realized that she had done the worst thing she could have done for someone intent on keeping him at bay. How was she supposed to do what she needed to do after that night? That kiss?

Well, he was gone now, and she would have a few days, if not weeks, to come up with an answer.

She was wondering whether she should start hemming the new shift she was making for herself or go and see Godgifu at her market stall when a knock on the door made her jump. Who could that be? Osbert? Come to check if their visitor was gone?

No.

The door revealed a tall, blond Norseman with braided hair. For the space of a heartbeat, Eahlswith thought it was Sven. Then she saw that his hair was shorter, his clothes different— and the effect his proximity had on her, much less pronounced.

"Steinar?"

"Yes. Eahlswith, good morning."

What was he doing here? "Is it Cwenthryth?" she asked, as

fear suddenly seized her guts. She could only think of one reason for her friend's husband to come see her unannounced. "Is everything all right? With Liv?"

"Yes, they're both fine. Don't worry. It's just..." He sounded uncharacteristically hesitant. "Cwenthryth was wondering whether you could go to the hut for a few days. I might be absent and, with Liv hardly sleeping the night at the moment, she could do with the help. Not that it sounds very appealing, I understand, but she said you'd offered to help and well, to be honest, I was hoping you might still want to. It would be a load off my mind to know she is not alone."

She smiled at his confused explanation. It was endearing to see such a strong, self-assured man worried about putting her out and so committed to helping his wife.

Which was why she decided to put an end to his suffering quickly. "Of course. I did offer to help and I'm happy to come." Helping her friend would be the perfect way to distract her from her musings about a certain Norseman. She opened the door wider, welcoming him in. "Will you come in, have a drink while I pack a change of clothes?"

"I won't, thank you. I'm actually on my way to the harbor to meet a man," he said, glancing at a point to his right. "But my brother is here. I chanced upon him as I was riding into town. He will take you back to the village. I believe you met him when you last came to visit?"

Eahlswith's heart sank because the only other one of Wolf's sons she had seen during her visits to Cwenthryth was the one who'd just left her house. The one she was desperately trying to get out of her mind. The one she had hoped to get some distance from. When Steinar moved to make room for his brother, she already knew she wouldn't see the one named Torsten appear in the door frame.

"Eahlswith. Good morning."

Sven walked into the room, as assured as the predator she had likened him to only the night before. He was a wolf's son indeed. Never had she seen a smile so full of teeth. Perfect, straight teeth that had nipped at her skin. She placed a hand over her neck, remembering how he had nuzzled at her throat while he took her in long, fluid strokes. Did it show? Had he left a bite mark? Had Steinar seen it and guessed who had made it? Had Sven told him about the two of them?

The questions threatened to make her mind explode.

"I'm going to take you up on your offer of a drink, if you don't mind," Sven said, straightening to his full height. "I still haven't broken my fast. Would you have a slice of bread to spare, by any chance?"

The wretched man! He knew she'd been using the cutting of bread to avoid meeting his gaze earlier.

"I do, she said, refusing to dignify him with a glare though she was sorely tempted. "Please sit down while I get ready."

"Thank you again, Eahlswith. This means a lot to me," Steinar told her, before barking something at his brother in Norse. It sounded as if he was warning him not to inconvenience her. Had he noticed the tension in her body? She dearly hoped not.

"It's my pleasure," she told him.

A moment later Steinar disappeared through the door and Eahlswith was alone with Sven, who was looking at her with eyes aglow with mischief.

"So." He crossed his massive arms over his massive chest. "It seems that fate decided to be on my side. That was remarkably quick on her part, don't you think?"

What could she answer to that? Indeed she couldn't believe that he was back already. It was not as if he'd contrived this meeting as well. It was purely coincidental. Steinar had been coming to her and had walked into his brother, who was leaving her house.

There was no use fighting fate.

"I will s-see to my clothes," she stammered, wondering how she would deal with sitting on a horse with him all the way to the village. Could she ask to walk by his side? No, not with her boots in the state they were. Besides, Sven would never agree to it. And if she suggested he be the one to walk, he would refuse.

"No need to change," he told her. "What you are wearing is fine."

More than fine, the heat in his gaze said. *Except that it hides too much of your gorgeous body.*

How could he make her blood sing thus? Eahlswith felt as she would after a cup of particularly strong mead.

"I mean that I should gather some clothes to take with me to the village," she specified, turning to go to the chest where she kept her meager possessions. The packing wouldn't take long, as she didn't own much.

"Of course," she heard him say with what sounded like amusement. "Do you mind if I help myself to some bread?"

"No. It's on the table," she said, though he would know that already, having watched her cut slice after slice earlier.

"Is there any cheese left by any chance?"

Eahlswith gritted her teeth. Had she ever met a more infuriating man? He was taking pleasure in highlighting the connection between them.

"You'll find it where you put it last night."

"Of course. Silly me."

She took as long as she dared to pack her things but eventually, there was nothing left to do. Sven had finished his bread and cheese and was watching her with ill-concealed delight.

Eahlswith took in a deep breath.

"Shall we?" she said, refusing to give him the satisfaction of initiating a conversation which would make her feel worse—or drawing him into another soul-shattering kiss. She wouldn't make that mistake twice in the same day.

"But certainly. Your wish is my command."

She didn't answer. What would be the point?

8
———

Sven bit back a groan.

He had expected that having Eahlswith with him on Gulltoppr would be sweet torture but this was a hundred times worse than what he had anticipated. A hundred times better. He barely resisted the temptation to steer his horse the other way so as to prolong the ride for as long as possible.

When they finally came in view of the village, he stopped before they could be seen together and jumped down from the saddle. Fortunately, he still had a couple of planks in his bag. He'd been unable to use them as they were too short to be nailed to Osbert's roof, but they would be ideal for what he wanted to do. Fumbling in the bottom of the bag he extracted a particularly sharp nail and looked up to address Eahlswith, who was watching him, brow arched.

"Tomorrow I will bring you new boots," he said matter-of-factly. "We have an excellent cobbler here at the village. Bo is a friend. I'll go speak to him, see what he can do and—"

"No."

Of course he'd expected it, but her refusal still grated. Precisely because he'd guessed she would refuse, he would have preferred to surprise her with the new pair of shoes, thereby avoiding an unnecessary conversation. Unfortunately, that was not an option, as he needed to take her measurements.

"Listen, it is not a question of money," he said, guessing that would be the reason behind her objection. "You're here to help my family, look after my nieces, help my sister-in-law, set my brother's mind at rest. That is priceless. The least I can do I ensure your comfort while you're doing it." This time Eahlswith didn't reply but she still looked unsure. He hated it. "Please, let me do this."

To his relief, she took the hand he was offering and jumped onto the ground. Then she obeyed his silent instructions to place her booted foot on the plank and didn't move when he traced the outline of it with the nail. Then he drew the other foot on the other side of the plank. With this, Bo would be able to make her a pair of shoes that would allow her to walk in the snow without getting wet. The ones she was wearing really were good for nothing, and they had still not completely dried. The new pair could not come quickly enough.

"Thank you, he said, standing back up.

"I think I should be the one thanking you."

"No. I won't be the one making the boots."

"You know very well that is not the issue here."

Yes. He did. Still. He would have done much more for her. "If it were up to me, I would also get you a new pair of stockings and gloves so this is nothing." She reddened when he nodded at the ones she was wearing. He could tell she was fighting the urge to hide her hands behind her back. "Don't think I haven't noticed that they, too, are worn out."

"Please. You have done enough for me already."

No. Whatever he did for her, it would never be enough. Sven forced himself to move and put the nail and plank back into his bag. It was either that or give her another kiss and he could tell that, this time, she might well push him away. The explicit rejection would be too hard to handle.

"Let's go. Cwenthryth will be waiting for you."

They climbed back on Gulltoppr and a moment later they were in front of his brother's hut. Sven handed Eahlswith down, enjoying the feel of her in his hands. What was it about her that set his blood on fire? She was hardly the first woman whose waist he had held...

"Come to find me tomorrow night. I'll give you the boots then."

He could have brought them to the hut, of course, but he guessed she would prefer it if no one knew he'd had them made for her, instead pretending they had been in her bag all along. After all, the two of them were not supposed to know one another. The way she nodded indicated he was right. She didn't want to be seen accepting a present from him.

"Thank you, Sven. For everything."

Everything. The boots and the night of passion.

The wind had picked up since they'd exited the forest and was now whipping tendrils of hair about her face. He reached to remove an inky strand from her eyes. If she had been his wife he would have suggested she braided it around the temples like the people in his village did.

His wife.

He swallowed as the idea exploded in his mind. It was not the first time he had imagined himself married, of course, but this time it felt just right, not merely like wishful thinking. With the other women, his reason had prevailed. It had told him that they could perhaps fulfil the role of wife. With Eahlswith, his Alva, his heart was doing the talking. And it was urging him not to give up until he'd made her his in all the ways a man could make a woman his.

The door opened, preventing him from doing or saying

anything else. Cwenthryth beamed when she saw that her friend had arrived. Despite her obvious delight, though, Sven did not miss the dark circles under her eyes. If they worried him, he could not imagine what his brother would think when he looked at his beloved wife. No wonder Steinar had arranged for her to have help while he was gone. She looked exhausted.

"I was about to go to the well," she said, indicating the bucket in her hand.

"I'll do that." Eahlswith immediately volunteered. "You go—"

"No, *I'll* do that. You two get back inside, where it's warm. I'll bring the bucket back in a moment, when I've seen to Gulltoppr."

"Thank you."

Sven barely repressed a snort. No one had thanked him more than this woman had today. But he didn't want her to thank him for bringing in water for her, making sure she had dry feet or even giving her pleasure in bed. Any man, anyone could do that. Instead, he wanted her to accept what was between them and agree to see what it could develop into. Unfortunately, she didn't seem ready to.

Well, at least, she was here for a few days. He would make sure to make the most of this unhoped for opportunity.

Eahlswith watched Sven walk away, Gulltoppr following him like a pup would. The two of them made a striking pair. The true Heimdallr and his golden-maned steed could surely not look more magnificent.

"I should have guessed Sven would go to the well for us. He's very thoughtful, like his two brothers," Cwenthryth told her, leading her into the hut. Indeed, the wind was bitterly cold and she was glad not to have to have to worry about filling the bucket. In this weather, she wouldn't be surprised if there was a layer of ice to break to access the water.

"Yes, it was thoughtful of him to offer to go to the well."

What else could she answer? He was thoughtful, generous and patient, undoubtedly. She should know. Another man would have pressured her into accepting what they both knew she felt by now, or at least tried to convince her that if she didn't want him to become part of her life, at least she could allow him access to her body. He had done neither and she was grateful for it.

"How come he brought you to the village?" her friend asked, closing the door behind them. "I thought Steinar would have."

"Apparently your husband ran into his brother as he was reaching the town gate and, as he wanted to get to the harbor to meet a Danish merchant, he asked him to bring me to you instead."

"Mm. What was Sven doing in town that early in the morning, I wonder?"

Eahlswith busied herself with putting her bag into a corner of the hut to avoid having to answer—and hide her face, which had likely gone bright red. What would Cwenthryth think if she realized he'd spent two days repairing Osbert's roof? She would, understandably, wonder what could have motivated him to help a man he didn't know and who was connected to a woman he'd seen only once in passing.

"Now. Tell me what I can do to help," she said, straightening her back. They had better get to the important part of this conversation and stop talking about Sven altogether. She was here to forget about him.

Cwenthryth let out a sigh. "Having someone to look after the girls while I get the sleep I need would be wonderful."

"I will do much more than that. You are not to cook a thing or see to the animals or go into the forest while I'm here, do you hear?" Her friend did look exhausted, but hopefully, it wouldn't take too long for her to recover if someone else did what needed to be done. "The only thing you'll be allowed to do is feed Liv and give Sanna motherly kisses when she needs them. This I cannot do for you."

"Oh!" To her horror, since she had only meant the comment as light-hearted, Cwenthryth burst into sobs.

"What is it? What have I said?" Eahlswith asked, taking her into her arms. Panic flooded her chest. Was there something she should know about the girls? Liv was sleeping in her cot but she hadn't seen little Sanna yet.

"You've always b-been here for me. You were there when I— When the— And now you're here with me again, but this time I have two beautiful babes with me and though I'm t-tired, it's too much joy f-for me to—"

Unable to carry on, Cwenthryth tightened her embrace.

Eahlswith held her, understanding what she was referring to. Her own eyes filled with tears at the memory. Three years ago, Cwenthryth had lost her unborn babe. That this baby had been the product of a rape had not lessened the shock of it, and the loss of blood had endangered her life. Eahlswith had been the one to find her on her bloodied pallet and then help her to deal with the whole mess.

It had been awful and it did feel good to now be able to help her deal with the very real joy of having two healthy little girls.

"Hush, you're exhausted and need to rest, that's all. You will feel better after a nap, I promise. I'm here. I will always be here. After what you endured, I am delighted to help you look after your children."

"Thank you. I'm so glad to have you here. I've missed living next to you."

"Yes, me too."

Though she knew Cwenthryth had found her place in the Norsemen village, it did mean that they didn't see one another as often as she would have liked. A thought flashed through

Eahlswith's mind. Could she come live here also? She stilled. Of course not. The only Saxons living here were the ones married to one of the inhabitants and she knew that would never be her, even if she did know a Norseman who might—

Enough. She had come here to forget about him, *not* to think about marriage!

Just then there was a brief knock on the door. As if he'd sensed she was thinking about him, Sven entered the hut, bucket in hand. He froze when he saw the two women in the middle of the hut, hugging one another and crying.

"What happened?"

He was instantly on alert, placing the bucket down and scanning the hut for the source of their distress. Had he been wearing a sword at his belt, it would be in his hand right now. The image sent shivers all the way down to her toes. Sven with a sword at the ready and a look of thunder in his eyes... Heimdallr, god of war, indeed. The man had the body of a warrior, even if she guessed he did not have an aggressive bone in that chiseled body. He would, however, be the first to jump to his family's defense when needed.

"Nothing happened, don't worry," Cwenthryth told him, wiping at her eyes. "I guess I'm just overwhelmed and need to sleep."

He nodded, looking somewhat reassured. "You do, Steinar told me as much this morning. What can I do to help?"

"Nothing, you've done more than enough by bringing Eahlswith to me. Thank you." She smiled at him. "And thank you for the water."

"'Twas nothing."

Eahlswith stole a glance at the bucket at his feet. As she'd guessed, floating on top of the water were shards of ice. Brr. A shiver went down her spine and she shuffled closer to the firepit. She hated the cold.

"Well, I'll leave you to it then."

Eahlswith inhaled when their gazes met, hers black as a moonless night, his clear as a sun-filled day. *Until the morrow*, he seemed to tell her.

Yes.

Her plan to forget about him was destined to fail. She was going to spend the next few days at the village, in constant danger of running into the very man she had hoped to avoid.

9

Motivated by the substantial price offered to him, Bo, the cobbler, worked diligently and Sven was able to present Eahlswith with the new boots when she came to find him the following evening.

"I'm embarrassed," she said, taking them with obvious reluctance. But he hadn't missed the light in her eyes at the sight of the beautiful pair. She loved them. Something in his chest warmed. It felt good to bring her joy.

"Don't be. There is snow everywhere, you needed new boots." She didn't contradict him, as that was undeniable. "If you really want to thank me, make sure that when my brother comes back he finds his wife looking her usual self."

Eahlswith nodded, as if relieved to have been given a way to repay his generosity. "She does look tired. But I'm here now." She nodded and clutched the boots to her chest. "I'd better go. I left all three girls sleeping in the hut and the pottage bubbling. I don't want it to spoil. Thank you. I do love the boots."

With those words, she hurried back to his brother's hut.

Sven took to wandering around the village in the hope he would walk into her by carefully contrived accident but it was another three days before he saw her again. In the end it was pure chance that he met with her.

He was gathering wood in the forest when he happened upon her.

Delight was instantly replaced by confusion. What in the name of Odin was the woman doing?

Basket in hand, Sven came to a halt at the edge of the clearing, making sure to stay hidden from view so as to observe her. Eahlswith was standing under a snow-covered beech, her face raised to the skies. He watched, bemused, as she reached for the branch above her head and gave two tugs in quick succession. A shower of glimmering powder fell over her, dissolving like dust into the air. She laughed, the sound as crystalline as the flakes whirling around her, adorning her cloak with their diamond-like brilliance. It was a perfect vision of beauty and innocence, like her. His Alva. Never had she deserved the name more.

Before he knew it, he'd walked over to the beech.

At the sound of his crunching footsteps, she turned around, the laughter getting stuck in her throat when she saw that she was not alone. Or perhaps because she had recognized him, the man she was going out of her way to avoid.

"Sven." She sounded slightly out of breath, like someone caught doing something illicit—or a lover recovering from an intense release.

He stopped in front of her, utterly entranced, and put his basket down on the ground. She was breathtakingly beautiful and wet all over. Her inky black hair was sprinkled with rapidly melting snowflakes that glittered in the pale morning light. Her skin was damp, her eyelashes dotted with tiny droplets of water that clung to their silken ends.

"What are you doing here at this hour?" he asked, his voice raw with desire. If he kissed her now her lips would feel cool and taste as sharp as freshly fallen snow. The temptation was hard to resist. Perhaps he should have left her to her games and carried on gathering kindling for the fire.

"I was up for the best part of the night with little Liv and I found it hard to go back to sleep. So I didn't and went for a walk instead, leaving everyone to rest."

"I hope you are getting enough sleep?"

It wouldn't do for her to sport the dark circles that had started to disappear from beneath Cwenthryth's eyes. That had not been the plan. But she did look like a picture of health that morning.

"I'm fine, don't worry. It won't be too long before Steinar is back anyway."

No, unfortunately not.

He nodded at the boots peeking under her skirt. "How do they fit?"

"They're perfect," she answered, pleasure making her cheeks go the color of a wild rose again. So lovely. "With them, I didn't hesitate to come into the forest."

"So that you could shake snow all over you?" he teased, nodding at the branch she had just shaken.

The color on her cheeks deepened. "I couldn't resist. We used to love walking in the forest and getting drenched in powdery snow. It is a wonderful feeling."

Who was this mysterious person with whom she loved to get lost in the forest? "Who's we?" he asked, doing his best not to let his jealousy peak through.

Eahlswith winced, like someone regretting her words. Evidently, she hadn't meant to mention someone else, which only increased his curiosity further. Edwin. The name flashed through his mind and he knew he would have to ask her about him. She had told him she was not involved with anyone but it was clear that she had been at some point.

"My...friends and I. As girls we used to roam the woods. In

the winter we liked to get covered in snow. I haven't done this for more than ten years." Her eyes sparkled again. "I'll tell you what I haven't done in years either. Eat some freshly fallen snow. In town, it is best avoided."

Yes, in towns snow landed on all manners of filth you wouldn't want anywhere near your mouth. But out here in the forest it was as pure as it could be, white and unspoiled. In fact people often melted it to drink, a much safer source of water than ponds and even rivers.

"I did that too, as a child," he admitted. Feeling like a boy of ten again, Sven bent down and gathered a handful of immaculate snow from the padding covering the boulder by his side. "Shall we? Feel young and innocent again? I dare you."

He should have known Eahlswith would not be one to eschew a challenge. She scooped the top layer from the blanket of snow at her feet and cradled the precious flakes in her palm. Sven had to avert his eyes when she stuck out her tongue to lap at them with obvious delight. In that moment he felt nothing like an innocent ten-year-old boy, but definitely like the fully-grown, virile man he was. Never once had he thought he would regret not being made out of snow.

With more determination than grace, he crammed the snow he was holding into his mouth, hoping it would help cool his blood. The tiny crystals dissolved on his tongue, filling his mouth with a spoonful of liquid he quickly swallowed. The taste, slightly metallic, for want of a better word, had not changed in all those years, and he couldn't repress a smile. He should do that more often.

When he dared to look up at Eahlswith he saw that the melted snow had left a droplet of water at the corner of her lips.

"Allow me."

Before she could refuse or even guess what he was about, he reached to wipe it off with his thumb. She stilled, and watched while he brought the hand to his mouth to lick the drop. His cock jerked when his tongue made contact with the pad of his thumb. He wanted *her* to lick it, to lick every part of him. He could not forget the feel of her lips on his skin when she'd explored his body that first night, licking him all over before focusing on his cock. Her teeth, playful when she had nipped at his inner thighs, her tongue, soft when she had licked him like the most delicious treat, her throat, tight and hot when she had taken him to the root. Never had he allowed himself to spend in a woman's mouth before but with her it had been impossible not to. He had been so aroused by the notion that he'd remained hard enough to show her his appreciation afterward, lifting her onto his lap and making her ride him.

A shuffling noise overhead cut through the lewd memory.

"Oh, look, a wren," he said, a desperate attempt at distraction. He had to steer his mind away from thoughts of Eahlswith suckling the part of his body currently threatening to escape from his braies. Thank the gods it was winter and he was wearing a cloak. If he managed to keep his face impassive she would not suspect he was ready to burst.

Eahlswith turned her head so sharply the little bird took fright and disappeared in a flurry of feathers, leaving a trail of glimmering dust behind him as he wove through the maze of branches.

Sven expected Eahlswith to bemoan the lost opportunity. She didn't. Instead she paled, so much that her cheeks became almost the color of snow.

"I hope Steinar will be here soon," she said, looking at her feet. "I won't be able to stay much longer."

Sven's stomach fell. Why was she telling him that now, when they were sharing a moment that could only have been called intimate and pleasurable? There was no need to remind him that she was only here temporarily, unfortunately he knew it all too well. With Steinar not back home yet, she was still needed at the village, and anyway, Cwenthryth would not turn her out the moment her husband came back. Eahlswith wouldn't *have* to leave, she merely wanted to escape him, as she always did.

Why? What was he doing wrong? He didn't understand. At times she seemed to respond to his advances. They had been laughing together just now, sharing stories from her childhood. She had welcomed him back into her bed the other day. And yet every time he thought he was making progress, for no reason that he could discern, she drew away and fled like the startled little wren had just now. It was exhausting.

"I have to go. Cwenthryth will be waiting for me," she breathed.

Another excuse. Only a moment ago she'd told him her friend was asleep. He took her by the wrist before she could turn away.

"Before you go, I have one question." Taking her silence for a permission to ask it, he took in a deep breath and asked what that had been torturing him for days. "Who is Edwin?"

EAHLSWITH STARED at Sven for a long, agonized moment. He'd asked her the last question she'd expected him to ask and he'd mentioned the last person she wanted him to mention.

How on earth did he know about Edwin anyway?

She started to panic. *How* did he know? Had Cwenthryth mentioned him to Steinar who, in turn, had told his brother?

And then she remembered. Sven had pretended not to speak their language when she and Osbert were talking while he'd repaired the roof, but, of course, he had understood everything. And the old man had mentioned Edwin while they ate their soup that first night. She had managed to cut him short by spilling soup on her dress, so she had hoped that Sven would not have thought the name of any particular interest.

Obviously she'd been wrong.

"Osbert's son," she said as calmly as she could while she disentangled her wrist from his hold. His fingers were warmer than they had the right to be, considering that he was not wearing gloves and only a moment ago he'd been handling snow.

"Yes, I thought he might be. I mean, who is he to you?"

No one. Not anymore.

"He's...dead."

She turned to hide the tears that had sprung to her eyes at the terrible words. A moment later, she felt Sven's arms wrap around her and she didn't even think of pulling away. It felt too good. Eahlswith melted into the embrace and drew from his warmth and strength. After a while she was able to speak again.

"Why are you asking me this?"

"The first night I stayed in your house, you dreamed about him," he said in her ear. "You clung to me and kept saying I was back. Obviously, you'd mistaken me for him and I didn't have the heart to contradict you or wake you up. I held you and you fell back to sleep. You don't remember?"

Oh, she did remember. She'd had that exact same dream many times over the years. But usually, she ended up waking up to her own screams, not falling back to sleep in a man's embrace. She also remembered the sense of peace she had felt in the morning, as if she'd finally been granted absolution. Sven had done that for her? He had heard her call out for another man and yet he had comforted her? She wasn't sure what to think, except that it was one of the nicest things anyone had ever done for her.

"That's why I thought he might be your lover, someone you'd

had an argument with and wanted back," he carried on, keeping his hold tight around her.

She nodded slowly. If he'd thought she had a lover it would explain why he had asked her if she was free to be with him that second night in her house when he'd been poised at her entrance. He had not had any reason to think she had someone else in her life in the summer but after hearing her call out to Edwin in her sleep, he'd wanted to make sure he wasn't about to take a woman who was involved with another man.

He was as honorable as she'd suspected.

"No. Well, yes, he was my lover but he... It was more than that. He was supposed to be my husband."

She could tell from Sven's sudden stillness that she had rendered him speechless.

"Do you want to tell me about him?"

"Do *you* want me to tell you about him?" she countered. Why would he? Weren't men supposed to be jealous of other men? Didn't they prefer to pretend the woman they were bedding hadn't had anyone before them even if they knew it was not the case?

Sven had the honesty not to hide his discomfort but he met her gaze without flinching. "I will listen if you think it would help you."

It didn't take her long to see that it would. Odd as it was, she wanted to tell Sven about her lost love. "I think it would."

He took her hand in his. "Come then. Let's take a walk."

10

A walk had been the perfect suggestion. As they went deeper and deeper into the forest, Eahlswith found herself telling Sven everything about Edwin. Why, she wasn't sure. Perhaps because he was listening attentively, and his face betrayed no annoyance or frustration. Perhaps because she relished the chance to talk about the man she had never quite stopped loving. Perhaps because with the snowy world wrapping them in a silent cocoon, everything seemed unreal anyway, as if for a little while they were in a bubble of peace suspended above reality.

"I arrived in town five years ago, at the age of twenty, having decided to leave my native village for good." There she paused, not wanting to reveal the reason why. It was a painful topic and it had nothing to do with Edwin himself so there was no point mentioning it. Would Sven sense she was hiding something and ask her anyway?

To her relief, he didn't comment, even if she could tell he'd guessed some part of the story was missing.

She carried on. "At first I didn't know anyone, as you can imagine. The first few days were hard but I had been lucky enough to strike a friendship with a group of laundresses I had met at the river upon my arrival in town. Realizing that I had nowhere to live, they let me sleep in the room they used to boil the laundry at night. After about a week, I met Osbert. He saw me one day at the market, trying to convince the fishmonger to give me the crumbs of salted fish at the bottom of his barrel. He deduced from this that I had little, if no means of subsistence and he offered to house me until I found one. Though I had no way of knowing whether I could trust him or not, I agreed."

It was inexplicable and perhaps foolish, but she had known instantly that she had nothing to fear from the old man. In the same way, she had known as soon as she had seen Sven in the summer that she could act on the desire he stirred in her without fear of being hurt. And she had known just as clearly as soon as she had met Wiglaf that he was best avoided.

But what had happened with him was precisely what she didn't want to think about.

"I'm not surprised you accepted Osbert's kind offer. The man is as trustworthy as any I've ever met." Sven said, echoing her thoughts. "The fact alone that he wanted to help you says a lot about him."

"Exactly. Perhaps it was that he reminded me of my father, who had died not so long before that made me trust him. I know not. In any case, that night he brought me to his home. His son was there."

With those words, Eahlswith was instantly transported back in time. From the moment she had entered that house, her life had been irremediably changed.

Edwin had been tall for a Saxon, almost as tall as Sven, his hair slightly darker, his body slightly leaner. But he'd had the same masculine appeal, something that called to the part of her that made her a woman. As soon as she had seen the smiling young man welcoming her in, she'd fallen in love.

The feeling had not been dissimilar to what she had felt when she had seen Sven standing outside his hut back in the summer. Except that, since he had been bare-chested at the time, some might say she had fallen in lust, not love. Perhaps. But it mattered not. It had been the same immediate reaction, visceral. She had been struck by the knowledge that the person in front of her had a role to play in her life. Whether it was for one night or for the rest of her days was inconsequential.

Sven threw her a sideways glance and she was reminded that he was still waiting for the rest of the story.

"The two men lived together in the house you know, Osbert's wife having died the previous year and the other children having moved out. They helped me find a way to provide for myself and get a home. About a month after I'd met them, I moved into the house I live in now. Edwin kissed me for the first time that evening." She paused, lost in memory of that moment. It had been a sweet kiss, quickly followed by other, more passionate ones. "I think he felt too ill-at-ease to try anything while we were staying with his father."

Indeed, though physically there had been a certain resemblance between them, Edwin had been nowhere near as self-assured, as commanding as the Norseman currently walking next to her, especially where women were concerned. It might have been due to his age. Edwin had only been one-and-twenty at the time, a year older than her. Whatever the reason for it, he'd been shy. Though it had been obvious he desired her, it had taken him days to build up the courage to kiss her. He would never have invited her into his home mere moments after locking eyes with her or buried his head under his skirt as soon as he'd closed the door behind him.

Their lovemaking had been wonderful, but she would not have described it as wild. More as sweet and gentle. She had been his first conquest, and he hers, even if she had already kissed a handful of other men. It had been wonderful, nothing like her laundress friends described. If they were to be believed, men were only interested in their own pleasure and rutted like animals. Edwin had been nothing like that.

"He was your first lover, and showed you what pleasure could be had between a man and a woman."

As ever, Sven was following her thoughts. He didn't sound accusatory but all the same, he didn't doubt that he was right. Of course, he would have felt she was no virgin when he had possessed her and her behavior that day had not been that of an innocent. She had responded to his silent invitation, something an untouched woman might not have done, and afterward in his arms, she had shown no inhibition, exploring every inch of his body, doing to him what she had only ever dared do to Edwin.

"Yes. It wasn't long before we agreed to get married and we didn't see why we should wait until the actual wedding to share a bed. As he wanted his brothers and sisters to attend the ceremony, and they lived quite far away, that would have meant waiting for weeks. We loved one another, we saw no reason to deny ourselves the pleasure we needed."

Once again, Sven merely nodded. He clearly agreed.

"What happened to him?" So he'd guessed the wedding had never taken place. Not that it was hard. Her grim tone was hinting at a catastrophe.

Eahlswith came to halt and swallowed, as familiar guilt stabbed at her chest. How would she bear to say out loud what had happened? Knowing that there was no way to soften the blow, she delivered it in one blunt sentence.

"He was killed, less than a week before our wedding."

As if uttering the dreadful words had sapped her of all her strength, she collapsed on the fallen tree behind her and stared at her hands.

Yes, he had been killed, but that was not all. It had been her fault that Edwin had died, and no one knew it. She'd had to live with that awful burden all these years, pretending she wasn't responsible for his death. Even Cwenthryth, her closest friend, didn't know that part of the story. She knew what had happened to him, but not why. No one knew why. Least of all his poor father, who would hate her if he knew.

"He was killed…because of me."

And just like that, sobs started to rack through her body.

Sven allowed her to cry for a moment, then knelt in front of her, his face full of compassion. "I'm sorry, I didn't mean to upset you. If you don't want to talk about it, I'll understand."

Did she want to talk about it or not? Eahlswith didn't know. On the one hand, saying the words out loud at last could help her. On the other, knowing what had happened might make Sven see her differently.

Well, that was what she wanted, was it not? A way to fight the feelings he stirred in her? This seemed like an ideal solution. If he agreed that she had been unforgivably selfish, he would not want to have anything to do with her. It would make the task of keeping him at bay easier. And if her heart broke as a result of his rejection, then it was no more than she deserved for causing the death of a good man.

She took a deep breath and started to talk.

"One evening, as we lay in bed, I told Edwin about a carving my father had made on the door frame of our home." Had she known that this innocent comment would end up costing him his life, she would have cut off her tongue. "I told him that I had loved it from a young age and wished I could have taken it with me when I left, as it was the only thing I had that reminded me of my father."

It had not been an option at the time. Not only had she left in a hurry, barely taking the time to assemble a few essentials in a bag, but the carving was an integral part of the house. It would have taken more skill than she possessed to remove it. But Edwin had insisted that with the proper tools and some patience, he could probably lift it from the door frame. It had quickly become an obsession. He wanted her to have the one thing that reminded her of the father she dearly missed before she started her life as a married woman.

"He decided to go and get it before our wedding. I had twisted my ankle a few days previously and couldn't ride so I begged him to wait until a more propitious moment, when we could go together but he was determined I should have it in time for the ceremony. So, one morning, he left."

Eahlswith had often wondered what she would have done differently that morning if she had known he was riding to his death. Would she have made their last kiss more passionate? Would she have assured him that she would always love him? Would she have draped herself over him in bed and begged him not to go?

She had done none of those things. Silly her, she had assumed that they had their whole lives ahead of them and that there would be time for passionate kisses, heartfelt declarations and loving embraces when he came back. She had kissed him as she always did and watched him mount his gelding with her usual calm, never suspecting that this was the last glimpse she would ever get of him.

There had been no grim squeaking of a crow, no old soothsayer warning her of the terrible grief awaiting her, nothing.

"Osbert and I waited for days for his return. At first we didn't get worried, knowing it would take him at least four days to get to the village and back. But when four days turned into five, then six, I understood that something had gone wrong. The wedding was planned for the following day, and his sisters and brothers had all arrived by then. Considering the effort it had taken them to attend, I knew Edwin would have made sure he didn't miss the ceremony. It was impossible that he—"

She stopped as her throat had gone too tight to allow her to carry on.

"He was attacked on the road?" Sven said after a while. She nodded. Unfortunately, the story was too common for him not to have guessed.

"The day we were supposed to get married, a man came to the door to tell us what had happened to him. Edwin had been found in a ditch just outside my village. He'd been stabbed trying to stop three men from stealing his horse and he was dying. As he lay wounded, knowing he wouldn't survive his injuries, he begged the man who'd found him to go tell his father what had happened to him. And tell me, the wife he would never have...that he would always love me. Though it was a considerable journey, the man agreed to grant him this last wish, as he'd recognized my name as one of the former inhabitants of the village."

Tears were now flowing freely down her cheeks. The night that should have been her wedding night, she'd thought that she had shed all the tears that she was capable of shedding, alone in her pallet. She'd soon discovered that despair was a bottomless pit and that she would never stop crying over the loss of the love of her life.

"It was all my fault, you see," she said on a sob. "He'd gone to the village for me. If I hadn't told him about the carving, he would never have gone—"

"It's not your fault," Sven cut in. "You did nothing wrong by confiding in him about something you loved, and that meant a lot to you. That's what lovers do. And people are allowed to come and go as they please. That Edwin was traveling alone did not make it acceptable for anyone to attack him, steal his horse, stab him or anything else. That he had chosen to go to your village did not mean he should have died for it."

"Maybe not. But he did die. Can you imagine how that makes me feel?"

"No," he said with brutal sincerity. "I cannot begin to imagine the depth of your pain. No one can. Only you can know. But I can tell you, and repeat it as often as you need to hear it, that you did nothing wrong and that his death is not your fault."

There was such earnestness in his voice that somehow, she found herself believing it. Eahlswith took a deep inhale. Maybe today would mark the first step toward acceptance.

"Thank you."

Sven made a face she had difficulty interpreting. It was almost as if he would have preferred her not to thank him.

"Is that why you take such good care of Osbert?" he asked softly. "Because you feel guilty?"

Once again, he had read her mind. She did feel as if she had robbed him of his youngest son and wanted to compensate for that loss. "I feel genuine affection for him. He helped me when I needed it, and I would have wanted to look after him no matter what." Her voice wobbled. "But yes, I feel that without me, he would still have his son and the least I can do is do what I can to make him comfortable."

Sven's heart almost broke when Eahlswith looked up to the skies and inhaled deeply, doing what she could to compose herself. Her courage was inspiring.

He waited, knowing she would eventually calm down. Once she had herself under control, she dabbed at her face self-consciously. "Forgive me. I must look hideous."

Hideous? He barely repressed a scoff. Did she have no idea how dazzling she was? He wiped at her cheek slowly. "Believe me, you couldn't be hideous if you tried. You've been crying, which is not the same thing at all."

"Thank you, Sven."

Here she was, thanking him again, for doing nothing more than what anyone of sense would have done. He gave her a tight smile. "What are you thanking me for now?"

"For listening to me. For being here. For being you."

Oh. No one had thanked him for being him before. Perhaps he could make his peace with her endless gratitude if she were praising his character.

"It's no problem. Shall we?"

Their talk had taken them further from the village than he'd thought and he wouldn't be surprised if it didn't start snowing soon. They had better start going back.

They walked in silence for a while, then suddenly Eahlswith came to a stop.

"Look, someone's carved a moon, a sun and two stars in the tree," she told him, placing a hand on a mighty oak.

Upon closer inspection Sven saw that the moon appeared much older than the other three images, the layer revealed by the cut on the bark a different color.

"Ah, so this is it..." he said, delighted to have found it at last.

"What is what?"

"My sister Eyja told me a few years ago that she and her husband, Halfdan, whom everyone calls Moon, had carved a tree with such images but she refused to tell me where it was. Though I was curious to see it, as you can imagine, I didn't even try to find it."

In the middle of the forest, so far from the village, it would have taken him forever. He and Eahlswith had only seen it because their walk—and their talk—had taken them further than villagers went on a normal day. He was grateful to her for allowing him to see it.

"'Tis beautiful," Eahlswith said, stroking the radiant sun with a light finger.

"Yes. Apparently, they add a star for each of their children," he explained, showing the two stars flanking the moon. One for Emma, one for Frida. Mayhap more would follow. It wouldn't surprise him. The two of them were deliriously happy together, like every couple in his family. It struck him then that he was the only one without anyone special in his life.

Or at least, not someone he'd acknowledged publicly.

"What a wonderful idea," Eahlswith murmured. "A testimony of their love that will stand the test of time."

It was exactly that. Which gave him an idea. Reaching down to his boot, Sven extracted the dagger he always carried and held it out to Eahlswith.

"Do the same," he instructed her when she looked at him with an arched brow. "Choose a tree, and carve something like your father once carved the door frame for you, something that will stand the test of time and serve as a reminder of your love for Edwin."

For the longest moment she didn't move, didn't say anything. He thought that she might refuse, or even throw the knife in his face. Then slowly, she extended her hand and allowed him to place the dagger hilt in her palm.

He nodded and showed her a clump of bushes to his left.

"Take your time. I'll wait for you behind there. I promise I won't look. This is between you and Edwin only."

While he waited, Sven reflected on what Eahlswith had told him that day. Now he understood better where her reluctance to accept what was between them came from. Deep down, she was still in love with Edwin, the man she had wanted to marry and she didn't feel she had the right to betray his memory, didn't feel she deserved happiness. Something in his chest tightened. If that were the case, then wooing her would be even more difficult than he had feared.

It didn't take her long to join him. It was obvious she had

cried again, but she seemed at peace, as if it had helped her to leave a trace of what she and Edwin had once felt for one another.

Without a word, she handed him the dagger back. He replaced it in his boot and nodded toward the village. They didn't exchange a single word while they walked, but when he left her in front of Steinar's hut, he could have sworn something had changed within her.

Hope swelled within Sven.

Perhaps wooing her was not such an impossibility after all.

11

Sven moaned, trying to shake the torpor from his body and the last vestiges of sleep from his mind.

Unless he was having the most realistic dream of his life, someone's hand had taken possession of his cock. The hand gave a squeeze. No, he was not mistaken. Someone was indeed holding his cock, and stroking it. A woman. There was no mistaking the softness of the fingers and the gentleness of the grip. In any case, he couldn't think of a single man who might want to sneak into his hut and stroke him so intimately.

Whereas there was one woman who might want more of what he could give her.

Eahlswith.

He'd thought something had changed that morning. Was that what he had seen in her eyes? The decision to come find him in bed? His groin caught on fire at the thought. Finally, after their discussion, she had come to see that she didn't have to fight the attraction between them, that she could let go of her guilt and give the two of them a chance.

How long had she been in his bed, stroking him? He was hard so he guessed she had not just arrived, but had been here long enough to coax his limp member to tempered steel. He moaned, delight and anticipation flooding his veins. Should he let her finish what she had so boldly started? There was not much risk. Even if she brought him to release, the idea that she was finally acting on her desire for him would ensure he was hard again in moments, ready to take her. And in the meantime, he could return the favor and pleasure her.

Yes. That was what he would do. Her caresses felt too good for him to ask her to stop anyway.

When he opened his eyes, intent on enjoying the sight of her worshipping his cock, he didn't see anything. It was too dark in the hut and Eahlswith had brought her head down, her intentions clear. Except that the hair brushing against his stomach glowed in the moonlight, instead of blending into the shadows.

He bolted upright, too late to avoid the heat of a tongue on the head of his shaft.

"What the hell!" Scuttling away as fast as the tangled blankets would allow, he stared at the woman whose face he still couldn't see. The woman who'd been about to pleasure him intimately. "Who are you?"

Not Eahlswith, for sure, whose hair was as black as the surrounding darkness. Eahlswith, who would never have come to his bed uninvited. Of course, she had not. He really was a fool for thinking she might have done so.

The woman raised her head just when a moonbeam pierced through the window. And then he did see her. Very clearly.

"Freydis?"

He had bedded her for a few days two years ago, and had hoped to build something with her. But then she had left for Denmark, not having thought it necessary to tell him she'd decided to leave months before they started sleeping together. It had stung but, as he'd thought never to see her again, he had overcome his disillusion. And now, here she was, apparently ready to resume their affair as if nothing had happened.

"Sven." She beamed at him. "I've missed you. Did you miss me?"

Her naughty smile wavered when she saw that his shaft, rock hard a moment ago, was now too limp to stand straight. It wouldn't be long before it was completely soft.

"Does this answer your question?" he asked, nodding at it.

Her face fell. Admittedly, he'd been very blunt but really... What did she think she was doing, sneaking into his bed and taking possession of his cock without even letting him know that she was back?

"There was a time when me using my mouth pleased you," she whispered, looking rather stricken.

"Yes. But that was before you left without warning."

Even in the dark it was obvious that she'd paled. Sven sighed. Evidently she had no idea she had hurt him when she'd left. He had the honesty of acknowledging that she had not broken his heart, claiming so would be a gross exaggeration. But he had liked her, and he would have liked to be given a chance to see how things could evolve between them. Except that now she was back and she wanted him, he didn't care.

There was another woman he wanted in his life.

"I did leave, but Denmark was not what I had hoped for, so I came back," she said unnecessarily. He could see that she was here. "And I thought we could—"

"No, we can't." He would not allow any room for hope. She needed to know where things stood. "In fact, you need to leave now. But I promise we'll discuss this later."

Without knowing quite why, he couldn't bear the idea of Freydis being in his hut. At least she was still dressed so he wouldn't have to wait until she put her clothes back on. Not bothering to cover himself since she had seen his naked body countless times, he walked over to the door, opened it, and signaled that he was waiting for her to walk out.

At first, Freydis didn't move. Then, seeing there would be no swaying him, she reluctantly rose to her feet. She didn't make a scene, which he appreciated. Perhaps there would be a dignified way to end this. It had been a misunderstanding, nothing more.

"Go back home. I'll see you tomorrow and we'll..." he said, his voice quickly dying in his throat.

Standing in front of the hut was Eahlswith, her eyes huge with shock.

Fuck. Fuck. Fuck.

Oh, I'm so, so, so stupid!

Eahlswith could have kicked herself. To think she'd actually slipped out of Cwenthryth's hut in the middle of the night to go find Sven in bed in spite of her best judgment... And while she'd been tossing and turning, battling her conscience, wondering whether she could allow herself to see what could become of her feelings for this man, he'd been bedding another woman. It was so pathetically predictable that she wanted to scream. What an utter, utter fool she'd been.

There was nothing else to do but leave.

Sven's voice sliced through the predawn gray light. "Alva, wait!"

Wait? Was he serious? Did he really think she would want to listen to him now, when another woman's scent was still on him? She didn't start running, turn her head or slow down. She didn't indicate that she had heard him in any way. Let him come after her naked if he dared, she would not even dignify him with an answer.

There was a frightful curse in Norse and Eahlswith thought

for a moment that she had won, and he'd given up. This victory, if victory it was, left her hollow.

A moment later, however, she understood that he had not given up. He'd only taken the time to cover himself before setting after her like a wolf after his prey. Before she could pick up her pace, a hand closed around her elbow, stopping her retreat.

"Don't touch me!" she snarled. She, too, could bear a resemblance to a wild animal if need be.

Sven let go of her instantly, his attitude unusually earnest. "Alva, please—"

"I told you not to use this name!" Not now, not when she was already fighting tears. She didn't want to be reminded that he was the only person other than Edwin who had given her a special name.

Seeing that there would be no escaping him, she turned to face him.

Dear Heavens, despite the freezing weather, he was barechested, bare-legged and barefoot. The only piece of clothing he was wearing, if one could call it that, was a piece of fur wrapped around his loins. It was a sight to behold, one of pure decadence and savagery, utterly dangerous, an attack on her womanly senses and a challenge to her reason.

Under her cloak, she shivered. His bare feet were half buried in the powdery snow and his hair was already crowned with tiny snowflakes. Forget Heimdallr, at the moment he was the very image of the god of the cold and darkness. Höðr, was it? Right now she struggled to remember.

"So, who is she?" she asked, lifting her chin. His beauty would not be allowed to sway her in any way. She was angry, she reminded herself, she had every reason to be. Instead of ogling him, she should make him feel guilty for hurting her.

To her relief he didn't even pretend he had no idea who she

was talking about. "Her name is Freydis. But I swear I had no idea she was in my bed. I was sleeping and I woke—"

"No idea? You were naked!" He still was, more or less.

"I always sleep naked. You of all people should know that."

She did know that. But she had forgotten. In any case, that was not the issue right now. "I heard you tell her that you would go to see her tomorrow," she accused. Surely he wouldn't deny that?

"I do want to see her." Once again he did not even try to lie. "Because I want to talk about what she did, make her understand that I'm not available anymore. She thought I might be, which is why she came to me. But she needs to be told in no uncertain terms that I'm not and I didn't want to do that while I was naked and angry at her presumption."

Her heart missed a beat. There was such earnestness in his voice that she could not help wanting to believe him. Despite herself, she was impressed by his attitude. He was not trying to pretend she had misread the situation or minimize what had happened. He was even doing his best not to place any blame on Freydis. What if it really had been a misunderstanding?

"Did you—"

"Eahlswith. I'm sorry but could we please do this inside?" He glanced at his feet. No doubt his toes would have lost all feeling by now. "I promise I will answer all the questions you have but, to be perfectly honest, I can't feel my feet. Or my fingers. Or my… nose."

She blushed. He'd said nose but he'd meant cock, she was sure of it. Oddly his effort at politeness caused something in her chest to melt.

Would it serve any purpose to let him freeze to death? No. She wouldn't even derive any satisfaction from it. Besides, she wanted answers because she was starting to suspect she might have jumped to conclusions and this was not as bad she had first thought.

"Let's go back in," she said, nodding toward the hut.

Relief seemed to sweep over Sven, as much because she'd accepted to listen to him as at the prospect of going back to the warm interior. "Thank you."

Eahlswith led the way, not sure she wanted to look at him just yet.

Once he'd closed the door behind them, Sven put on his shirt, braies and boots faster than anyone she had ever seen. Then he threw two medium-sized logs into the fire and crouched down to warm his hands over the flames.

Refusing to feel guilty for causing him discomfort, Eahlswith waited. Eventually, he spoke.

"The woman you saw is Freydis, as I told you. She was born in the village, like me. We dallied a few months ago."

A few. What did he mean by that? Eahlswith's heart skipped a beat. Four or five?

"Please tell me you weren't seeing her in the summer when I… When we—"

"No. I say a few months, but it's been more like two years. Long before I met you, she left for Denmark, putting an end to what had been between us."

Two years. Yes. She could live with that, even if she suspected he'd had other lovers since.

"I'm not sure she would agree that what was between you is over. She's obviously back for more."

Only women who wanted to sleep with men thought of slipping into their beds at night. Eahlswith should know, as that was exactly what she had planned to do herself. Shame flooded her. *What* had she been thinking? This was not like her. She was not a wanton!

"Yes, it would indeed seem that she is back for more." Sven

ran a hand through his hair, looking as sheepish as a man of his stature could do. This alone would have convinced her he was telling the truth. A guilty man would brazen this out, tell her she was imagining things. But he was admitting that she was not. "But she won't be getting it."

"Why not?" Eahlswith asked with sudden, uncharacteristic ferocity. Why should he not give in to temptation, considering she was fighting the attraction between them and not giving him what he wanted? No one would blame him, not even herself, for bedding a willing woman when they had not promised anything one to the other.

But the idea of Sven in bed with a beautiful, lithe Norsewoman who was her opposite in every way had torn at her heart. Stupidly, she'd thought she would have time to deal with her confused feelings and come up with a decision before he moved on to his next conquest. Now she was being shown that she didn't have that luxury. If she didn't want him, there were plenty of women who did.

It was only a matter of time before she lost what little advantage she'd had.

"If you once wanted her and she still wants you," she forced herself to say, "then what is stopping you now from—"

He straightened back up and silenced her with a murderous glare.

"Don't even say it. Don't say that I don't owe you anything, because all we're doing is fucking." He sounded dangerous, on the edge of an outburst that would reduce her to cinders. "Oh, Alva, how can you even ask me this? How do you not see what we have, what we could have? Is a hard fuck all you want from me, just like all the others?"

She wavered at the harsh words but managed to murmur. "I... I told you not to call me Alva."

"And I asked you a question. Answer me."

She saw the vulnerability in his eyes, the hurt she had caused him, and she hated it. He really thought she was only after his body and the pleasure it could give her, that she cared nothing for his feelings. That was not true. She cared, too much. That was the problem.

"No. That's not all I want from you."

Despite the assurance, he shook his head, like a man defeated. "But it is. Don't you see? You certainly don't want to get involved with me. After our discussion yesterday I even understand why. But you having good reasons to be wary of intimacy doesn't change facts. I thought you didn't want anything more from me because of who I was and it stung. Now I know you cannot accept what I want to give you because of what you feel toward another. It is not quite the same, I'll admit, and yet it makes no difference to me, because I actually want to try and build something with you."

What could she say to that? He was absolutely right. She was not yet ready to accept that she could have with someone else what she'd once thought to have with the first man she had ever loved—and who'd died through her fault. She didn't feel she deserved a second chance at a good life. Her reasons for keeping Sven at bay mattered not, for him the result was the same. Her doubts meant that they could not build anything together.

"Give me time, please," she whispered, unable to meet his gaze.

Time.

Sven almost scoffed at the request. They had already lost half a year, what more did Eahlswith want? He didn't need another season, much less another week to know this was the woman he wanted to be with. Hell, he didn't need another day, and yet he would have to agree. There was no other choice because refusing would only push her further away. If there was a chance she would ever accept that she could be with another man, even a slim one, he had to wait for it.

"Yes," he said through gritted teeth. "I will give you time."

Feeling more dejected than ever, he helped himself to a cup of ale. The cold of the snow had finally left his limbs but there was a strange emptiness in his chest preventing him from being comfortable, and no wonder. He was being denied what he most dearly wanted.

Again.

"What were you doing outside my hut at this hour, anyway?" he asked as he emptied the last drop of ale. It had been very early for a visit, which roused his suspicions. Except to come get her boots, she had not visited him once since she'd arrived.

Eahlswith flushed a violent red and avoided his gaze. Heat flared inside him, chasing away the last vestiges of ice in his veins because suddenly he knew. She had come to bed him. He *had* been right that morning, after all. Something had changed within her. She might not be ready to welcome him in her life, but she had at least come to acknowledge the desire burning between them. It was a start, better than nothing.

His fingers tightened around the cup. Had Freydis not chosen this night to try to renew their relationship, he would be buried deep inside Eahlswith's heat right now, giving her the only thing she was ready to accept from him at the moment—pleasure.

How unlucky could one get?

Because now the moment had passed, might never present itself again. The one time she had found the courage to act on her desire, she had seen him naked, in bed with another woman. It seemed that she had accepted his explanation that nothing had happened, but it mattered not. He could tell she would not risk doing such a brazen thing again, which he understood.

Damn it all.

"I think you know why I came," Eahlswith said in a breath. "But I see now that I shouldn't have."

"Fuck, Alva, how can you even say that?"

The moment he used the name he had invented for her he knew it had been a mistake. He was doing the one thing she had asked him not to do. But he couldn't seem to help it. She was Eahlswith to everyone else, and Alva, to him only. He liked it, liked that he had something of her no one else had.

She stood up. "I will leave you now."

He didn't answer. What was there to say?

Yes, she was leaving. As usual.

12

"Could you open the door for me please?" Cwenthryth called out from the corner of the hut. She was fastening her dress back up after having fed her daughter. "I'm afraid 'tis not quite the right moment for me to do so."

"Of course." Pleased to hear the laughter which indicated that her friend was well and truly back to her usual happy self, Eahlswith went to the door.

The woman waiting outside stilled when she saw who had opened to her.

"Forgive me, but I was told that there was a Saxon healer living in this hut," she started, visibly ill at ease.

"There is but it's not—"

"Yes. I would understand if you didn't want to see me."

Eahlswith was more confused than ever. Why would she refuse to see the woman if she'd truly been the healer? And then it dawned on her. The petite Norsewoman was none other than Freydis, the one who'd gone to find Sven in bed earlier that morning. That explained her embarrassment. It was no wonder Eahlswith had not recognized her. In the dark, she had not seen her clearly and all she had been able to concentrate on had been Sven's nudity, and what it meant—or rather what she'd thought it meant.

The woman cleared her throat, not knowing how to proceed.

Yes, Eahlswith thought with unusual ferocity, *you can be embarrassed after what you did.*

"It is not my place to accept or refuse you," she said more crisply than she'd intended. "I'm not the healer. My friend Cwenthryth is."

"I'm here," Cwenthryth said, coming to the door. Had she sensed the tension between the two women? Probably. "Forgive me, I was just seeing to my daughter."

"I will wait outside," Eahlswith mumbled. Though it would be cold out in the wind, anything was preferable to hearing personal, feminine complaints from a woman determined to have Sven in her bed. Why had she come? Did she want to ensure their couplings didn't have any issue in case she decided to leave again? Was she after a love potion to slip into his drink to make him accept her?

She headed straight to the vegetable patch, hoping that some weeding would help calm her nerves. Fortunately, nature had ensured she was not short of plants on which to focus her attention. Such was life. One was constantly trying to remove unwanted seeds from the soil—and block unwanted thoughts from entering one's mind. It was often a losing battle. The only way to win was to keep at it and focus on the beautiful and nutritious plants you could cultivate thanks to your efforts and enjoy the peace of mind you earned by keeping negative feelings at bay.

Eahlswith fell to her knees and tackled the corner where the leeks grew. It was the one most in need of attention but it only served to remind her of the soup she had made for Sven the day he had repaired the roof for Osbert. It seemed so long ago now.

She had the odd impression he had always been part of her life, and always would be, even if she never saw him again.

After a while, the door opened again. She heard Freydis thank Cwenthryth and a moment later, her friend joined her. She nodded at the pile of limp weeds by her side and smiled.

"My. You've been ruthless."

"Sometimes it is the only way to get results. What did Freydis want, then?" Eahlswith asked, sitting back on her haunches. Despite the weather, she wasn't cold.

Her friend arched a brow. "You know her name?"

Eahlswith waved a hand. There was no easy way to explain how she did and it was hardly important. "Did she want a potion that makes men hard against their will?" She was still seething from what Sven had told her that morning, she realized. How could the woman go to an unsuspecting man and all but rape him?

"Erm. Wait. *Do* you know her?"

"You mean that's actually what she asked you?" Another handful of weeds joined the pile.

"No, of course not, no one would come to me for something like that. I'm only a midwife." Cwenthryth looked pensive. "But you do seem to hold a grudge against her. I don't understand why, or even how, since she doesn't even live in the village."

I do hold a grudge, because she tried to seduce my man, against his will, no less.

Eahlswith shook her head. She couldn't say that, and anyway, Sven was not *her* man, was he? She'd told him only that morning that she needed time, and she meant it. Claiming him as hers was hardly the way to handle this.

So what could she say to explain her animosity toward Freydis? Cwenthryth had no idea her best friend and her brother-in-law had exchanged more than the occasional greeting—much, much more. Heartfelt confessions, fiery kisses, pleasure beyond imagining, not just once but over and over again, and against her better judgement.

She sighed. "I'm sorry, that was nasty, I know, it's only that she was not very pleasant to me when I opened the door and she mistook me for you." The lie was the best she could come up with.

"Mm, because you're a Saxon? I'm sorry, some people here are like that."

"Might have been. Anyway," Eahlswith stood up and walked back to the hut, eager to change the subject. "It matters not. I guess I'm tired, that's all."

Cwenthryth made a face. "I'm sorry. That's my fault, I—"

"No," Eahlswith cut in, feeling both foolish and guilty for making her friend feel bad. "Worry not. I'm glad to help. But I might need a nap this afternoon."

"Of course."

When they rounded the corner of the hut they saw a man waiting at the door. He looked like almost all the men here, tall and broad, with gleaming blond hair. Objectively stunning. What would she have done had she happened upon him bare-chested back in the summer, Eahlswith wondered? Would she have followed him inside the hut for a tryst? Perhaps. But would he have invited her? That was far from certain. She still wasn't sure what had motivated Sven to ask her.

"Good morning," he told her friend, smiling. "I was looking for you. I was at the harbor yesterday and I have a message from Steinar. He's very sorry but he's going to need a few more days to conclude his business with Gorm's men. He hopes you and the children are well."

"We are." Cwenthryth nodded. "Thank you, Knut. I expected he might need more time than he thought. How is Brenna?"

The man's smile, already more compelling than most,

became dazzling. "Better, now that the morning sickness has passed."

"I'm glad. Tell her I'll visit tomorrow."

With one last nod, Knut walked away. As soon as they entered the hut Cwenthryth went to check on Liv, who was still asleep in her cot. Then she turned to face her, looking contrite. "I would have asked you to stay longer but if you're already tired, I—"

"No. Don't worry. I told you I was fine. I will stay until Steinar comes back," Eahlswith said, refusing to think that she was jumping on the opportunity to be near Sven a bit longer.

Yes, Sven. He was all she could think about. Had he been anyone other than Cwenthryth's brother-in-law she might have confided in her, asked her opinion. But he was Steinar's brother and it did complicate matters.

The two women started making dinner together. Once they had eaten, they would go to get Sanna, who had spent the night at Wolf and Merewen's. As they were clearing the vegetable peelings from the table, Liv woke up. Eahlswith, who'd just cleaned her hands, went to pick her up.

"She's such a happy, beautiful baby. Do you think her irises will keep that amazing shade of blue?" she asked, peering into the little girl's eyes.

Cwenthryth beamed and gave her daughter a stroke on the cheek. "I know not. She certainly looks nothing like Sanna."

"No." The eighteen-month-old was the image of her Saxon mother, whereas Liv was a real Norse baby.

She remembered Sven's outrage when she had doubted his Saxon origins. But it was hard to blame her when he looked like the epitome of the Norse warrior.

"Her eyes are just like Steinar's," she said, smiling at the little girl.

Cwenthryth pursed her lips. "Mm, actually, I think they're

more like Sven's, his younger brother. You might not see the difference because you've only seen him in passing, but I spend my time looking into my husband's eyes so I know." She smiled at the mention of him, as she always did. "Sven's eyes are slightly darker, with a sort of star shape around the pupil, just like Liv has."

Yes. Eahlswith did in fact agree that the little girl's eyes were just like her uncle's but she hadn't wanted to say as much because she was not supposed to have noticed the exact shade of Steinar's brother's eyes or the gold star making the middle shimmer.

"Sven is a good man."

"Is he?"

"Of course he is," Cwenthryth chided. "He's Steinar's brother, so what do you expect? Torsten is also a good man, one of the best."

In truth, Eahlswith's comment had not been meant to express doubt, rather she hadn't wanted to give the impression that she was interested one way or the other in the kind of man he was. Why was Cwenthryth even mentioning this? Was she suspecting something?

"Forgive me, I did not mean to insult him or his family, simply to say that I don't know anything about him."

This was not strictly true. There were many things she knew about him. She knew the taste of his kisses and the scent of his skin. She knew he was kind, patient and capable of the most astounding gestures. She knew he was the most incredible lover. Still, it was shockingly little, all things considered, and she was suddenly curious to know more. This seemed as good an opportunity as any.

"What kind of man is he?" she asked, settling Liv on her lap.

"He is thoughtful, reliable and caring. He loves his brother's children fiercely, and they love him just as fiercely. He might seem easy going on first acquaintance, and he is more carefree than most but I would trust him with my own life. When Steinar was arrested after we met, he stayed with me at the hut, making sure no one came to bother me, all without making me feel oppressed or weak."

This was the first Eahlswith had heard about that. She knew Steinar had been arrested after being wrongly accused of killing his wife, but she had not known Sven had protected her friend during that time. A pang of jealousy stabbed at her gut because she couldn't think of anyone better suited to play the role of a protector and she dearly wanted him to play that role with her.

"And nothing happened between you during that time?"

"Of course not!"

Cwenthryth sounded, if not horrified, at least shocked that her friend could entertain the possibility. But considering that she, herself, had ended up in Sven's bed mere moments after having set eyes on him, it seemed all too possible that her friend should have been tempted by the Norseman sleeping under the same roof as her.

"I was already in love with Steinar then," Cwenthryth specified. "Even though they look eerily similar, I wouldn't have looked twice at him or anyone at that point."

"I see." Indeed, a woman already in love with the man who would become her husband would not have paid that kind of attention to anyone else, however attractive he might be.

"Anyway, as I was saying, he is a good man, but too handsome for his own good sometimes."

"What do you mean?"

Cwenthryth couldn't know about the incident with Freydis. So, was she saying that what had happened last night was a regular occurrence, that women tried anything to end up in his bed? She wouldn't be surprised if that were the case. Hadn't she been one of those irresistibly attracted women?

"I mean that it is all people, and women in particular, can see. He attracts them like honey attracts flies but they don't seem able to get past his appearance, see that he's not just a wicked lover they could boast about having had. They don't see that he could also be a wonderful husband, loyal and reliable. Or if they do, they are scared to be married to a man who will have to battle temptation every day. I think this is why he has never had any relationships that lasted more than a few weeks." Cwenthryth sighed, as if genuinely concerned for him. "Everyone in the village thinks he's enjoying this dissolute life, for want of a better word, too much to ever want to settle. I thought the same at first but now I know him better and I wonder if it's that simple. I believe that he is less opposed to family life than people think."

Eahlswith placed a kiss on the baby's head to hide her expression and give herself time to think. What should she make of her friend's assessment? Sven certainly seemed loyal and reliable to her. Could it be that he was trapped by his appearance, unable to convince women he could be trusted not to succumb to the many solicitations he received? Yes... Perhaps he was less opposed to starting a family than people thought. At least he seemed determined to build something with her and despite her numerous hints that she was not ready herself, he was not giving up.

But she could not deny being confused.

She would have understood Sven's insistence to fight for what they had if they had known one another for a while. But it was not the case.

They had come together in a wild explosion of lust. Neither had considered the other's character before surrendering to the desire burning between them, only their appearance. Every time he'd reached his release he'd made sure to withdraw and spill his seed anywhere but inside her. All this didn't point to a man ready to settle and have children, rather to one with too much experience and control to be caught unawares. One who didn't want to be forced to face his responsibilities after a night of passion.

Yes... Except that there had been that last time in her house.

In the middle of the night, once they had caught a few hours of well-earned rest, they had woken up at the same time. After kissing her with exquisite tenderness, Sven had taken her in long, languid strokes that had melted her bones one by one and stripped away what had been left of her sanity. And when he had finally followed her into unimaginable bliss, he had not withdrawn. At the time she had been too spent and too lost to pleasure to fully register the importance of the fact, but he had definitely stayed inside her while pleasure overtook him. And he had not panicked. On the contrary. She'd heard him mumble something before falling back to sleep, his arms wrapped tightly around her. She was now wondering if he had not promised to look after her should his lovemaking have consequences.

Dear God.

She had gone to Sven in the summer, thinking that she could allow herself this folly once in her life because a man who responded with such readiness to women's advances—not that she had done anything to lure him in except stare at him—could never be a threat to her heart or want to be part of her life.

It seemed she couldn't have been more wrong.

"Are you ready to go get Sanna?"

"Yes." Eahlswith took Liv in her arms while her friend put herself to rights. The little girl had just drunk her fill and was half asleep again. It was utterly adorable. "Ready when you are."

She could tell Cwenthryth missed her daughter, though it

had been less than a day since she'd entrusted her into her grandparents' care. How wonderful it must be to feel such unconditional love for another person. A person you'd created deep inside your own body.

"I will carry Liv if you don't mind," Eahlswith said, smiling as she placed her baby against her shoulder. "I love feeling her fall asleep against me."

It was a new experience to her, and surprisingly soothing to one who had never been in close contact with a newborn before. In fact, she reflected as the little girl's weight settled in the crook of her neck, she felt very content in the village, more than she had in years. Perhaps she should rethink her current situation. She could not go back to her native village, but with Edwin gone she had no real reason to stay in town.

Well. All that could wait until a more opportune moment. For now they were going to see Sven's parents and, though they had no idea what she and their youngest son had done together, she could not deny being nervous at the idea of meeting them.

Taking in a deep breath, Eahlswith followed Cwenthryth out of the door.

The day was glorious, the sky blue and cloudless, the air crisp and fresh. Yes. She was happy here, she realized, happier than she had felt since Edwin's death.

They were reaching Wolf and Merewen's hut when a woman approached them, a graceful woman that looked uncomfortably familiar. Freydis. Eahlswith's heart sank, her new sense of peace quickly evaporating. This time it was clear the Norsewoman had come to speak to her, not a midwife.

A midwife.

As the word crossed her mind, a thought suddenly struck her. What if...?

Eahlswith tightened her hold on the little girl asleep in her arms. If Sven's seed had taken root in her womb that second night in her bed, she would be even now—

No. She refused to think of the possibility. Refused to hope that their night of ill-advised passion would have consequences. Refused to—

"Excuse me. Can I have a word?"

Jolted out of her thoughts, Eahlswith came to an abrupt halt. Freydis was standing by the well, looking at her expectantly. Cwenthryth, having realized that this time, the woman didn't mean to talk to her, reached out to her daughter. Then she nodded and veered toward her parents-in-law's hut without a word, leaving the two women alone.

Eahlswith waited.

"Forgive me, I just wanted to tell you..." Freydis swallowed and started, her speech halted. "To tell you that Sven came to see me today and he explained everything. He was furious at me for going to find him in his bed but it wasn't the first time I had done that, you see, and he had always quite liked the surprise... I didn't know that this time he would not... I thought he would b-be available for—" By now she was stammering dreadfully and unable to finish a single sentence. "I guess I'm trying to say I'm sorry. I had no idea he was involved with someone else."

Eahlswith didn't know whether to be angry, horrified or simply incredulous. Sven had told the woman they were a couple? How dare he, when she had made her opinion clear and asked for more time?

"He told you the two of us were involved?"

"No. Not in so many words. But I saw how he reacted when you saw us and thought... what you thought." Freydis shook her head. "He was horrified because he feared you would never forgive him for betraying you. He would never have reacted that way if you meant nothing to him. I'm sure he already told you as much, but I swear nothing happened. And I'm the only one responsible for the mishap. I slipped into his hut, thinking I could just slip into his bed uninvited , even after all this time. Silly of me, I know."

No, not so silly. Eahlswith had tried to do exactly the same.

"He did tell me you had taken him unawares," she eventually said, though it was hard to talk past the ball lodged in her throat. Another woman might have thought it a convenient story, but she had believed him. She now congratulated herself for it because she had the proof that he'd been telling the truth. But how could she have doubted him when there had been such sincerity in his voice, in his eyes?

"Well, anyway, I came here to say that I will not stand in your way." As if to illustrate the point. Freydis took a step back and shook her head again. She seemed full of regret at her behavior. "Take care of Sven. He's a good man. I was a fool for leaving when he wanted me and go after a dream that only brought me disillusion because now he doesn't want me anymore. He wants you and I see what I have lost."

Dumbfounded, Eahlswith watched the woman walk away. It was safe to say that this conversation had taken her completely by surprise. And the more she thought about it, the more she found herself feeling sorry for the Norsewoman. Her only crime had been to want a man any woman would want.

Eahlswith took in a deep inhale. Would she one day reflect back on this period of her life and think, like Freydis, that she had been a fool for leaving a man who wanted her, and this to chase something that only brought her disillusion?

She could only hope not.

13

"Good morning, Sven."

Sven bit back a groan of relief when Eahlswith's voice reached him from the corner of the smoke house. Busy filleting fish, he hadn't seen or heard her draw near. But it seemed that she had finally decided to come to see him. It had been two days since she had walked in on Freydis exiting his hut and they had not met once. She'd been helping Cwenthryth with the children, of course, but he guessed that she wouldn't have made any effort to see him. Well, she was here now, and he wouldn't let her go until they had spent at least a moment together.

He turned around and saw her standing by the door in her fur-trimmed cloak. She wasn't carrying any basket, wood, buckets or anything. Why was she here? Had she come to get smoked meat for their meal and thought she might as well say hello when she'd seen she could not avoid him or had she come specifically to speak to him? It mattered not. Now that she was here, he would make sure they did speak.

"Eahlswith, good morning. Do you have a moment?"

"I... Yes. I-I suppose I do."

"Let me just put the fish into the smoke room and I'm all yours," he said, already lifting the wooden sticks over which the fillets were draped. His mind was no longer on the task at hand, however, and he placed the sticks rather more haphazardly than he usually liked to. No problem. There would be other fish, but he didn't want Eahlswith to disappear if he took too long, as she was wont to do.

To his relief, she was still here when he exited the door again.

"Come. I need to wash my hands."

She followed as he led the way to the river. It was one of those rare sunny winter days, crisp with cold and glittering with ice, beautiful and pure. On such a day it was easy to believe that everything would be all right. He dipped his hands into the water, relishing the bite of cold, and straightened back up. When Eahlswith looked up at him expectantly, he realized that he didn't know what to say to her. He'd only wanted to secure a moment with her.

Then, as if to help smooth over the awkwardness, Torsten and his wife appeared on the other side of the bridge. His brother was holding their newborn daughter in the crook of his left arm and his right was wrapped around Aife's waist. Though the two of them had been married for over a year now, seeing his brother with their childhood friend and their baby was still something of a novelty for Sven, one he wasn't sure how to handle. Perhaps because it hammered the point home that he was now the only one of his siblings without a family.

"Good afternoon," Aife said, looking at Eahlswith as if expecting an introduction. When none came she added, "forgive me, but you look familiar. Have we met?"

"I don't think so," Eahlswith replied, smiling at the baby, who was yawning in the most adorable manner. "But I have been in the village for a few days, helping my friend Cwenthryth, which might explain you having seen me?"

"Maybe."

Because, unlike Eahlswith's, his attention was not on little Thyra, Sven didn't miss the look passing between Aife and Torsten. They seemed to have remembered at the same time where they had seen the Saxon. It was then that he guessed they had seen her slip out of his hut back in the summer. His brother had told him that the two of them had spent many a night outside the hut, because Aife could not settle, too heavy with child, and they lived not far from him. It was very possible they had seen her. And with her distinctive look, they wouldn't have failed to remember her.

If only they had stopped her at the time!

He looked on at his Alva and his sister-in-law as they started talking together. The contrast between the two women was stark. One small and slender, the other tall and luscious, they had nothing in common. Aife's hair was as fair as flax fibres, while Eahlswith's head was crowned with a riot of midnight curls. People always compared Sven to his eldest brother, commenting on how similar they looked, adding that Torsten was nothing like them. It seemed that he and Steinar had similar tastes in women as well, having both chosen outsiders, dark-haired Saxon women to share their lives.

He started. Was that what he wanted from Eahlswith? Share her life?

But of course it was. Why else would he persist in catching her attention otherwise? He wanted her in his life, permanently, not just for a night, or even a month. Perhaps that was what he had meant to tell her earlier.

"If you'll excuse us," Torsten said after a while, taking Aife's hand in his. "We were actually on our way to the beach. My wife woke up in the mood for cockles."

Sven blinked. Had he heard that right? The last syllable of the word "cockles" had been uttered so quietly that for a moment he'd thought his brother had said something else. Something very naughty indeed. Aife's cheeks went crimson red, proving she had heard the same thing as he had. Perhaps the two of them were going to the beach for a purpose that had nothing to do with shellfish. He smiled, pleased to see that their desire for one another was still vibrant even after the birth of their daughter.

"Don't listen to your brother, he's a fool," she mumbled, before taking the baby from Torsten and heading straight to the field where the horses were doing their best to find patches of grass amidst the lingering snow.

A moment later Sven was alone with Eahlswith again. She had lowered her gaze to the ground as soon as Aife had nodded her goodbyes, as if unsure whether she should stay with him. To avoid an uncomfortable silence settling between them, Sven seized on the most obvious topic of conversation.

"Little Thyra is growing so fast," he said, looking at the family in the distance. "Did you see her yawn and smile? Yet I can still remember the day she was born."

"Thyra. That's a beautiful name, not one I've heard before. Mind you, most of the names I've heard here were new to me. Does it have anything to do with your god, Thor?" she asked, looking slightly ill at ease. Was she worried he would think her ridiculous for asking? He did not. Rather the opposite. He thought her endearing. "Only... It would make sense, I suppose, since her father's name is Torsten."

Sven couldn't help a smile. She really seemed interested in furthering her knowledge of his people's beliefs and language. He liked that, because it showed interest, if not exactly in him, at least in his community. It was a start.

"Yes," he confirmed. "Thyra means 'Thunder Fighter'."

"With such a name, I guess she will have no choice but to become a fierce woman," Eahlswith mused. "Otherwise she might feel inadequate."

He smiled again, for he had thought exactly that when his brother had told him his new niece's name. "Indeed, she will. But I'm not too worried. She has one of the strongest grips I can recall feeling on a newborn. I'm sure she will be just fine."

There was a pause, during which Eahlswith seemed to absorb what he had told her. He waited with bated breath for her next comment.

"You seem at ease with children," she observed eventually, looking at him from under her lashes, a lethal look.

"I hope I am. l love children. I can't wait to have my own."

The scoff escaping her lips made it clear she didn't quite believe him. No surprises there, why should she when the people who had known him all their lives would not? Not only would she have heard about his reputation but the two of them had slept together mere moments after they'd locked gazes. It would not appear as if he were looking for commitment.

Except that it was exactly what he was doing, even if not many people knew it.

He took in a sharp breath and decided to be honest. With her he couldn't help but expose his most vulnerable side. "I know it does look like I don't care about settling down but the opposite is actually true. It's only that I go about it in a different way than others."

"By sleeping with all the women you can find, you mean?" Though he could tell she had done her best not to sound accusatory, there was an unmistakable note of disbelief in her voice.

"Not all of them." He gave a side grin, deciding that teasing her might be the best way forward. She always seemed to respond well to it. "I sleep only with the ones that interest me, the ones I think might be a suitable match for me. It's not my fault there are so many of them."

"I... That's..." He could tell Eahlswith wanted to laugh at this provocation but dared not, in case he was actually serious.

But the truth was, he hadn't slept with half as many women as people thought. Still, because he always acted on his desire with decision, taking his conquests to bed as soon as he wanted to, everyone assumed there were many others they didn't know about.

"Freydis was one of them, I take it," she said, clearing her throat.

"Yes. I really liked her. But then she left without warning, not telling me she'd planned to go to Denmark all along, proving she wasn't ready to commit, like so many others."

Women didn't seem to think he had the makings of a good husband. An indefatigable lover, yes, but more? No. When it came to marriage and stability, they turned to other men.

Eahlswith reddened, but didn't comment. "She came to speak to me the other day," she said instead. "The afternoon after I'd seen her leaving your hut."

He arched a brow. This was unexpected—and potentially problematic. Just what had the woman told her?

"Did she?" he started cautiously.

"Yes. It is clear she regrets leaving you."

Well, this much he had already guessed from their own conversation. But it was too late for them. Years had passed, and he was now intent on wooing another woman, the most reluctant yet fascinating one he had ever met, as elusive as a fairy and just as beguiling.

"Unfortunately, Freydis is not the woman for me. But I know there must be one somewhere."

"So you are ready to settle? Cwenthryth told me she suspected as much."

He leaned against the bridge and crossed his arms over his chest. Yes, this was why he had asked Eahlswith to come for a walk, to make her understand the kind of man he was, and the kind of life he wanted. Whether that would be enough to sway her, he didn't know. But he had to try, so he began his explanation.

"Steinar married Astrid, his first wife, when he was twenty. They married after having spent only one night together, the day they met at a feast organized by my father. They spent a fiery night together and never thought they would see one another again after that." He stared at Eahlswith, willing her to see the similarities with their own situation. If the way she flushed was any indication, she did. Satisfied, he carried on. "A few days later, Astrid reappeared, explaining that her father was forcing her to marry a man who scared her and Steinar didn't hesitate. He married her to spare her having to wed the man she was promised to. Less than a year later, he was welcoming his first child. I was fifteen years old then and, oddly enough, I got jealous. It seemed like the perfect story to me."

"So, you tried to do the same."

He shrugged. "Not tried, exactly. You keep the men you sleep with at bay because you're afraid of losing your heart to them, while I sleep with the women I feel an attraction to in the hope that this promising start will lead to a more permanent arrangement. Ironic, is it not?"

Yes, that was one way of putting it.

Eahlswith blinked. "So you really are telling me that you sleep with the women who fire your desire in the hope that the lust you feel for them will turn into love and that the trysts will evolve into marriage?"

Unsurprisingly, she sounded dubious, but that was exactly what he was telling her.

"Can you blame me? I have seen that it is possible to find a life partner in that way. So when I do feel desire for a woman, why should I go against it? As long as she is willing, what harm is there in trying? Besides, I am a man, with men's urges. Bedding someone I desire seemed to be the best way to satisfy those urges while giving the two of us a chance to see what can happen."

To his delight, she swallowed, betraying the fact that she was remembering the day they'd met. One look had been enough to persuade her to join him in bed. She had certainly not gone against the desire she'd felt for him either.

For a moment it looked as if she would tell him that she agreed his method had merit, and perhaps they should go to his hut to see if the heat between them was still burning as bright as it had in the summer. His groin tightened at the thought because he already knew the answer. But then she shook her head and seemed to change her mind.

"You are aware, of course, that this marriage you envied quickly became a nightmare?" she said instead.

He was not surprised she knew about the rift between his brother and Astrid. Cwenthryth would have told her all about Steinar's first marriage and how it had ended.

"I am. But marriages where the couple court for months and take their time deciding can also end up that way. I can give you half a dozen examples just here in the village. There is no guarantee that being overly cautious will ensure the success of a union." She nodded but he had no idea if she agreed or not. "Love and dedication can spring from many a source. My parents' story proves it. They are probably the strongest couple I know, yet they met when *Faðir* bought my mother at a slave auction."

"I'm sorry?" Eahlswith's eyes went as round as coins, just as he'd imagined they would. "Did you say that he *bought* her?"

"Yes. It's a long story."

He'd hoped to lure her into an even longer conversation with a retelling of the unusual meeting between the Icelander and the Saxon, but she resisted the temptation. Damnation. She really didn't want to get involved with him.

"Another time, perhaps. I think it is time for me to go back into town. That's what I came to tell you."

It was all too easy to read her mind. She had been in the village for a week already, longer than she had anticipated, and she was feeling things for him she didn't want to feel. Desire, understanding. She needed to leave before she allowed these feelings to sway her. She wasn't ready to let go of all her doubts. Unlike him, she was being overcautious.

"Steinar is not back yet."

"I know, but he sent word that he would be there before the end of the day," Eahlswith answered, already making her way back to the hut. "And Cwenthryth insists that she is back to her normal self."

"I will accompany you then," he declared, nodding toward the field where they could see Gulltoppr grazing next to Grendel.

"There's no need, I can very well—"

"I'm not letting you go alone," he cut in. What did she take him for? "We can walk or we can ride if you prefer. If you don't want to ride with me, you can borrow my friend's horse, Grendel, and I will bring him back home holding the reins afterward," he added before she could point out that she didn't have a horse. He wouldn't put it past her to use this as a reason to refuse his company.

"There is no need to put you out."

"You're not. It's not a problem."

The silence stretched between them, neither prepared to back down. Then, Magnus, the blacksmith called out from behind the fence.

"Forgive me, but I couldn't help but hear your conversation. Agnes and I are going into town now, so you're welcome to ride with us on the cart if you want."

"That would be wonderful," Eahlswith said, beaming at him.

Magnus nodded. "Let me finish loading the last of the tools and we'll be ready to leave."

"Thank you. I'll get my bag and meet you at the forge."

Sven glared at his father's friend but the man was already heading back toward the forge. Damnation, why had Eahlswith accepted his offer so readily when she'd refused his? How much longer would this go on for? Every time he thought they were making progress, she pulled back. Months after their first, fiery lovemaking she had welcomed him back in her bed, only to behave as if she regretted it the following morning. The other day she had opened up to him, revealed the reasons behind her reluctance to get involved with a man, but it had led nowhere. She'd been sensible enough to listen to him after seeing him with Freydis and she had asked for time, making him think she was trying to come to terms with what she had come to feel for him. And yet now she was fleeing again, not even allowing him to escort her home, preferring to go with two strangers.

It was maddening, but there was no other choice but to follow her to Steinar's hut.

He stayed outside while she said her goodbyes to Cwenthryth and the children, then accompanied her to the forge.

"We're ready when you are," Magnus called out a moment later. His wife had already taken her place on the cart's seat.

"Thank you, I'm coming," Eahlswith replied before turning to face him, her eyes huge with unspoken emotions. "Goodbye, Sven."

She made the two words sound so final that he couldn't bear it. Before he knew what he was doing, he had drawn her into a kiss. Though at first she stiffened in surprise, it was not long before she melted into his arms and kissed him back with all the passion she was trying to ignore. Hope flared inside Sven's chest. No one kissed like that without feeling something for the person in their arms. Perhaps all was not lost, whatever she said.

They drew away, panting slightly.

"You promised you would give me time," she said, whispering too low for Magnus and Agnes to hear.

"I am giving you time." Why else would he let her go back into town with other people? Why else would he allow her to leave without any guarantee that they would meet again? "But I never promised not to kiss you."

She shook her head as his hold around her waist tightened and he thought he detected exasperation mingled with tenderness in her eyes. Finally, he let her go and she headed toward the cart. Magnus helped her up and then took his place in the driver's seat.

"I'll see her home safely, don't worry," he told Sven, picking up his agitation.

"I know you will." That wasn't the problem. The problem was that she was going back home.

Without him.

As the cart pulled away, Sven felt his resolve harden. He'd promised to give Eahlswith time and he would, but he would win this woman over if it was the last thing he did. His sanity might well depend on it.

14

"Torsten. Would you make a comb for me?"

His brother arched a brow in surprise at the request. "I gave you the last one I made barely a fortnight ago. Don't tell me you've broken it already?"

"I haven't. This one is not for me."

It was for Eahlswith.

She had been gone for six days now. The longest six days of Sven's life. He'd never thought himself an impatient man, but he had discovered many things about himself of late. It seemed that when it mattered, he was impatient, jealous, high-handed, unreasonable. Eahlswith had better start accepting what was between them because he didn't like the man he was turning into. Once his future with her was assured, he would hopefully revert back to the carefree, whimsical person he'd always been.

"The comb is not for you? Who then?" Torsten, the wretched man, crossed his arms over his chest and smiled, appearing delighted. "As if I couldn't guess. Cwenthryth's Saxon friend, the one with the dark hair. I saw the way you were looking at her the other day and wondered if you—"

"Nevermind that. Stop wondering and just make a comb, will you?"

"You are such a charmer, you know that?" Torsten chuckled. "No wonder so many women fall for you, brother mine."

Yes. Many did, to the point of coming to find him in his bed, but the one he really wanted was proving less easily seduced. Which was the problem.

"Well, I don't exactly talk to them as I talk to you, do I?" he snapped. "Or about the same things."

"I hope not. They would not appreciate—"

"Listen, will you do the bloody comb or not?"

Perhaps he had gone to the wrong person. Perhaps he should go to Eirik and ask for a drinking vessel instead. Eahlswith had seemed to like the bowl-shaped cup the day she had drunk from it. Had she not broken it he would have gifted it to her. His decision had already been made when she'd dropped the cask of ale on her foot. By the gods, but it should not be so complicated to woo anyone, make her accept what she already felt for him. It was not as if she didn't like him, or desire him or want to know him better. She did all that.

She just didn't want to act on it.

His desperation must have shown, for his brother finally stopped smirking and sighed. "As it happens, I do have one already made. The other day I found the whitest bone I've ever seen in the forest and I could not resist putting it to use. You know I like to keep my hands busy."

At any other time, Sven would have made a bawdy jest, winked and told him that his wife should be the one benefiting from his inability to keep his hands still but this time he just wanted the comb.

"Can I have it then?" he asked instead.

"How can I refuse such a gracious request?" Torsten's grin was back.

Damnation, his brother had become insufferable since his wedding to Aife, happier than any man had the right to be. Not that Sven had liked seeing him so despondent, but still... As his own mood was deteriorating, he found himself losing patience with people who had everything he wanted to have. Envy. There was another, new aspect of his personality he was not proud of.

"So?"

"Of course, you can have it. The only thing missing is the decorative carving. Unless you want it plain?"

"No, decorated would be perfect, thank you." That it was not yet carved meant that he could make the gift even more personal. "Do you think you could make an image of an elf? A female elf?"

Torsten tilted his head. Sven knew what he was thinking, that never before had he gone to such lengths to woo a woman. Well, no, he had not because there had been no need. A smile and a wink, usually sufficed. If not, a whispered promise in their ear was sure to win them over. But Eahlswith, the infuriating little elf, was different.

"I'll see what I can do, even if I am better at drawing leaves and shapes than people. Come back tomorrow evening."

"Thank you, brother, I'm truly grateful."

"I know. Not that it particularly shows." A scoff, and Torsten slapped him on the shoulder.

Sven made to go, then came to a halt and peered through the door of the hut. "Actually, while I'm here, could I have a word with Aife?"

"She's gone to take some fish to the smoke house. If you wait a mo—"

"No, it's fine, I'll go meet her there," he said, nodding his goodbyes. The conversation he wanted to have with her would be better had away from Torsten's ears.

He did find her at the communal smoke house, washing her

hands in the bucket of water she'd taken with her. She smiled at him when he handed her the piece of cloth she'd placed next to it to dry her hands.

"Sven. Good afternoon."

"Good afternoon."

Now that he was in front of her, he wondered if he would find the courage to do what he'd thought to do.

"Was there something you wanted?" She tilted her head, basket already in hand. Of course, she had work to do and was ready to go.

Sven swallowed. There was something he wanted, but how should he say it?

"Forgive me, I don't know how to ask this tactfully, so I'll just come out with it." They were friends, hopefully she would not resent him for being too blunt. "Have you ever been attracted to me?"

She stared at the floor, which gave him all the answer he needed. She had.

"I-I... Why would you ask me that?"

"I'm not going to tell Torsten if that is what you're worried about," he hurried to specify.

His intention was not to create problems between the two of them. They had just had a baby and everyone could see that they were a perfect match. But knowing she had married his brother in such a hurry only made him more eager to understand why she had not thought to act on what she had felt for him.

"I'm not worried about that. And Torsten knows."

"Oh?" This was the last thing he had expected her to say.

"Yes. In fact, it was because I was attracted to you that the two of us ended up marrying."

He could only stare at her, hoping she would explain what she meant because this was decidedly odd.

Aife deposited her basket on the ground and gave a sigh. "I began to feel attracted to you, as you say, the summer before I married Torsten. But I could see that you had no interest in me. I didn't know what to do to attract your attention. Do you remember the day I told you about little Emma putting sand in my pottage?"

"Erm...yes," he said, though in truth he could not recall. His niece was a veritable imp, like her mother, and he had been told many such stories over the years.

"Well, that day, Torsten was with us. You walked out in the middle of the conversation to go see Freydis, who you wanted to talk to, as you called it."

Ah, yes. *That* he did remember. Vividly. It was the day he and Freydis had slept together for the first time.

"I still don't see what—"

"I got jealous, and thought that if you saw me kissing another man you might start seeing me as more than a friend, as a woman men were taking an interest in." The color on her cheeks became alarming. "It was silly, of course, and I ended up hurting Torsten with my scheming, but he forgave me eventually and we..."

She bit her bottom lip, embarrassed. Sven could all too easily guess what was making her blush—and what form Torsten's forgiveness had taken.

"Wait, was that why he challenged me to a fight one day out of nowhere?" he blurted out. He'd always wondered what had made his usually measured brother behave so rashly. "Because he wanted to impress you? Because he knew you were attracted to me?"

"No, it's more complicated than that. Anyway, why are you asking me that now?" She seemed worried he was about to ask her to his bed, convinced as he was that she had once wanted to seduce him.

"I'm not about to pounce on you, Aife, don't worry. I was merely wondering why you lost interest in me," he said quickly, like someone swallowing a dish they knew would help satiate their hunger but was highly unpalatable. "Is there something about me that women sense is wrong, something that makes them doubt my ability to be a good—"

"There is nothing wrong with you, nothing at all," she cut in, all embarrassment vanishing in her earnestness to have him believe her. "You are a man any woman would be lucky to have. The problem was all mine. I was going through a bad period in my life at the time. I became attracted to you because...well, because I defy any woman not to be. But then, as soon as Torsten and I kissed, I knew he was the man for me. It was inexplicable."

"Yes." Odd as it was, he thought he understood exactly what she meant.

That first night with Eahlswith had been like that. Though she had hardly been his first conquest and he, unlike what people assumed, never bedded women he was not, at least in some measure, interested in pursuing further, what he had felt in her arms had been, just as Aife had said, inexplicable. He had known from the start that he would want more of her after that one night. He had known there was something worth pursuing.

But then she had disappeared, and for months on end he'd thought never to see her again. Had he not felt that strong, inexplicable pull, surely he would not have obsessed about her for so long? When Freydis had left, even though he'd been convinced that they could have had something together, after a few weeks, he had come to terms with the ending of their relationship.

His beautiful Alva, on the contrary, had stayed on his mind. He had not bedded another woman in months, not even felt he was missing out. Then, against all odds, they had been reunited.

And yet this second chance at wooing her was being denied to him, all because he was competing against a dead man who could do no wrong. Sven sighed.

In those conditions, he might never win.

"Forgive me, I have to go," Aife said, picking up her basket again. "It's getting dark and Thyra will need feeding soon."

Above them, the winter sky had turned a heavy purple, ominous. It might snow again tonight.

"Of course. Go to your husband. You and Torsten are made for one another. And I'm sorry I never saw—"

"No need to apologize." She placed a hand over his arm and smiled. "We were friends. There was no reason for you to start seeing me differently. And I hope you find the woman who makes you as happy as Torsten makes me."

"Yes, so do I."

Except... He thought he already had.

He watched Aife walk back to her husband and daughter. The family that had been created because, too blinded by Freydis, who'd only been after amusement, he'd not seen that a good woman was interested in him.

Well, at least something positive had come out of the whole mess.

15

The merchandise on offer on the last stall in the row caught Sven's eye. He'd wanted to buy a new purse for a while and the man had at least a dozen. Perhaps he should have a look while he was here.

He walked closer, congratulating himself for choosing market day for his visit to town. Not that he had come for that. He was here to see Eahlswith. But the two could be combined, could they not?

"What will it be today, my friend?" the seller enquired, when he saw him finger a dark leather bag that was decorated with, of all things, a wolf's head. A sign?

"I'm looking for a purse. What do you have?"

"Here let me show you. I have just the thing for a man like you."

Just then a woman appeared in the street to his left. Eahlswith. She was doing her best to shield herself from the wind with the hood of her cloak and her walk was less gracious than usual, no doubt due to the mire of half-melted snow and mud at her feet, but he had watched her too often to be mistaken. That hair, those curves... They could only belong to one woman.

It was her.

And she was just a few yards away. Luck was with him, because he'd been wondering if she would be at home. With no warning of his visit, there was no guarantee he would actually see her. But now he knew he would not leave town without having met with her.

"Wait a moment," he told the Saxon, taking two steps to the side. The purse could wait, but she could not. "Alva," he called out, gesturing in her direction.

At first she pretended she had not heard him. He called again. When she finally turned her head, the look in her eyes betrayed no recognition. Sven's eyes narrowed. Pretending they had never met, was that how she hoped to avoid a conversation with him?

He took another step toward her but she shook her head.

"My name is not Alva," she said, before turning her back to him and disappearing into a narrow alley, leaving him thunderstruck.

My name is not Alva.

Yes, she had told him many times she didn't want him to use the name. And she had told him she needed time. And she had fled his village twice without saying goodbye. But never had her rejection been so brutal, so complete. She had behaved as if he were a stranger, no less. A week after her departure, she had obviously decided it was time to put what they had shared behind her.

This last blow was enough to stun him.

"So? Have you made your decision?" the Saxon behind his stall asked.

At first Sven had no idea what he meant. What decision? And how could he possibly know about him and Eahlswith?

Then he understood the man was talking about the purse he wanted to purchase.

"Sorry," he grumbled. "I'll have to come back another day." It was fair to say that right now, his mind was not on the wares on offer.

Body numb, he made his way to his horse which was tethered in the corner of the market square. In the last two days, while he'd waited for the comb to be ready, he had imagined all kinds of reaction to the gift he'd chosen for Eahlswith. What he had not thought for a moment was that she would pretend the two of them were strangers. Damn the stubborn woman! Well, if that was what she wanted to do, she didn't deserve another moment of his time.

This time, *he* would disappear and let her deal with the consequences of her refusal to accept what was staring at her in the face.

Vaulting on Gulltoppr's back, Sven thundered out of the gate and started galloping back to the village. But as soon as he'd reached the forest, he came to an abrupt halt.

No. He would not be so easily defeated.

If this was to end, it would be ended on his own terms. He would not be ignored, not when he had done everything she'd asked—except stop using his special name for her, hardly a crime worth mentioning. She'd asked for time, and he'd agreed. He'd given her a whole week, damn it. It was not as if he'd gone to her to bed her either, to try and take advantage of the desire he knew he could provoke in her, he had only wanted to give her a present. She thought she could walk past him in the street, but if he cornered her in her house, there would be no avoiding him.

Sven shook his head, disgusted with himself. Since when did he think of cornering women, or anyone for that matter? He really was turning into a different man because of her. Well, that man would not be deterred, and he would go get what he deserved.

An explanation.

He turned Gulltoppr around and headed back into town. As he arrived back on the market square, he saw a familiar figure cross the street in front of him. Osbert. Sven cursed his luck. The old man did not see very well but a strong Norseman atop a white stallion was hardly inconspicuous. The Saxon's attention might well be drawn to the unusual pair. Indeed, Osbert turned his head toward him and frowned, as if trying to remember where he had seen him before.

Sven nudged his mount into a trot before the old man could stop him and start asking questions. Not only were the two of them not supposed to be able to converse, but he didn't want someone of Eahlswith's acquaintance to know he'd visited her. There were limits to the level of humiliation he was prepared to endure.

He turned a corner and a moment later he was in front of her door. She opened on the first knock, which surprised him. After their encounter at the market, he wouldn't have put it past her to pretend she was not in.

"Sven. You're in town."

"I am," he answered, not impressed by her feigned surprise. "We met at the market earlier, by the stall selling leather goods. Don't you remember?"

A frown. "I'm sorry, I did go to the market this morning but I didn't see you."

The blatant lie caused him to clench his teeth. "I was right in front of you." With those words he walked into the house, not giving her the opportunity to refuse him entry on some false pretext. "Perhaps I'm not big enough for you to see?"

She swallowed as she let her gaze roam over him. "You are big enough. But I swear I didn't see you."

"Apparently not. You didn't hear me or speak to me either, I gather?"

Her brow furrowed. "I'm sorry, I—"

"Leave it," he said, reaching for the door, to close it.

This was going nowhere. If she was going to pretend she had not seen him, then there was nothing he could do to force her to admit she had and insisting only made him feel like a fool seeking attention.

"Why did you come to town?" she asked, as if she agreed with him that this conversation was pointless.

Everything within Sven crumpled because with sudden clarity he realized that his efforts would be in vain. Never had he worked so hard at convincing a woman to let him woo her. In fact, he had never thought that wooing could require such determination. Why was he even persisting? It was clear she didn't want him. Hadn't she ignored him earlier today, hoping he would take the hint and leave?

"If you really have no idea why I came to a place where you're the only person I care about, if you don't understand why I cannot seem to stay away from you, why I allow you make a fool out of me time and time again, then you're right. I don't know why I came." He bunched his hands into fists. "Nor do I see why I should stay."

Without another word, he turned and made for the door. This was it. He'd given it all his might and he had failed. Eahlswith didn't want him. She would never accept what she felt for him. The reason why mattered not.

He had lost.

There was nothing to do but leave. And never come back.

A hand landed on his shoulder as he was ducking his head to pass under the low door frame.

"Sven. Please. Don't go. I'm sorry. It's not you. It's me."

Eahlswith paused, giving his shoulder a slight squeeze. "This is very hard for me and...you know why."

She sounded about to cry, more vulnerable and honest than he had ever heard her. Though it gutted him, he didn't turn around. If he didn't immediately comply, if he didn't immediately assure her that he understood her dilemma, she might finally gather the courage to explain what was really going on in her mind.

He closed the door again, signaling he would listen, and waited. After a moment, she carried on.

"It's Edwin. I can't... No other man made me feel like he did until you. I didn't even think it was possible and I had made my peace with it. But then...then you came along and everything was turned inside out. I want to be with you, but I feel like I'm betraying him simply by wanting this and I cannot bear it."

At last, he turned to face her. She was not a small woman, but he still loomed over her and it did odd things to his insides. It made no sense because he towered over other women as well, and yet it had never provoked any special feeling in him.

"I know." Yes... Didn't he know it. "And I'm not asking you to forget the man you loved and wanted to marry. Only to give me —and yourself—a chance."

They looked at one another, emotion swirling in the air. Eahlswith's amazing eyes were brimming with tears. When one fell on her cheek, he was surprised to see that it was transparent. For a brief moment he'd had the impression it would be as dark as liquid ink, as black as a moonless night.

"Why did you come, Sven?" she asked, her voice completely different.

"Because I wanted to give you something."

Her eyes lit up at that, an involuntary reaction that warmed the part of him he'd thought broken beyond repair only a moment ago. As painful as it was to her, she wanted to give him

—and herself—that chance he was talking about. She just didn't know how.

He would have to help her, starting with the gift.

He put his hand in the leather pouch at his belt and extracted the comb Torsten had given him that morning. The elf design had taken longer than the usual decorations but it had been worth it.

"Here. This is for you," he said, handing her the present. His brother had even made a case for it, decorated with a simple pattern of leaves.

Instead of taking it, she stared at the comb. No wonder she was entranced. It was one of Torsten's best pieces. White and smooth, with thin, regular teeth, and a beautiful carving on the handle, it was the perfect gift for her. "You made this?"

"No." He couldn't help a smile. Once again, she was hoping he'd made a delicate object. But just like the cup and the wicker basket, he had not. "I wish I had. But Torsten is the talented artist."

What he wouldn't have given to have half of his brother's talent in that moment. But he had never been artistically inclined. Torsten could carve whatever he wanted, Eirik was skilled at pottery, Moon could have woven a basket in his sleep, but he was only good where strength was required.

He took her hand and, seeing that she didn't seem brave enough to take it, placed the comb into her palm. She turned it this way and that, examining it.

"Is that a woman?" she asked, awe in her voice.

"Yes. Or rather, it's a female elf. Alva means elf in Norse, so I thought it—" He stopped, remembering how she always insisted that it was not her name, that he should call her something else. "I know you don't want me to call you Alva, so perhaps I should have asked Torsten to carve something else. I'm sorry. I didn't think."

Eahlswith cleared her throat. Her chest had gone too tight for comfort but she forced herself to talk, and reassure Sven because he looked like someone who thought he had made a terrible mistake. *I didn't think*, he'd said. But she knew that the opposite was actually true. He'd thought long and hard about how a comb destined to her should be decorated to make it meaningful and he'd found the perfect answer.

"Thank you. I love it as it is, with the elf." Closing her fist around it, she brought it to her heart. It was perfect. Perfect for them.

How much she had hurt him, she realized, by asking him why he had come. It was as if the light in his eyes had been snuffed out. It was time to stop being silly and give herself another chance at happiness. She was only five-and-twenty, she could not realistically spend the rest of her life alone.

In her house right now was a man who wanted her, who wanted to see where things could go between them, a man she wanted as well. Edwin had once been the man she wanted, the man she should have married, the man she loved but he was dead. She was not. Wasn't it time she started to live again?

Yes. If living meant being with Sven.

He wanted commitment, he loved children, he gave her thoughtful gifts, he made her laugh, he lived in a place where she would be happy, he was ready to love and protect her, he knew how to give her body and her soul what they needed. The list went on and on. Why was she even hesitating?

Eahlswith went to the window and took in a deep inhale. It was time to let go. Edwin had been a good man, she knew he would have wanted her to be with someone who was so determined to be with her, someone who bestowed beautiful gifts on her, someone who listened to her without judging, someone who wrenched indescribable pleasure out of her.

Someone who wanted to give her a special name.

Someone like Sven.

"It's snowing again," she observed quietly. Would he understand what she was hinting at? He could not ride back to the village in this weather. "It will not be pleasant to be outside."

She had barely finished her sentence than two hands closed around her waist and two arms drew her against a strong chest.

"No. Let's get to bed, then, shall we?"

Eahlswith could not repress a smile. Not only had he understood the hint, but he had jumped on the opportunity she was offering. This was her fierce warrior, unashamed of his desire and refusing to be denied the opportunity to give her what she needed. What they both needed.

"Yes. Let's go to bed."

No sooner had she given her agreement than he swept her feet from under her and started to carry her to the pallet in the corner of the room.

"Put me down!" she protested. "I'm not really an elf, despite what you say."

"We've already had that discussion once, I believe. I refuse to have it a second time. especially now, when I'm barely hanging on to my control. I'm carrying you to the bed, and that's all there is to it." He gave her a truly wicked smile. "Or would you like me to pin you against the wall again and make you forget your ridiculous notions of being too heavy?"

It did sound tempting but no, not today.

For now she had other ideas.

Sven almost lost his seed when Eahlswith bit her bottom lip and shot him a lethal look from under her sooty lashes. That look told him she had an idea in mind, an idea he already knew he would love. Good, for he had never been that hard. Or rather, it had never hurt that much. Or...something.

All he knew was that from the moment the light in Eahlswith's eyes had changed and he'd understood she would welcome him back into her bed, if not into her life just yet, he'd not been able to think. Tonight would be like none of the other nights they had shared. He would not just take her body, he would make sure to take possession of her soul in the same way as she had taken possession of his.

He made to deposit her on the pallet of furs, like a precious gem in its nest of furs but a hand on his chest stopped him

"No. Not here," she surprised him by saying.

"Where then?"

Surely she didn't want to go outside, in the street and in the snow? He would not have her body exposed to people's curiosity or her skin to the cold for the world. Or perhaps she wanted to be seated on the table so he could lick her like he had done that first night? If that were the case, he would be only too happy to comply.

"There is a little storeroom there, through this door," she said, nodding to the other end of the room.

A storeroom? Well, why not? As long as he could have her.

The door was so small he had to put her back down and duck to get through.

In there it was pitch black. Muttering what sounded like a curse at the unforeseen inconvenience, Eahlswith went to get the tallow candle from the main room. She came back with a fur in the other hand. Once the candle had been placed on a wooden box to the left of the door, he was able to see. Better. Now he would be able to see her gorgeous, naked body.

She placed an empty sack that might once have contained root vegetables or flour on the floor, and then covered it with the fur she'd brought along with the candle.

"Here. Lie down here."

Not needing to be told twice, Sven lay onto his back and drew Eahlswith atop of him. His breath caught in his throat.

Straddling him, with a naughty gleam in her eyes, she had never looked more beautiful.

"Now what?"

"Take your tunic and shirt off," she ordered, her voice just as husky as his.

Well, if she wasn't in an authoritative mood today. His shaft went from stone to granite as he hurried to obey her instructions. He liked a woman who knew what she wanted, especially if what she wanted was him naked. In the blink of an eye, he had disposed of his clothes.

"Alva, forgive me, I know this is a bad moment to tell you this, and I'm not even sure you'll want to hear it but I think I'm falling in love with you," he said, the words he had never pronounced before leaving his mouth with shocking ease.

Her reaction was not the one he had hoped to see, quite the opposite. She blinked in incomprehension.

"Do you think you could say that again in a language I can understand?"

It was his turn to blink. Then he understood. Damnation, he'd spoken in Norse. Of course, he had. He always did that when he spoke from the heart. From a young age, he'd associated his mother's language with everyday, useful exchanges, reserving his father's native tongue for what was more personal, what really mattered.

Like his feelings for this woman.

He swallowed. "I...can't."

It had been one thing telling her in the heat of the moment, but now, while she was looking at him expectantly? He wasn't sure he could. Would she be displeased? Fortunately she didn't seem to be.

"Perhaps you can tell me later?" she breathed, giving a small smile.

Yes, later, once they lay panting on the floor, exhausted by the most intense release of their lives, *then* he knew he wouldn't be able to keep the words to himself.

"Your turn to undress," he said, heart in his throat.

Slowly, she tugged at her bodice and lowered her shift to expose the most beautiful breasts he had ever seen, the breasts he had fantasized about from the moment he had seen them back in the summer, bathed in the silver moonlight. They were just as perfect now, gilded by the golden candlelight.

"Do you want to taste me?" she asked, lifting the two perfect orbs in her hands as if to offer them to his gaze. Forget the mischievous elf, in that moment she was the goddess of temptation herself. And he, mere mortal, didn't stand a chance.

"Yes," he rasped.

She smiled and leaned forward, bringing one nipple to his lips, pinning his wrists above his head. Despite the light pressure, he could not have freed himself in no time. He didn't want to, as he was right where he wanted to be.

"Suckle me, Norseman."

Never had a man delighted more in his task. She tasted so sweet, her nipples were so tight he could have come just from filling his mouth with the most delicious treat he'd ever had and imagining what would happen next.

With her breast in his mouth distracting him, it took Sven a moment to understand what was happening. Eahlswith was tying his wrists together. Before he could ask anything, she put the length of rope through a loop fastened on the wall and yanked, forcing his arms to straighten, holding him in place.

What the fuck?

It didn't hurt but all the same, he couldn't help a pang of discomfort. Just how many men had she tied to the wall thus?

"This loop has annoyed me from the moment I moved into the house," she said with a smirk, observing her handiwork. She didn't seem to have noticed his reaction, or think he would mind being at her mercy. Which he didn't exactly. "I almost asked my neighbor to remove it the other week. I'm glad I didn't, as I've finally found the perfect use for it."

Now that he knew she had not used the annoying loop on anyone else, his body relaxed. This was maddeningly arousing. Not one of his lovers had dared to tie him up, or even asked him to tie them up. Just the idea that Eahlswith wanted to have her way with him was enough to send fire coursing down his veins.

She placed her lips at his neck and gave a teasing bite. "Mm. You taste just as delicious as usual but this time I'm thinking we'll need honey."

Honey. To be spread all over him and licked in slow, sensual swipes of her tongue. For the second time that evening, Sven feared he had unmanned himself.

"Yes. Go get the honey," he rasped.

"It's in the other room." She straightened back up and restored some order to her bodice. "Wait here, Heimdallr."

Bloody hell, if hearing that name in her mouth didn't reduce his loins to cinders. How was he going to survive this? He wasn't sure.

"I'll not be going anywhere."

Even if he had not been tied up to the wall, he would not have wished himself anywhere else for the world. Finally, his Alva seemed to have accepted what she felt for him, allowed desire to dictate her actions.

Today would mark a turning point, he could feel it.

16

"Get her, quick."

Before she could understand who had spoken and what they were doing in her house, Eahlswith found herself with her mouth trapped under a filthy hand and her arms pinned to her side by an iron arm. She could no more talk than she could move. Behind her was a man as solid as a boulder, impossible to shake off.

In front of her was the living image of herself.

Ealawynne.

Her twin sister.

The sister she had thought never to see again.

Eahlswith froze as everything suddenly made sense. Sven had told her earlier that she had ignored him when he'd placed himself in front of her at the market. Silly her, she'd thought he had lied or been mistaken. She should have known something was amiss, Sven was not the sort of person to lie or make such glaring mistake. He had seen her twin, who had not recognized him, it was the obvious explanation. She should have guessed from what he'd told her that Ealawynne was in town but she'd been so confident she was safe—and so bewildered by Sven's visit—that she had not even taken that possibility into account.

Why was her sister doing here? And, more to the point, how had she found her? Eahlswith had made sure to vanish without a trace when she'd left the village, and to choose a big town days away to hide.

Well, she had failed because her twin was definitely here, and she was not alone.

"Sit her down on this chair," Ealawynne instructed the man who was holding her. "Tie her up, and gag her mouth."

A moment later Eahlswith was trussed up and unable to do anything other than glare at her sister and turn her head to try and catch a glimpse of her accomplice. She had still not seen him and had no idea who he might be. Not many men she knew were that huge. Except one.

One who would no doubt take exception to the treatment inflicted on her.

While the Saxon had tied her to the chair, one thought had helped her to keep panic at bay. Unlike what her attackers thought, she was not alone. Sven was in the house. He would never let the ruffians take her away, or even hurt her. With the filthy rag stuffed in her mouth she couldn't call out to him, ask for his help but that was no issue. He was not too far away, he would be able to hear the threats issued to her. He might think she had visitors at first and not wish to interrupt but it would not take him long to understand that she was in danger and come to her.

Thank God he had chosen today of all days to come give her the comb. Thank God he had not given up on her, despite her efforts to push him out of her life. Eahlswith closed her eyes. As soon as she was free, she would have to ask herself some serious questions and make some decisions. She had already concluded that she wanted to give him a chance but she might even have to accept that she wanted to fight to keep him in her life.

"I bet I know what you're thinking," Ealawynne said once the man had joined her. He *was* huge, at least a head taller than her and he would have been handsome if a spark of intelligence or compassion had warmed his gray eyes. As it was, he just looked like a brute. "You are wondering to what you owe this visit."

Visit.

Eahlswith would have scoffed if she'd been able to. Since when did visitors tie their hosts to their chairs? Seeing as she couldn't answer anyway, she waited for the explanation that was sure to come, because she was curious. What was her sister doing here, and why had she asked a mountain of man to attack her?

"Fuck, Ealawynne, she looks just like you."

"I know." Her sister didn't seem to like the comment. Eahlswith shared the sentiment. "We are twins, I told you."

"Yes, but there's twins and twins. This one is definitely a twin, if you know what I mean, not just a twin."

Mm. The man definitely did not have the sharpest mind. Good. Muscles were one thing, but they would be useless against a man who had muscles *and* a brain.

Eahlswith kept glancing at the door to the storeroom, knowing that Sven would emerge any moment. Placed where she was she would be able to see everything. The fury on his face when he saw what had been done to her, the fear in her sister's eyes when she realized she would not get away with her little scheme, the confusion in the brute's mind when he found himself on the receiving end of an irate Norseman's blows. She would relish every moment of it.

It was when she tried to move her arm and felt the rope dig into her flesh that it dawned on her.

Sven was indeed here in the house but, just like her, he was tied up.

~

AT FIRST SVEN thought Eahlswith was talking to herself, trying to locate the honey. It made him smile. Then he understood that there were people in the other room with her, two and possibly a third, silent one. How had they not heard that someone was entering the house? Because they had been too busy kissing and tasting one another, that was why.

By the gods! Why did the visitors have to come today, when he was waiting for her with the most painful erection of his life?

Not wanting anyone to see him tied up, bare chested and hard as a lance, he remained silent and listened, hoping to hear the intruders make their excuses and leave. But what he heard froze the blood that had been boiling in his veins when Eahlswith had straddled him.

"Listen to me, sister mine. I need you. Or rather, I need you to die."

The woman in the other room was Eahlswith's sister? And she wanted her dead?

His first instinct was to shout and promise the woman thunder and hail for daring to threaten Eahlswith. Then reason prevailed. If they realized someone had heard their plans, the two people would want to silence him. And tied as he was, he would be powerless to stop them. One quick thrust of a blade and he would die. Then his Alva would be at their mercy.

No, he had to be smarter and free himself before the two ruffians understood that she was not alone in the house. Thank the gods she had taken him into the storeroom, out of the way. Or perhaps it would have been better if she'd simply let him lie her down on the pallet. Then he would have been able to defend her when the two bastards entered the house instead of tied to a hook.

Well, it was what it was.

A quick tug at the rope holding his wrists to the hook indicated that he would not be able to free himself that way. Eahlswith had made too fine a job of restraining him. He needed to cut it, but how? He was alone and unable to—

His boot.

He had a dagger in his boot, the one he had given Eahlswith so she could carve the memory of Edwin in the tree. She had asked him to take his tunic and shirt off earlier but he had kept his braies and boots. If he could somehow reach his dagger, he could use it to slice at the rope. Eahlswith had tied his two wrists together, not each to a separate loop, which meant he actually stood a chance.

Careful not to make any noise and alert anyone to his presence, he started to move. Using the rope tying him to the wall to brace himself, he rolled backwards to bring his legs above his head. Yes. It might work, if he could hold himself folded up long enough to reach into his right boot and draw out his dagger. It would not be easy but fortunately, he was strong enough, supple enough—and determined enough—to make it. In any case, there was no other choice but to keep on trying. He could not just lie there, waiting for the two bastards to put their plan to action.

Silently, he tried again, this time for real, making sure to remain still, with his ankles hovering next to his hands.

It took four attempts but he finally managed to extract the dagger.

Sven took in a deep breath. He had the blade in hand. Now for the truly difficult part. He had to saw the rope despite the awkward, almost impossible angle. It would also be slow, because he had to make sure not to drop the dagger as he worked. It was his only chance to free himself—and save Eahlswith.

～

"Let me tell you why I'm here."

Eahlswith swallowed, pushing the idea of Sven being unable to come to her aid to the back of her mind to listen to the explanation she had been waiting for.

"It's quite simple. I cannot remain married to Wiglaf," Ealawynne said, grimacing. "He's a pig with no idea how to treat women, how to treat me. He thinks I'm happy cooking his meals by day and enduring his rutting at night. Well, I'm not. Godstan is the man I want in my life and in my bed."

Godstan.

Presumably the man by her side, grinning like an idiot.

Eahlswith had no idea what her sister, or indeed any woman, could possibly find attractive in a man who did not seem to be in possession of all his faculties, even if she was not surprised that Ealawynne didn't want to remain married to Wiglaf. He was indeed a pig. She had tried to warn her about him at the time, only to be told she should mind her own business.

The falling out with her sister—and what had happened after that, the night before the wedding, of course—was the reason Eahlswith had left their village, never to go back.

She still didn't understand what her sister's wish to take a lover had to do with this attack, however. How was hurting her going to help?

"This is where you come in," Ealawynne said. As girls, the two of them had been able to read each other's minds, in the mysterious way twins usually could. Then, as her sister's behavior had started to become more and more erratic,

Eahlswith had found it hard to make sense of what Ealawynne was thinking.

Like now.

"'Tis quite a brilliant plan!" Godstan guffawed. "You are quite brilliant. I like that about you. I also like your tits. They're perfect."

"Thank you."

And with those words, she kissed him

Eahlswith blinked. Was she dreaming? Had the man just said that? Had her sister then thanked him and drawn him into a heated, highly inappropriate kiss? At any other time, she might have laughed but this was serious. Her life was in the hands of a madwoman and a man who had the intelligence of a cabbage.

Once she had extricated herself from her lover's embrace, Ealawynne turned to face her again, her expression serious.

"You have to understand that Wiglaf will never let me go. If he suspects I want to leave him for another man, he will kill me. If I try to escape on my own, he will come after me. Even if I flee to the other end of the country, I will never know peace, I will always be looking over my shoulder. He has connections. Since you left he's become quite a powerful man in the community." A pause. "But if he thinks I'm dead, he will not think of looking after me, will he? It is the perfect solution. The only solution."

And now Eahlswith understood exactly why she was being attacked.

For her plan to work, her sister needed to fake her death. For that, she needed a corpse to pass off as hers. A corpse that looked exactly like her would make any doubt impossible.

Apart from their mother, no one had ever been able to tell the two sisters apart. Even their father had had difficulty. Once her face was scratched and bruised and her body dislocated from her fall from the cliff—without being told, she sensed this was the death her sister had planned for her—no one would suspect that the dead woman was not who she was supposed to be. Eahlswith had left the village more than five years ago, never to be seen again. Who would assume that she was the one being buried, if Ealawynne was no longer anywhere to be seen?

Yes, it was quite brilliant, in a twisted, ruthless kind of way.

Fear descended down Eahlswith's spine. This was a hundred times worse than she had first thought. Everything had been meticulously planned, there would be no talking them out of it. She was, contrary to what she had first hoped, alone. Because Sven might be in the house but he was unable to come to her aid.

Should she try to call out to him, make her two captors understand that she was not as defenceless as they thought, make them realize that someone had heard their plan and would come after them as soon as he was able? Thinking themselves alone, they had not tried to lower their voices or hide their intentions.

No. Even if they removed her gag, she would not call out to him. If she alerted the two ruffians to Sven's presence they would hurt him. He was bound and unable to defend himself. One stab from Godstan's blade and his life would be over. They were plotting her murder so it was reasonable to think they wouldn't let a powerless man stand in their way. She would have to rely on herself.

If she couldn't save herself, at least, she could save him.

By some miracle, Ealawynne and Godstan had arrived in the house moments before she'd walked into the main room and they had not heard her talk to Sven in the storeroom. Because she had been intent on seducing him, she had kept her voice low, whispering in his ear rather than talking out loud. In doing so, and taking him away from the main room in the first place, she might have saved his life.

Her mind somewhat reassured where Sven was concerned, Eahlswith started to think.

From what Ealawynne had said, it was quite obvious they planned to take her back to the village. No sense in killing her here, only to present a half-decomposed corpse to Wiglaf and his friends. That meant she had a few days ahead of her to come up with a plan. And she would come up with a plan. Nothing would be beneath her, if she thought it had a chance to work. She would beg, she would reason, she might even try to seduce the oaf Godstan and have him take her side.

The only two things she wouldn't do were to give up and place Sven in danger.

"Now, we are going to wrap you in this piece of cloth and take you to the cart waiting outside the door," Ealawynne said, sounding mightily pleased with the success of the first part of the operation. "At this hour, the street might well be deserted but I advise you to keep still and silent. If you wiggle to try to attract attention or moan, Godstan will be forced to silence you and he doesn't always know his own strength. With your face hidden, he might not know what he's hitting. You don't want to die just yet, do you?"

No. Or ever.

Eahlswith shook her head, wishing she could speak, so that she could say something to tell Sven where they were headed. He would have understood they were going to her native village but he had no idea where that might be. Stupid her, she had not wanted to share any more information about herself than necessary, thinking it would help her fight the attraction she felt for him. Even Cwenthryth didn't know where she had spent her childhood and wouldn't be able to help if he went to her. When Sven finally managed to free himself, how would he know where to look? Would he even bother to come for her after all she'd put him through?

Of course, she thought, tears stinging her eyes. Even if he didn't feel anything for her, he wouldn't let a woman be carried to her death without lifting a finger. The problem was, it might well take him weeks to find out where she'd been taken.

By then it would be too late.

"Good. As long as we understand one another." Ealawynne nodded and helped herself to a cup of ale, which she emptied in four long gulps. "Godstan, if you please."

FINALLY!

When the last shred of rope fell away from his wrists Sven barely repressed a shout of triumph. He doubted anyone would hear him now, but he could not be too prudent. This was a life and death situation.

He stilled and listened. Nothing. The house had been silent for a while. What if he was too late? He'd heard everything while he'd been slicing away at the rope preventing him from storming into the other room and cutting through the two bastards holding Eahlswith captive. He knew they would have taken her away in a cart, bundled up at the back like a bolt of fabric. Fortunately, he had his horse, Gulltoppr, which would be faster and allow him to catch up with them. The snow would further aid him. All he would have to do to find them was follow the cart's tracks, black against the white landscape.

But there was still one problem.

To catch up with them, he would have to know which direction they had taken. Out in the fields, the tracks would be easy to see but here in the mud-splattered street they might be impossible to spot. Had they turned left or right? Had they gone north or south? Neither of Eahlswith's captors had mentioned where they might take her or which direction they wanted to go.

Well, there was only one way to know.

Though there was no time to lose, Sven forced himself to get dressed again before heading out into the cold night. Riding out bare chested in the middle of winter was pure madness. He would need all his strength to rescue Eahlswith.

Gulltoppr was saddled in record time. Now for the most nerve-racking part: choosing a destination. If he got it wrong, precious time would be wasted. And if he delayed for too long he would lose the advantage the snow was giving him, other travelers would muddy the tracks and make it impossible for him to follow the cart.

He'd made up his mind to try and go West first when he heard a commotion at the end of the street, which surprised him. Like Eahlswith's sister, he wouldn't have thought anyone would be out and about at this hour and in this weather. Vaulting onto Gulltoppr's back, he headed toward the people. With luck, they would have seen the cart depart.

"Did you see that?" a woman wailed as he approached. "They almost killed poor Richie and they didn't even slow down."

"A dark-haired woman in a cart driven by a big brute, you mean?" he asked, assuming that was what the man called Godstan looked like. He'd certainly sounded as if he'd been selected for his size rather than for his intelligence. The comments about his lover's tits had not been in the best taste.

"Aye, they set off at a mad pace and cared not what or who was in their way."

"Did you see which direction they took?"

The woman blinked. "That way, they went toward the North gate."

The gate. Damnation, of course. With night falling, the town gates would be closing down soon. How had he forgotten about that? Would he be stuck inside the walls, unable to set off in pursuit?

"Why, are you going after them, young man?"

He didn't answer, as he'd already launched his horse into a canter by then, but yes, he was definitely going after them. As he rounded the bend, Gulltoppr's hooves skidding in the fresh snow, he heard an ominous creaking, the very sound he didn't want to hear.

"No!" he shouted, thundering toward the gate. He couldn't get locked in, not now. "Hold it, I'm coming through!"

The men who were pushing the big wooden doors shouted and jostled out of the way. Sven flew past them, shooting out of the walls like an arrow let loose by a mighty archer. A moment later he was racing through the snow-covered fields. As he'd hoped, it was easy to follow the track leading to the cart. At the speed he was traveling, it shouldn't take him long to reach it, even if they didn't stop.

Except... Once he entered the forest, the traces disappeared. Under the cover of the trees, the layer of snow was too thin to show anything and there were many paths they could have taken to exit the dense woods. Had they carried on straight or veered off North at the earliest opportunity? Had they decided to get out of the woods and use the moon to light their way? It would take him days to explore all the possible options. And then, as if that were not enough, he saw through an opening in the trees that it had started to snow. The tracks, out on the fields, would disappear in no time.

Sven looked around, despair seeping into his bones.

This time it was over. He'd lost them.

17

After what felt like an eternity of jostling, the cart came to a stop. Eahlswith waited, hoping to be freed from her bonds now that they were out of the town. Surely her captors didn't think she would run, alone in the wilderness, in the snow and at night? Even she had the presence of mind to understand that it would be useless. Then she heard Ealawynne and Godstan argue from their place on the driver's seat.

"Why did you stop?" Her sister sounded more than a little annoyed.

"Why do you think? In this snowstorm I can't see where I'm going," was the equally curt reply. "I'm not risking breaking my neck when we fall into a ditch or worse. A little delay will not hurt. No one will find out your sister is gone before the morning and when they do, they will have no idea where she went or that she was abducted. They will simply think she's gone out of town for a day or two. I say there is no rush, so we might as well sleep under the cover of the trees instead of getting back out in the open fields."

Eahlswith closed her eyes, relieved beyond words. The longer it took them to reach their destination, the better.

Wrapped as she was, she had not noticed that it had started to snow but indeed, she agreed with the man. No sense in risking their lives if the conditions were treacherous.

Besides, he was right. No one would worry about her disappearance for days, if not weeks, instead assuming she had gone to the Norseman village to see Cwenthryth. Even if the cart had been seen leaving her house, people would remember seeing "her" in the driver's seat with a friend, just like she had been seen the other day with Magnus and Agnes. There would be no cause for concern.

A moment later, she felt someone, Godstan judging from the strength of his grip, lift her into a sitting position and then remove the cloth covering her head. Meeting his gaze, she nodded and looked down, hoping to make him understand she wanted him to untie the cloth that was digging most uncomfortably into the sides of her mouth.

"I think she wants us to remove the gag," he told her sister, who was climbing down the cart in turn. "I say 'tis quite safe to do so."

Ealawynne made a sort of grunt that could have passed as an agreement and a moment later, Eahlswith's mouth was freed from the tight bond. The relief was indescribable. She moved her tongue gingerly, tried to close her mouth and found that everything hurt.

"How did you know where to find me?" she asked, her throat so dry that her voice came out like a croak. It was all she had been able to think about as they'd traveled and yet she had not been able to come up with a suitable explanation.

"You thought you were quite safe, didn't you? Well, you're not as clever as you think." Her sister smirked, not even trying to hide her satisfaction. "A few years ago a man from our village was asked to deliver a message to you by a dying traveler, I believe?"

Eahlswith's blood froze in her veins. Edwin. Of course. How had she not thought of this? Indeed, as he lay dying he'd asked the villager who'd discovered him, the priest's nephew, to go tell her about his death. How had she not thought it meant that someone knew where she had gone to live?

"That man is one of Godstan's closest friends," Ealawynne carried on, clearly enjoying herself. "Last month during an innocuous conversation, he let slip that he'd last seen you in a distant town once, when he delivered the dying man's message. That's what finally allowed me to put my plan into action. I got the idea to use you to feign my death months ago, but I didn't know where you had disappeared off to. Thanks to Cuthbert's innocent comment, I was able to find you."

What a stroke of bad luck. Eahlswith gritted her teeth, refusing to cry, when it would serve no purpose. She had to find a way out of this mess instead.

"Give me something to eat and drink," she begged. She was thirsty but that was not the only reason for the request. If they untied her hands, she might be able to loosen the ties on her ankles while they were not looking. Then when they retied her hands, she would wait for an opportunity to flee. Even with tied hands, she could run.

Ealawynne laughed, the sound jarring. "Do you think we have food to spare on a dying woman? You can have a few handfuls of snow and be happy about it." She turned to the man who was tethering the horse to a nearby sapling. "Godstan, bring her some snow."

Snow... The memory of the day she had eaten snow with Sven assaulted Eahlswith and this time tears did roll down her cheeks. Where was he now? Had he heard what was in store for her? Had he managed to free himself? Very few people visited her at home. The ones who did would not insist and leave when they knocked on the door and she didn't open. Would he die of thirst in her storeroom, when he could not get out of the rope she'd used?

Dear Lord, please let him be safe. He had done nothing to deserve being involved in this nightmare.

"Here."

Her sister placed a heap of snow on a sack of cloth next to her head. There was no other option but to bury her face in it and try to catch as much of it as she could before it melted. Once Eahlswith had lapped at a few mouthfuls of snow that did little more than wet her lips, Ealawynne put the gag back in place.

"It wouldn't do for you to call to any passerby, would it? Not that I expect many in this weather and at this hour but you never know." She settled herself in the cart, making a nest amidst the various bundles and furs. At least they had everything they needed to make themselves comfortable. As consolations went, it was a small one. "Now, we are going to get some sleep so we can set off tomorrow at first light. Hopefully it will have stopped snowing by then."

Sleep. Eahlswith closed her eyes. Did they really think she would be able to sleep with her body trussed up and her mind in turmoil?

But to her surprise, she soon found herself drifting off into oblivion. Then suddenly she was jolted awake when a hand landed on her breast. A hand belonging to Godstan, who had elected to lie between the two women when he'd joined them for the night.

"Awake, little captive?" he whispered, bringing his mouth to her ear.

She shook her head, more a way to indicate that she didn't want him to touch her than to answer his question. But yes, she was now most definitely awake—and dreading what was about to happen.

The hand over her breast gave a squeeze. "Mm. I love tits."

Yes, unfortunately she already knew that. And if he thought her sister's were perfect then he would like hers also, as they were identical.

Please, please, she silently pleaded. *Ealawynne, wake up. Save me from this nightmare.*

"I could loosen your bonds, you know," Godstan carried on, "if you allowed me certain...liberties, shall we say. I could even remove the gag from your mouth." He allowed a finger to stroke her cheek, the gesture almost tender and all the more terrifying for it. "I bet it is hurting you. I could help, slip something far more pleasant between your lips, something warmer than snow."

Eahlswith fought the nausea roiling in her gut. With her mouth gagged the last thing she wanted was to be sick. Dear God, she'd thought her situation dire earlier today but it had just taken a dramatic turn for the worst.

She started to squirm, hoping to wake her sister up. Surely Ealawynne would object to her lover touching another woman? But even if she did not and agreed he was owed some reward for helping her, then Eahlswith would be no worse off. She had to try. She arched her back and let out a scream that came out as a moan.

"Eager, are we?" the man chuckled. "Don't worry, I'm—"

"Godstan, what are you doing?"

Thank the Lord. Ealawynne had finally woken up. Eahlswith stopped moving. With bated breath, she waited to see what her sister would do. Anything was possible coming from a woman intent on killing her.

"I'm warming myself up with our captive's lovely body," the man answered, not in the least worried that Ealawynne might find this explanation unsatisfactory. "It is not often a man finds a lover with a twin sister that looks so much like her. I think I should be allowed to see whether fucking her will feel the same as fucking you."

Oh Lord.

"That's not why I brought you here."

"No. But now we are here, and my balls ache something fierce. This is every man's fantasy." He sat up and gave a grin. "I'll tell you what. You don't have to be left out. You two could pleasure me, and I can return the favor. I swear I won't leave either of you wanting. What say you?"

If Eahlswith's gag had been removed in that moment she would have spat in his face. Fortunately, for once, her sister seemed to agree with her.

"I say that you're mad," she said, sitting up in turn to look at him. "If you want to rut, it will be with me, no one else."

Godstan let out a frustrated growl then reached out to his braies. "Open your mouth then," he ordered, his voice gruff. "And you had better make sure you put your heart into it so that when we're done I don't feel like I'm missing out."

Wishing she could block her ears, Eahlswith screwed her eyes shut.

SVEN TIGHTENED the girth on Gulltoppr with renewed determination. Last evening instead of bemoaning a situation he could not change, he had made sure to get some rest while the snow was swirling around the forest, doing its best to pierce the cover of the trees. No point in wasting energy lamenting his situation, he simply had to find the cart today and free Eahlswith from her abductors. The alternative was too dire to contemplate.

It was not all bad, though. The snowstorm of the night meant that the two captors had probably stopped as well and on the fresh layer of white the cart tracks were sure to show. Now that it was daylight, if he exited the forest and found a high point from which to scan his surroundings, he might well see something.

Choosing to stay on the most direct path from the town, he carried on until he had left the last tree behind. Then he cantered to a nearby hill, where he would get a good view of the area. Nothing. He was starting to think that he had exited the forest in completely the wrong place when he saw what he wanted to see.

A cart, over there, next to a river.

Two people were in the driver's seat, one tall and one with dark hair. It had to be the right one. They were obviously riding along the river bank in search of a bridge, which meant that they would not get farther from him until they had found one. He could catch them up in no time. Barely repressing a growl of triumph, Sven launched Gulltoppr into a gallop.

As he drew nearer, he brought the animal back down into a trot so as not to give the impression he was giving chase. If the two ruffians took him for a simple traveler about his business, they would not get suspicious until it was too late. Surprise would be his best weapon, not that he expected any serious issue. He felt more than ready to take on a clumsy fool, however heavy he might be, and a woman, however vicious. They would pay for what they had done and what they intended to do.

Atop his mighty stallion, he quickly gained ground on the heavy cart. Soon, it slowed down and then came to a complete stop. The reason why quickly became obvious. The man, who was driving it, had gone into the bushes to relieve himself.

Perfect. Sven would deal with him first, while he was distracted.

This time he did gallop, confident the man would not see him, from his place in the bushes. A moment later he was behind him.

"Bloody Ealawynne," Sven thought he heard him grumble as he tucked himself back in his braies. "Why can't she understand that a hot-blooded man is—"

Not waiting to hear what the man thought Eahlswith's sister didn't understand, Sven pounced, placing his trusted dagger at his throat, forcing his head up.

"Make a move and you're dead."

There was no mistaking the earnestness in his tone and the man instantly stilled. "What do you w-want?" he stammered. "I have no money."

I don't want money. I want my Alva back. She's more precious to me than all the gold on this earth.

"Yesterday you abducted a woman. *My* woman," he growled into his ear. "That was your first mistake." If he had hurt her, that would be his second.

"Listen, this has nothing to do with me. I only obeyed Ealawynne's orders. She's the one who wanted to abduct your woman and she needed a strong man to do it."

He thought he was going to save himself by placing the blame on someone else and claim he had no knowledge of the fate his lover had in store for her sister? "Yes, she needed a dumb brute to abduct her so that she could kill her. And you agreed. Tell me, you piece of shit, if she had asked you to abduct a child or rape a nun or kill your own brother or anything else equally as foul, would you have done it?"

"She didn't ask me any of this, I swear. It was not me."

Was the man really that dim or was he hoping to escape retribution by playing the role of an idiot? Either way it wouldn't work. Sven had had enough of this. He had to go to Eahlswith.

"Sorry, not good enough," he told the man, as he plunged the blade into his shoulder.

"Ah! You bastard!"

"I'm not the bastard around here. If I were, I would have

plunged the blade into your heart. At least I gave you a chance." With those words, he knocked him out. Let fate decided what would happen to him.

When he turned around, Sven found himself staring straight into the dark eyes he had fantasized about many a time. His heart exploded. At first he thought Eahlswith had freed herself and relief swept through him. Then the woman—for it was not his Alva but her twin sister, of course—ran to the man at his feet. Blood had already started to soak the snow under him.

"You monster, what did you do that for? We have nothing of value." She placed a hand on the man's cheek. "Is he dead?"

Sven shrugged. "Not at the moment, but he might die if no one sees to his wound soon. Still, if he didn't want to get hurt perhaps he should have thought twice about abducting innocent women with the aim of killing them."

The woman understood then that he was no mere passerby looking to rob them, as she'd initially thought, but Eahlswith's champion, come to free her. With a cry of rage she stood up and started to run. Sven rolled his eyes. Did she really think it would be that easy?

"Not so fast," he said, catching up with her in a few powerful strides and restraining her against his chest. "You're coming with me. Your sister might have some questions for you and she will be allowed to ask them. Then, once you've spoken to her, you can go to hell for all I care."

Sven dragged the woman back to where Gulltoppr was grazing. There was a length of rope in the saddlebag. Thank the gods he was always prepared for the worst. In less time than it took to tap a cask of ale, he had tied his captive to the nearest tree. It was odd, unsettling even, to treat a woman thus. That she looked exactly like the woman he loved only made the task harder. But he had to be sensible and remember that this was not his Alva, but a dangerous woman who had been plotting her murder. She might well strike her out of spite when she saw that her plans had been foiled if he did not incapacitate her before he went to free Eahlswith.

"You can't do this!" she protested. It was as if she had read his mind and tried to appeal to his sense of honor. "I'm a woman!"

"You're nothing but a snake," he hissed in her ear. "Now stay quiet or I will have to silence you and I don't always know my own strength. I might hurt you." Repeating the words she'd told Eahlswith the evening before was immensely satisfying.

As soon as he was sure she was securely bound and gagged, he turned away from her and hurried to the cart. Eahlswith would be wondering what was happening, and probably getting scared. He wasn't sure she would have understood someone had finally come to her rescue. From a distance, with noises being muffled under the cloth, she might just have assumed his captors were arguing. She had no idea he was coming for her.

And he refused to give her a moment of anxiety.

18

"Sven!"

Eahlswith's whole body felt weak with relief when the cloth was removed from her face and the familiar face of the Norseman was revealed.

She'd thought she'd heard raised voices but as there had been no sound of a scuffle she had lost hope of being rescued. Ealawynne and Godstan were only arguing again, she'd concluded, probably because he'd reiterated his desire to bed her. Thankfully she'd been wrong, and someone had indeed come for her.

The man she most dearly wished to see.

"Sven," she repeated, weak with a mixture of emotions amongst which relief and exhaustion played the most part.

"Alva, thank the gods," Sven answered, removing the gag from her mouth with gentle hands. It was obvious he didn't want to hurt her further. "Are you all right?"

Was she? Yes, now she was. He was here, so she would be fine. "I'm all right," she said, fighting a sob.

Sven grimaced when he heard how cracked her voice was. "Here. You need to have a drink." He handed her a wineskin and at last, she could take long gulps of cool water. Never had anything tasted sweeter.

"Thank y—"

"Don't thank me. By the gods, I'll kill the man. Look how bruised your mouth is."

It would be, considering she had been gagged all night but she ignored the pain throbbing at the corner of her lips to ask instead. "How are you here?"

His nostrils flared as if he appreciated her not asking *why* he was here. But she had known he would come for her if he could. She simply could not understand how he had freed himself and found out where she'd been.

"I always keep a dagger in my boot," he told her, extracting the weapon in question to cut the cloth holding her captive.

Though she could easily guess that his curt explanation did not do justice to the difficulty of the operation she didn't press him, because there was something she was dying to do. As soon as the top half of her body was free and her wrists unbound she threw herself into his arms and gave him the most heartfelt kiss she had ever given anyone. To hell with the pain it caused her bruised lips, she needed this. And it was clear from Sven's response that he needed it also. His hands had fastened around her waist, holding her tight against him.

"You came for me," she said when they finally drew away.

"Always." He spoke with his lips against hers. "I'll always come for you."

She blushed at the evocative words. What was wrong with her? She shouldn't be thinking of such things after having escaped death. He groaned, indicating he'd understood what he'd unintentionally said, and his tongue licked along her bottom lip.

"Yes, and that as well. All in good time. I will come for you as many times as you like, in whichever way you want."

Oh. Had she not been sitting down, her legs might well have given way. She forced herself not to think of the next time they were in bed together. For now they had to see to the situation they were in.

"What happened to Ealawynne?" Eahlswith asked, looking around. There was no trace of her abductors that she could see. "Godstan?"

"You mean your sister and her brute?"

"Yes."

All trace of teasing vanished from Sven's expression. His eyes became as hard as cut glass and almost as transparent. "*He's* probably dead. *She's* tied to a tree while we decide what to do. You don't have to see her if you don't want to. I wanted to give you the option but I can go untie her and join you on the cart. We can be gone in a trice."

"No. I do want to see her."

They couldn't leave like that. She hadn't had the chance to tell her what she wanted to tell her earlier.

"My Alva. I knew you would be brave."

Sven placed a kiss on her forehead before helping her disentangle herself from the cloth holding her legs together. Once she was back on her feet, he selected the biggest piece he could find and wrapped it around her shoulders. How thoughtful. Bundled up in the cart, amongst the balls of wool, she hadn't been cold, but now the chilly wind was biting at her most unpleasantly.

"Thank you."

"Would you rather have my cloak?" he asked, already making to remove it.

"No." The piece of cloth was fine for her but would be too small for him.

"Wait." Sven planted himself in front of her and took her by the shoulders. "Before we go, tell me this. Did the man touch you?"

Eahlswith swallowed. How had he guessed Godstan had wanted to assault her? Had the man told him as much before being dying?

"No," she said as firmly as she could. In the end, though he had put his hand on her breast and whispered his vile intentions to her, he had not done any of the things Sven was imagining. That was all that mattered.

He nodded, looking only marginally reassured. He'd obviously guessed she was hiding something from him but, to her relief, he didn't press her. "Let's go see your sister then."

Ealawynne was, as Sven had said, tied to a young tree and gagged in much the same way she herself had been last night, though she could see that the piece of cloth didn't dig as deep into the sides of her mouth as hers had done. The point had been to stop her from calling for help, not to hurt her.

As soon as Sven removed the gag, Ealawynne snarled at him. "Untie me, you bastard!"

Neither she nor Sven dignified the request with an answer.

"When we release you, I don't want to see you again," Eahlswith said, planting herself in front of the woman who had once been her closest friend, who had once shared a womb with her. "If you're unsatisfied with your life, you only have yourself to blame. I warned you Wiglaf was not a good man. I told you he would make you unhappy. I told you he was a lecher. You ignored me."

"Yes, you told me all this, and then you just left, instead of trying to make me see reason. You abandoned me. You didn't even come to my wedding!"

Everything within Eahlswith bristled. How dare she put the blame on her? "I didn't abandon you! I did try to make you see reason, as you say, but you refused to listen to my warnings, no matter how many times I repeated myself." She took in a deep breath and decided to tell her sister what she had sworn never to tell her. "And I didn't go to your wedding because the night before Wiglaf had come to me. He was about to marry you, and he tried to bed me. Do you hear? That is why I left."

By her side, she heard Sven growl. If the man had been in front of them now, she was certain his corpse would have joined Godstan's in the snow.

"It will have been a mistake," Ealawynne spat. "Or have you forgotten that we look alike? He would have thought to—"

"A mistake!" Eahlswith cut in, feeling her heart break anew. How could her sister persist in her folly when confronted with facts? How could she place a vile man's word before hers? "He knew, as did the whole village, that you and your friends were in Mathilda's hut, getting ready for the ceremony and wouldn't see him. Trust me, he knew exactly who was under him that night."

Another growl. Sven turned her to him so she could meet his gaze. His face was a mask of fury such as she had rarely seen. "Tell me that bastard didn't succeed in—"

"No." She could see the intention to go hunt him down flash in his eyes. There was no doubt in her mind that if she told him Wiglaf had raped her, he would make sure the man didn't see another day. But, mercifully, she had not been raped. "I managed to escape his clutches thanks to a friend," she said, addressing him instead of her sister. "He heard my screams and prised Wiglaf from me."

Sven nodded, jaw still clenched, seemed to will himself to calm and eventually released her.

"You never wondered why Wiglaf's face was scratched on your wedding day?" Eahlswith carried on, addressing her sister once more.

"He told me he had fallen into a ditch on his way back from the tavern."

"And you believed him?" This from Sven, who apparently

had decided he could not contain his hatred any longer. "Just how stupid are you?"

"I had no reason not to believe him. It can happen."

"No reason, you say! You had your sister's testimony that the man was a lecher and yet you chose to disown her instead of seeing the truth. She's right. If you're unhappy now, you only have one person to blame for it. Yourself for not heeding Eahlswith's advice."

"How dare you—"

"Eahlswith said what she had to say. Now it is my turn. She wants you out of her life and you will do as she wants. You will disappear, and we will never see you again. Speak to her again and you'll suffer. Touch her again and you will die. Slowly." Sven had never looked or sounded more lethal. "Woman or not, I will come for you. You being Eahlswith's sister will not protect you, not when I know how dangerous you are. Hurt her in any way and you will suffer the consequences. Do you understand me?"

"Yes." Ealawynne sounded half dead with fright, and Eahlswith could not blame her. Had she not known Sven for the man he was, she might have taken fright herself.

"As to the bastard you call your husband," the voice, icy a moment ago, had gone positively glacial, "should he even attempt to see her, he will find himself under *me*. And he will not be allowed the mercy of death until I am finished playing with him."

It was clear from the way Ealawynne blanched that they would not hear from her or Wiglaf again. "Y-yes," she repeated, though no questions had been asked.

"Good. Because I will know it if you dare set foot in town ever again. I too, have connections, more than that pathetic Saxon. And I will make sure you regret ever remembering you had a sister."

With those words he set about undoing the ties holding her

to the tree. Eahlswith watched on, happy to let Sven take charge. She had tried all she could to get through to her sister, and finally understood that she was never going to succeed. But at least she wouldn't have to worry about hiding anymore.

"Go," Sven told Ealawynne once she was free.

Eahlswith noticed that she didn't make a single move to go to her lover, who was still immobile on the ground. There might still be a chance, slim though it was, to save him but her sister did not seem interested in stemming the flow of blood or going to find help. So much for claiming to love him. Had it been Sven bleeding to death in that meadow, Eahlswith would have tried anything to save him.

Thankfully, he seemed whole—and in full command of the situation. His gaze flicked back to the cart by the river.

"This has been stolen, I gather?"

She confirmed it, having heard Godstan say something to that effect earlier that morning. "From a wool merchant, if I understand correctly."

He turned to Ealawynne, who still hadn't moved, as if wary of his reaction. It was clear she would wait until they were gone to do anything. "It goes without saying that we will take the cart and horse and bring them back to their owner."

"So I'm to walk the rest of the way in the snow?"

His answer was terribly blunt. "Walk, crawl, stay where you are even, I care not. Neither Eahlswith nor I are wasting another moment on you."

19

After retracing their steps to the forest where he had spent the night, Sven brought the cart to a halt in a sheltered meadow. Gulltoppr, who was following them as faithfully as a dog would, stopped also.

"We need to rest," he declared. "I didn't get much sleep last night."

Eahlswith could only agree that a rest was needed. She hadn't slept well the previous night either, which was little wonder. Being abducted and threatened with rape and murder tended to do that to a person.

Sven alighted and let the horse loose from his harness. Eahlswith was so weary she remained where she was, watching his every move. He was so strong, so dependable… He had come for her, freed her from her tormentors, saved her from certain death and he was acting as if there was nothing extraordinary in the fact. How could she ever repay him for what he'd done?

Once the horses were tethered, he held out his hand to help her dismount. Eahlswith gasped, shaken out of her torpor by what she saw.

"But...your wrist! You're bleeding." How had she not noticed it before?

Sven did not even spare a glance at his arm, he just shrugged. "I probably bled but it's stopped now."

"How did you get hurt?" She didn't think Ealawynne would have been strong enough to injure him and he doubted he would have been clumsy enough to let an oaf like Godstan cut him.

"I had to cut at the rope to free myself and come after you," he explained. "Considering how tightly it was bound, I suppose it was inevitable I should cut myself as well in the process. 'Tis no problem."

No problem? To think only a moment ago she had congratulated herself on the fact that he was whole. He was not. He'd been hurt. Worse, it was through her fault. Had she not tied him in the first place he would never have had to cut himself.

"I'm so sorry." She lifted his wrist to her mouth and kissed the place just next to the raw skin. "I promise I will never do that ag—"

"No, Alva," he said, eyes aglow with lust. "Don't make any promises I will force you to break sooner or later. We will definitely finish what we started last night and for that I will need to be tied up and at your mercy. I can't wait."

Eahlswith felt herself grow crimson. He still wanted her, even after what he had gone through . He still wanted her to tie him up to use as she saw fit.

"Yes. We will finish what we started," she murmured. "In the meantime, we need to clean your wound."

Not giving him the opportunity to protest, she tore a strip from the piece of cloth she was wearing as a cloak and crunched it in a patch of fresh snow. When it was soaked, she used it to wash the blood away, being careful not to rub too hard. Once his skin was clean, she ripped another piece of cloth and wet it the same way, before wrapping it around his wrist and covering it with snow. The cold would help numb the pain, or so she hoped.

"Better?"

"Yes." He had not taken his gaze from her during the whole proceedings, not throwing a single glance at his wrist. He either wasn't interested or it did not pain him at all. "Finally, it is my turn to thank you."

"Don't. And now, we'll get that rest we need," she declared. "We'll sleep in the cart, it will be warmer than the frozen ground."

Mercifully, Ealawynne and her lover had stolen a wool merchant's cart, not a blacksmith's, which meant they had everything they needed to cover themselves up and create a comfortable bed. Eahlswith nestled in Sven's arms, doing her best to forget that the last time she had lain in the cart next to a man, that man had wanted to rape her.

It was over. She could relax.

It was over. He could relax. Sven tightened his hold around Eahlswith, inhaling her familiar scent. He had made it. Finally, he could breathe.

"You see, Alva, I think there is a lesson to be learned from this," he said, speaking with his mouth in her hair. "If you hadn't relented and allowed me back into your bed, you would have been alone when you were abducted."

Against him, he felt Eahlswith shiver. "Yes," she whispered. "And I would have been dead before the week was over."

Sven kicked himself for his clumsiness. Why did he have to tell her that? He hadn't meant to frighten her or make her think of the ordeal she had escaped. Just to show her that she was better staying with him. He would always protect her.

He placed his forehead against hers. "Forgive me. That was not well done of me. I didn't mean to—"

"No, I know, and I'm saying that you're right. Without you I would still be in the hands of my sister and her abominable lover. And they would have killed me."

His hold around her tightened when she started to tremble. "It's all right, in the end I *was* in your bed. And now you're free. You won't die at their hands."

"No," she said in a sob. "I don't know what I would have done without you. It was— Dear God, it was awful, I thought…"

Sven frowned when she started to mumble to herself. She was getting upset, a normal reaction after what she had gone through. It was the shock, inevitable now that everything was over, and realization had sunk in. He rolled her to the side gently, until she was flat on her back.

"Hush. Lie down, sweet. Let me take care of you."

Eahlswith lifted enormous eyes to him, finally recalled to the present moment, and him, rather than reliving the ordeal of the night. "Yes. Hold me."

"I will do more than hold you." Of their own accord, his fingers found their way under her skirt. "Let me pleasure you, Alva. I need to touch you. Please."

He fully expected to have to beg some more, but she delighted him by agreeing immediately. "Yes. I need you to touch me."

When his fingers reached the apex of her thighs, they met scorching heat. Ignoring the need pulsing in his own body, Sven started to tease her, running a finger along her seam while his thumb settled on her most sensitive part. She moaned and started to roll her head from side to side. Then she stilled and opened her legs wider. Staring at him straight in the eye, she placed her own hand on top of his and licked her lips.

"Ah, you're so bloody perfect," he purred in her ear, before nipping at her lobe gently. "I do feel like one of the gods when you're in my arms."

A finger entered her and then two when she arched her back in supplication. Never had he been so attuned to a woman's reactions. Her body was merely an extension of his, making it easy to know exactly what she needed and when she needed it.

She was so soft he could have stroked her all day, but it didn't take long to coax her into the release she needed. Her raw cry sent a jolt of pure satisfaction through his veins. Yes. He was made for this, to give this woman what she needed, be it protection, confidence, or pleasure.

"Alva," he rasped, feeling her sheath contracting with beautiful abandon around his fingers. Her release seemed to last forever and he relished every moment.

Eventually she gave a long exhale and grew limp, like someone drained of all energy.

"You didn't have to do that." She sounded dazed and her eyes were glazed with satisfaction. "I just wanted... When I asked you to hold me, I meant—"

"I know what you meant. And I did as you asked. I held you. But you didn't say I couldn't stroke you at the same time." Thank the gods she hadn't protested, hadn't done anything to stop him.

"You're impossible," Eahlswith sighed, speaking with her lips at the crook of his neck. He smiled.

"I know I am."

"I've never met anyone else like you."

"Thank you."

Another sigh, just as he'd hoped. "I don't mean it like that and you know it." Her words were slurred. She was falling asleep fast, which was exactly what she needed, what he'd hoped to achieve by giving her release. "You're not going to give up, are you?"

This time it sounded like a plea.

"I'm not." He settled back down and drew her against his flank. "Not when I know I need you in my life."

There was a silence, so long he thought she had fallen asleep. Then she said, her voice a mere whisper. "Thank you, Sven, for what you did today. For coming after me, for saving me."

He gave another smile. "Sven, is it now? What happened to Heimdallr?"

She shook her head slowly. Had she not been on the verge of falling asleep, he thought she would have laughed. "Don't tell me you actually prefer me to call you that?"

"As long as you call me, Alva, I'm happy." He placed a kiss on her forehead. "Now, sleep."

The sun had started to dip below the horizon by the time they were ready to set off again.

"We will never make it to your house tonight," Sven declared. "I think that when we reach town the gates will be closed."

Eahlswith agreed. "There is a farm just outside the walls. The family there know me. Their daughter, Gedla, is a good friend. I'm sure they will let us sleep in the hay loft."

He nodded, satisfied, and steered the cart in the direction she was indicating. Gulltoppr, who'd gone to the stream to have a drink, started trotting back to them.

"I've always wanted a horse, you know," Eahlswith said, looking at the splendid animal, with his gold mane flowing in the wind. Why was she telling Sven this? She had no idea. Perhaps because she was finding it hard to go back to normal after what had happened earlier, when he had gifted her pleasure without asking for anything in return. Choosing an innocuous topic of conversation would help restore the ease between them. "Only, we could never afford to have even a mule when I was growing up and, living in town, there is little cause to have a mount."

"If you want a horse I will get you a horse," Sven said without even looking at her. She stilled. He would get her a horse. He'd made it sound so simple... She didn't know what to say. "My father has a sweet chestnut mare which has just finished her training. The men at the village, being rather large and full of energy, prefer to ride sturdy geldings or stallions full of spirit themselves so we weren't quite sure what to do with an animal that is as graceful as it is gentle. We've called her Amber for now but you can give her one of your animal names if you prefer. Doe would be a perfect name for her, actually, on account of both her coloring and personality. All the animal names don't have to be fearsome, do they?"

Eahlswith stared at him. He was talking as if all this was very reasonable, making plans for the mare and not thinking for a moment that she could refuse his all too generous offer. But though she wanted to accept, she knew she could not.

"Sven, you cannot give me a horse," she said feebly.

"Why not?"

Why not? "It's...well..."

This time he did look at her. "Are you telling me you would mistreat her?"

"Of course not!" She was horrified that he would even entertain the idea. Was he teasing her? "But a horse is too precious a gift... Besides, I cannot really ride." She had only ever ridden ponies and donkeys and never even attempted to trot.

He waved the objection away, the gesture surprisingly elegant for such a strong man. "That's no issue. I can teach you to ride."

Again. So easy. "To teach me, you'd have to see me often."

"Yes. I would. But that is not an issue either," he answered her with a piercing look. "Alva, make no mistakes, there will be no disappearing ever again. You are part of my life now. And I think you know it."

Her body started to heat. Indeed she knew it. When she'd been abducted she had been about to make love to him in the most scandalous manner for that precise reason. But she wasn't sure she was brave enough to say it out loud just yet, not here in the cold, while they were going back home after her near abduction.

Fortunately, the farm was now in view, providing a welcome distraction. She guided Sven on the quickest path to reach it and moments later they were at the door of a well-maintained and spacious hut. Eahlswith knocked.

The farmer's daughter, a girl a few years younger than her, opened and stared.

"Eahlswith? What are you doing here at this hour? 'Tis almost nightfall, I—"

The sentence was cut short when Gedla spotted Sven behind her, a tower of male strength. Despite the fading light, it was obvious that her cheeks had become quite flushed. Wonderful. Yet another victim to his charm.

"I know it's late. That is precisely why we are here," Eahlswith said, doing her best to regain the girl's attention. How had she not anticipated the effect the Norseman would have on her friend? No doubt it would play to their advantage, as the girl would be eager to help, but she couldn't help a pang of jealousy. "My friend and I were caught in the snowstorm yesterday and made it home too late to get back into town. Could we make use of your hay loft for the night?"

"Of course. Of course. Let me get you something to eat and drink as well."

"That would be much appreciated, thank you."

With those words Sven handed Gedla a silver coin he'd

extracted from the purse at his belt. She took a step back and started to protest.

"Please, that is not necessary, Eahlswith is a friend and we would always—"

"I know. Nevertheless, you will allow me to insist."

No woman could resist Sven when he decided to use his charm. The farmer's daughter, who'd already been struck, didn't stand a chance.

"Very well," she said, taking the coin. "You know where the loft is. Go there, get yourselves comfortable, I will be back in a moment."

While Sven saw to the horses, Eahlswith climbed the wooden ladder and started to create two nests in the sweet-smelling hay. She guessed Sven would not have objected to sharing a bigger nest with her but a strange shyness had invaded her. Perhaps because she felt uncomfortable lying in his arms when people knew that was what they were doing. Up until then, every time she had shared a bed with him, no one had known about it. It had been between them only. The idea that Gedla would be lying in bed tonight, wondering whether her friend was being pleasured by the strong Norseman was too much to handle.

Besides, after her ordeal, she felt dirty, and she was aching all over. She wanted to be herself the next time they came together, because she already knew it would be the start of something new. She wanted it to be special.

"There you are. Sorry I didn't bring any candles but you know, in the hay, it wouldn't be the best idea."

Gedla's face appeared above the wooden floor. She was holding a loaf of bread in one hand and a basket filled with food was perched on her arm. As soon as she climbed off the ladder and landed on the platform, her eyes started to search the near darkness. There was no prize guessing what—or rather, who—she was looking for.

"Your friend..." she started when she saw they were alone.

"Yes?" Eahlswith said, already knowing what the girl would ask her.

"Is he, by any chance, free to, you know... What I mean to ask is... Does he have someone special in his life?"

He did. Or at least, she thought he did. Everything he had done since they had found one another again pointed in that direction. What could she answer? That she thought he did have someone special, and even if he didn't, she wanted to ensure she still had a chance with him because she thought she was finally ready to accept what was between them? Could she tell someone else what she felt before she told him?

The only possible answer was no.

"I'm sorry, but he does indeed have someone special in his life."

The deep voice caused the two women to jump. Gedla gave a squeak and dropped the loaf at her feet when Sven's head appeared at the top of the ladder.

A moment later, he was standing in front of them, his head almost touching the ceiling. Eahlswith swallowed. Indeed she was not willing to have anyone come between them now. He was hers.

"I will leave you t-to it then," Gedla stammered.

"Thank you, you've been a great help."

There was no answer. A moment later, they were alone, Sven looming over her like another of his Norse gods, though this time Eahlswith's mind was too addled to think which one. *Was there even a god of lust?*

"You made two beds." It wasn't a question, or even an accusation but an observation. "A waste of time if you ask me. We both know you are going to sleep in my arms, Alva."

"I—"

"If you don't want pleasure, I won't give you pleasure." Oh, God, the way he said those words was almost enough for her to throw herself into his arms and beg him to do just that. And she wasn't saying that she did not *want* pleasure, exactly. "But I won't let you freeze to death, so you will sleep in my arms."

"Just sleep?" she asked in a breath.

"Just sleep. You know that even if I want you, I can keep my hands to myself when you've made your wishes clear." His voice had never been deeper, his masculine appeal more obvious.

"It's not that I don't want...ever again, you know, b-but I—"

"You're confused. I understand. You need time. I know. You're embarrassed because you think your friend will spend the night imagining us together. Don't be. Nothing will happen in this hay loft."

How could he be so understanding? Her legs suddenly felt about to fold from under her. Unsurprisingly, before she could worry about collapsing to the floor in a heap, a strong arm had scooped her up, holding her against a solid, warm chest.

"You're n-not angry?" she stammered. What had she done to deserve this man?

"Angry?" He let out a snort. "No, I'm not angry. I'll only have you when you want me."

"I do want you, just—"

"Just not tonight. It's fine." He settled her into the hay and reached to the basket at his feet. "Now, let us see what there is to eat."

20

The following morning, Sven and Eahlswith were amongst the first people to pass through the North gate.

Relieved to finally be able to take Eahlswith to the comfort of her home, Sven steered the cart into her street. He would see to her comfort before starting his investigation about the theft of a wool merchant's cart. Perhaps he would ask the help of the reeve. The man was a friend of his father's and would no doubt—

"It's her!"

Sven's head snapped to the side—and his stomach fell. Eahlswith looked as well, worry etched on her face. She had no idea who had shouted at her and why, but he had recognized the woman shouting the accusation.

Richie's mother.

She and the two men she'd been talking to placed themselves in the middle of the road, blocking his path. There was no other choice but to stop, at the risk of doing exactly what Godstan and Ealawynne had done the other night and run them over.

"Well, done, young man, you got her!"

"I know how it looks, but it is not her, I swear," he said before she could say anything else.

He had to admit it was damning, though. Not only did Eahlswith look exactly like her twin sister, but they were riding in the very cart that had ran over the youth. What could the people think other than that he had gone in pursuit and finally caught her? They would think he had brought her back into town to be punished. By the gods, not now! Would they be thwarted, threatened at every turn?

"What is going on?" Eahlswith asked, looking at him and the three Saxons in quick succession. "Could anyone explain?"

By now a crowd had assembled in the street, making any retreat impossible. The only advantage they had was that, sitting on the cart, they were higher up than the hostile mob who could turn violent at any moment. Sven kept an eye on the assembled men and glared at the ones who dared get too close to Eahlswith.

"Go get Richie and his brother," the woman said. "Someone carry him if need be. They will both confirm this is the culprit."

While the Saxons organized themselves, Sven leaned over to Eahlswith. "When your sister and her lover left town, they ran over a poor youth, breaking his leg in the process. They never stopped to see what had happened and now the woman is convinced you are her, and will demand retribution."

"Oh, no, this is awful. Poor man."

It was awful, but at the moment he was only worried about her.

"Look, it is as I say," he told the Saxons. "The woman next to me is not the one responsible for the accident. As you can see, she has no idea what you are talking about."

Predictably, they were not impressed. The man next to the woman, who Sven assumed to be Richie's father, answered.

"Well, obviously she's going to pretend she has no idea what this is about, so she can avoid punishment. That proves nothing."

It did not. And yet, they were telling the truth.

"She was attacked and abducted by her twin sister and her lover. That was why they were so intent on fleeing the town. Look at her mouth. Where do you think she got those bruises from?"

The man shrugged. "You? You wouldn't be the first man to—"

"I do not hit women!" Sven exploded. "I have, however, been known to hit idiots who refuse to listen to reason."

"What reason? We saw her clearly when she ran over poor Richie."

"For the last time, it wasn't her! I know she looks like her but—"

"Sven. I can understand their distress." Eahlswith placed a hand on his arm. "Imagine it was your son who'd been hurt."

Yes, he could understand their distress. But that didn't change facts. "You didn't do anything wrong and I will prove it to them."

He had hoped never to set eyes on Eahlswith's twin sister again, but it seemed he would have to get her back. It was the only way to prove her innocence.

"Let us go and see the reeve."

The man was used to dealing with the Norsemen community. He was not exactly a friend, but he was fair and would listen before acting. The family agreed to the proposition, thinking that their revenge was assured. At their request, the crowd parted to allow the cart to pass. Sven had refused to get down. He had to protect Eahlswith at all costs. Only when they reached the tall building did he allow her down.

Using his body as a shield, he guided her to the door where two men were stationed. They didn't ask questions when he asked to see the reeve, they just allowed him in. Evidently, they were used to such requests. Once he, Eahlswith, and the Saxon family, had entered the great hall, a dozen more men pushed through their way in and spilled into the room, shouting and grumbling.

Sven's temper was about to explode when a door at the back opened on the reeve, a tall man with a natural authority that would not be denied.

"What is the meaning of this?" His voice boomed though the vaulted room, mercifully putting an end to the chaos.

"We are seeking retribution for our son, Richie," the old Saxon woman started. "He was—"

Sven placed himself between the reeve and the Saxon, cutting her short. "I beg your pardon but the woman they are trying to blame is innocent."

A rumble answered the two declarations. The reeve gestured to the three men by his side, ordering them to usher everyone out save the people involved in the story. In surprisingly little time, everyone was sent out and the door closed. The men placed themselves in front of it, preventing further interference. Sven took in a deep breath. He would be allowed to expose his problem calmly.

Of course the family had other ideas. They all started to talk at the same time, forcing the reeve to interrupt them before too long. "I cannot make sense of this and will have to speak to you one by one. I will hear the Norseman first. Follow me."

Sven was loath to leave Eahlswith in the company of the family but she nodded to him. "I'll be fine."

Before leaving, he glared at the Saxons, signifying they had better not do anything they would regret and followed the reeve into a small room at the far end of the hall. A table occupied the middle of the space. It was covered with rolls and ledgers and there was a single chair at one end. This was obviously where the man worked.

Away from the unreasonable family, it didn't take Sven long to explain the situation.

"I'm not asking for anything other than a chance to prove Eahlswith's innocence," he concluded. "But I need to protect her from harm while I go in search of the real culprit. Will you detain her here for me? Keep her safe? I don't trust the family not to do justice by themselves."

The man tilted his head in consideration. He seemed almost amused. "You know, you're the third son of Wolf's I've had to deal with since I was elected three years ago. How many more are there? I'm starting to worry I will have to help one of you every year until someone else replaces me."

"I'm the last one. Then there is just our sister, Eyja." Sven's mouth quivered because the imp was worth two men, and he wouldn't be surprised if she ended up having to ask the reeve for help herself. But that was not why he was here. "Please. Eahlswith should not be punished for a deed she is innocent of and there is an easy way for me to prove she didn't do anything wrong."

The reeve nodded. "If you find this other woman, then Richie's parents won't have any other choice but to accept you are telling the truth. Now. Who is she to you?"

How to answer this question? And why was the man asking it?

"It matters not who she is to me, all that matters is that she is innocent."

"Indeed. Indeed." The reeve's eyes gleamed. He *was* amused. "Come," he said again, this time leading the way back into the hall.

To Sven's relief, Eahlswith appeared unharmed. She was even smiling a little. It wouldn't surprise him if she had half-convinced the family of her innocence already. Certainly they seemed calmer than before. He placed himself next to her while the reeve announced his decision.

"This woman will be detained here until Sven the Norseman brings proof that she didn't commit the crime she is accused of. Does that satisfy you?"

"Aye," the father said without hesitation. "But if he's not back before the month is out, we'll consider he's lied and disappeared to have to avoid proving the veracity of his claim. Then the woman will have to pay. It's only fair."

Sven's blood shot straight to his skull. Why was the man so determined to think ill of everyone? "For the last time, I'm not lying, you piece of—"

The reeve raised a hand. "It is agreed. Sven, son of Wolf, you will bring us the proof of this woman's innocence before the end of the month. In the meantime, she will remain here, under heavy guard."

The family started to thank the man for what they took as a form of punishment but Sven ignored them. Eahlswith was looking at him with eyes shiny with emotion. Was she grateful for his help? Worried he wouldn't make it back in time?

"Don't go. Please, don't go all alone, not for me." Her voice was little more than a breath. "It's not safe. I couldn't bear it if anything happened to you."

Ignoring the people around them he drew her into a fierce embrace, stopping just before he could kiss her. She was thinking of Edwin, who'd been set upon on the road and killed. But he wouldn't let anything or anyone stop him. She wouldn't have to carry the burden of a second death, he would make sure of it.

"I will be careful. And I will be back before the month is over, I swear."

21

In the end, it took Sven almost a week to find Ealawynne.

Asking everyone along the road if they had seen a dark-haired Saxon, he had no difficulty establishing her route, but to his intense annoyance she had traveled much further north than he'd thought. It seemed that she had thought it prudent to put as much distance between them as possible. A wise precaution, but it wouldn't be enough. She had to pay for what she had done to poor Richie.

When she saw him appear through the mist one morning, determination evident in his every step, she fainted dead away. Sven smiled to himself grimly. She had just made his job twice as easy.

Marveling at her resemblance to Eahlswith when malice was not distorting her face, he lifted her into his arms and onto Gulltoppr's back. When she came to a moment later they were already riding back. It would take another week, maybe slightly less, to reach town. There was not a moment to lose. He would not let Eahlswith in her cell a moment longer than necessary. Not that she would be mistreated, but still.

As soon as she saw where she was—and who with—Ealawynne started to scream. Sven ruthlessly clamped his hand over her mouth, having no intention of alerting anyone to what was happening when he was in a hurry. "Hush. I'm not here to hurt you."

She threw him a panicked look. *Why are you here then?* The question was plain to see in her dark eyes. He answered it, hoping that knowing she had nothing to fear would put an end to her protests.

"When you left town with your lover and your damned cart, you ran over a young man and broke his leg in the process. I believe you know what I'm talking about?" It would have been impossible for her not to notice Richie's screams or his parents' shouts. She gave no indication that she knew who the man was, however, or that she felt guilt over the accident. Why was he not surprised? The woman was as evil as her sister was kind. "Well, when Eahlswith and I rode back into town in the same cart, the young man's family obviously mistook her for you and demanded retribution. I'm here to ensure they do get it, but from the right woman, the one actually responsible for the youth's injury."

He relaxed his hold over her mouth, hoping she would have understood by now that she had nothing to fear from him, since he needed her. To his relief, she didn't utter a sound and for a while they traveled in silence.

They soon reached a stream. Having had to cross it the day before, Sven knew it was shallow enough to allow them to ford it without mishap while staying in the saddle. He slowed Gulltoppr right down, ready to guide him through the rocks. Taking advantage of the fact that his attention was wholly on the managing of his mount, Ealawynne jumped down to the ground before he could stop her and caught a large stone in her hand.

With a cry of rage she threw it at his head. It missed him by an inch but hit the stallion's right ear. The beast reared, more in surprise than pain and by the time Sven had him under control, Ealawynne was running toward the bushes.

Silly woman. Did she really think he would let her escape now? With a roar Sven jumped down from the saddle and gave chase. Seeing he was coming, Ealawynne changed her mind and headed toward the river, her intention clear. Not knowing it was too shallow to swim, she meant to use it to escape.

He caught her before she reached the water and pinned her against his chest.

"Try anything like this again, injure me or my horse in any way, and I will break your puny neck," he hissed in her ear. "The reeve and the family of Saxons need to see that Eahlswith does indeed have a twin sister so they let her go. But you don't need to be alive for them to see that. Your corpse will suffice. I believe you know exactly what I mean, having meant to use your sister's corpse to your own end."

It was odd to threaten a woman with murder, but he would have done much worse for Eahlswith. She had done nothing to deserve what her sister had done to her.

His words had the desired effect and Ealawynne stopped struggling.

A moment later, they were back on Gulltoppr, and her hands were tied behind her back with a strip of cloth he'd torn from her dress. It would be uncomfortable to travel thus but Sven didn't care. He had not asked her to assault her sister, injure an innocent man or try to kill him with a rock. His priority was to reach the reeve in the allocated time, not her comfort, and he was not going to waste another moment.

"So you're fucking my sister, I take it?" she said much later, as they dismounted for the night. Allowing her gaze to wander over him, she licked her lips. "Lucky her. I wouldn't mind having a man like you between my—"

"Shut your mouth," Sven growled, settling himself on the mossy ground, gesturing that she should do the same. It was dry at least, if rather cold. "What I do or don't do with her is none of your concern. We'll get some sleep."

Her question had made him uncomfortable, not that he would admit it to the vile woman. Yes, he and Eahlswith were fucking, as she'd said. Would it ever lead to anything more, as he hoped? There had been a moment in the storeroom when he'd thought it might. But so much had happened since then... What was she thinking, alone in her cell for days on end? Would she regret a decision taken in the heat of the moment? Would she prefer to leave town once this was over, and place herself out of her sister's reach? What would it mean for them? Would he be ready to follow her wherever she wanted to go, leave his village and his family?

He didn't know.

"I'm cold, Norseman," said a voice in the darkness. A voice that was eerily similar to his Alva's. His body responded to it before his mind reminded him who was really talking. "Why don't you come over here to warm me up with your big body?"

Unable to resist, Sven turned toward Ealawynne by his side. She was lying on her back, arching her spine, looking at him through heavy lidded eyes, a conquest ready for the taking. Though he knew she was not really the woman he wanted in his arms, he couldn't help a moment of confusion. His reason knew he should not respond, but his senses were fooled by the sight in front of him. Dark hair spilling over the ground, luscious hips undulating in invitation, the woman in front of him, doing her best to entice him, resembled the one he was desperate for so much that he almost reached out to her.

No, by the gods, no! He could not.

Sven ran a hand over his face. Had any man ever been subjected to such torture?

Finally, he stood over her, watching dispassionately. Her wrists and ankles were tied, to prevent her from escaping in the night. "You're cold, you say?"

"Yes. I need you."

"If you're cold, I can dump you into that ditch over there. You will be protected from the wind that way. I can even pile dead leaves over you if you wish." Her wide eyes made clear what she thought of this idea. He smirked. "No? Then I suggest you stop talking and just go to sleep."

The rest of the journey was just as hellish. Ealawynne alternated between throwing insults at him and trying to entice him into her arms. He did his best to ignore the former and resist the latter. Not that he was tempted any longer. It had been confusing at first but the woman was so unbearable that it didn't take long for his body to align with his reason and stop responding.

At long last they reached the town. Unfortunately, they arrived too late to pass through the gate, so once again he had to prevail on Gedla's family's generosity for the night. The girl was only too happy to help, even if she was shocked to discover that her friend had a twin, a twin that looked very much like her but was her opposite in every other way.

This time Sven made sure to prepare two nests in the hay loft, one as far away from the other as possible.

The following morning they were amongst the first people stationed outside the walls. Sven had to wait longer than he would have liked for the gate to open but he trotted straight through it as soon as it did. A moment later he was outside the reeve's house.

"Here," he said, bringing Ealawynne in front of the man. "As you can see. Eahlswith's twin sister, and her perfect replica."

The reeve nodded, taking in the extraordinary sight. "I didn't doubt you for one moment, you know. But this is incredible."

Sven nodded. Indeed the resemblance between the two women was frightening. "She's the one who injured the poor lad, as I told you. I trust you will explain it to the Saxons and they will leave Eahlswith alone."

"Yes. They will be sent for forthwith."

"Good. Now, take me to Eahlswith." It was all he had been able to think about this last week.

"This way, the room at the end of the corridor."

As they neared the door, Sven's heart started to beat a fierce drum. Finally, the ordeal was over, finally he was going to be reunited with Eahlswith, finally he would be able to reassure her, show her he had made it, tell her she wouldn't have to endure a punishment she didn't deserve. He had raised his hand to the handle when he heard the unmistakable sound of someone retching. It was coming from inside. From Eahlswith.

No! What was happening in there?

The reeve was just behind him. He seized him by the collar and barely resisted the urge to pin him against the wall. The wretched man had been supposed to protect her and he had left her here alone for almost two weeks. Had she taken ill, left in a cold, dank cell? Was she retching from hunger cramps?

"I told you to keep her safe!" he roared, his face an inch away from the reeve's. "I trusted you. I thought you'd look after her. What have you done to her, you maggot?"

"I haven't done anything to her. I think *you* might have, though."

"What is that supposed to mean?" he growled. "I haven't seen her for more than a week, as you well know."

"No. But I wager you saw her about a month ago."

"What the fuck are you—"

And then it hit him.

A month ago.

Yes, he had definitely seen her then. All of her. He'd made love to her all night. On his last possession he'd even found it impossible to leave her heat before exploding in pleasure.

And this was the result. She was not retching from hunger or lack of warmth, of course not, what was he thinking? This was a different kind of ailment. He let go of the reeve's collar and fell with his back against the wall. His legs no longer supported his weight.

"She's with child," he whispered, collapsing to the floor. He'd pushed the notion that his loss of control might have consequences to the back of his mind because he wasn't sure what he thought of the possibility but there was no choice but to face it now. And he was...elated. What would Eahlswith think, though? This might well scare her or she might be furious. Or both.

She might never forgive him.

Oh, what had he done?

"I cannot be sure, but yes, I think she might be with child," was the reeve's answer. "This is the third morning in a row she's been ill, when the rest of the day she's fine, if a little bit tired."

"I need to see her."

"Yes. Worry not, she's not been put in a dank, dark cell, nor is she starving. I made sure to give her all the comfort I could without appearing suspicious. It was important the family saw I was taking this seriously. But I promise you she has not suffered."

"No, I know. Of course. I brought her here because my father trusts you." Sven sighed and ran a hand through his hair. "I'm sorry for barking at you. Only, for a moment, I didn't think."

The man scoffed. "Don't worry I've endured far worse. Will you be able to stand, though?"

Everything within Sven bristled. He had never been accused

of being a weakling before, and he was not going to start now, when he was about to be a father. A father!

Sven shot back to his feet, invigorated at the thought.

"Yes. Take me to her."

EAHLSWITH WAS RINSING her mouth with ale when the door behind her swung open. She was not surprised. The reeve regularly came over to visit her and she knew he had noticed her bouts of morning sickness. Was he starting to suspect what she had come to accept? She was with child, there was no doubting it. It was not just the sickness, though this was rather damning. But she hadn't had her courses since that night spent with Sven in her house, that night he had spilled inside her. Secretly she had come to hope that his seed might have taken root.

She smiled to herself. It was as if someone—perhaps Edwin himself, from wherever he was—was making sure she accepted her feelings for Sven. A child was the best way to ensure that he became part of her life.

"I'm fine, don't worry," she started to tell the reeve, before she was swept up off her feet by a huge, hulking Norseman. "Sven!" she squeaked. No one else would be strong enough or bold enough to do this.

Their faces only inches apart, she stared into his amazing eyes and was shocked to see them shining with what looked suspiciously like tears. Her own were burning. He'd made it, he was back. He hadn't died. She could breathe again.

"Alva. Thank the gods you're safe."

"Of course, I am," she said, trying to smile. "How could I not be, when you made sure to take me somewhere safe?"

With her still in his arms, he sat down on the stool behind him. His hold around her was firm but careful. Then he glanced at her stomach, awe and pride lighting his face. That look could only mean one thing.

"You know," was all she said, her voice barely above a whisper.

"I know," was his answer, pronounced in the same husky tone.

"Are you not—"

"I'm happier than I've ever been."

Everything within her relaxed. He knew about the child and he was pleased. It was all she wanted to know for now.

She assumed that he had found her sister and brought her back to face her punishment. He wouldn't be here otherwise. She didn't need to know more. Ealawynne was dead to her. The reeve would do what was necessary, all she needed to know was that Sven was safe and that he wanted this baby. If truth be told, she had worried about his reaction. Though he had explained to her that he was ready to settle, considering his past, she couldn't help being dubious. There also was the possibility of him doubting the paternity of the babe, since he knew she had welcomed men to her bed on occasion. But he hadn't even asked any questions, taking for granted that he was the father of the babe she was carrying.

"I'm not completely sure yet," she forced herself to say. She didn't want him to be too disappointed if she turned out not to be with child after all. But why else would she be sick in the morning and feel fine the rest of the day? This was no illness, she felt it in her bones. And of course there was the fact that she had missed her courses. They should have arrived two weeks ago.

"No, I know 'tis not always easy to know for sure. But we'll find out together."

"Yes."

"And..." He made a face. "I'm sorry for that night in your

house. I didn't mean to trap you into anything. Only you felt too... It was too... I could not stop myself—"

Eahlswith cut him with a quick kiss on the lips. She had never thought he'd done that on purpose, to force a decision out of her. "I don't feel trapped. I know exactly how it was that night, as it was the same for me. And I'm not sorry." Quite the opposite, she loved this child already. "All I felt when I started to suspect I might carry your babe was joy."

He kissed her in much the same way she had done earlier. "Thank you for saying that." He placed a loving hand over her stomach. "Still, I'm sorry it took me so long to get back to you. You should not have faced such a discovery alone."

No, perhaps not. But what was done was done, and he was now back.

"What was the delay?" She knew he would have done everything as fast as he could.

"Ealawynne had traveled further than I thought, so I had to chase her all the way to the village where she had taken refuge and then ride all the way back."

"I'm sorry, it cannot have been pleasant to travel with her."

The tight smile he gave her was an answer in itself. "No," he said tersely.

Had Ealawynne tried her wiles on him, Eahlswith wondered? She wouldn't be surprised if the woman had thought to sway him from his purpose that way. Surely he hadn't been tempted? Then she remembered Godstan's fascination for the fact that the two of them looked so much alike. Wiglaf too had told her as he'd pounced on her that the idea of bedding twin sisters intrigued men. Did Sven agree? Had he been intrigued also? Should she ask him what had happened during their travel?

No. After what he'd done, after the trust he'd just shown her, she decided that trusting him back was the least she could do.

Her sister might well have done her best to tempt him, but that didn't mean he'd succumbed. She had made a fool of herself once already, with Freydis, assuming the worst, she would not do the same mistake twice.

"It was even more trying than you can imagine but it isn't all bad news," Sven told her with a gleam in his eyes she could not account for. "Because we actually rode past your native place on the way back. And we made a small detour."

"Oh?"

He stood back up to deposit her on the stool and knelt at her feet. Then he extracted a piece of wood from the purse at his belt. It was more or less square, a little bigger than her palm. One side was carved with a familiar image she had thought never to see again. Her heart stopped at the sight.

"I take it that's the one?" Sven asked, looking full of hope.

"You…It is. But how…?" Though he was handing the piece of wood to her, she didn't dare take it.

But it was indeed her father's carving, the one he had done on the door frame of their hut, the one Edwin had wanted to get for her. The carving that had cost him his life. Seeing it brought her so much joy and so much pain that Eahlswith couldn't handle it.

She started crying. She couldn't help it. Whether the child she was carrying was responsible for this sudden flooding of emotion or the memory of Edwin's death or the realization of what Sven had done, she couldn't say. Probably a bit of everything. She hid her face into her hands and dissolved into tears.

"Don't cry, please Alva. I'm sorry, I didn't mean to make you cry." Sven sounded almost panicked.

"I'm not crying," she said through her tears. "Not really. It's only… I love you."

He stilled and then buried his head into her lap, holding her tightly by the waist. "Oh, I love you too. Both of you."

Eahlswith placed a hand over his head, feeling blessed and indescribably happy to have finally put her doubts and fears at rest. It had been high time.

"I love you, Sven."

Sven already knew he would never tire of hearing those words. Finally, he had overcome Eahlswith's scruples and won her heart. And now he was holding her and their child in his arms. His chest felt fit to burst with happiness and gratitude. Finally he had found the woman he would spend the rest of his life with. And he knew it would not be anything like between Steinar and Astrid. Even if it had started in lust, their union would never turn sour.

"You asked me to tell you what I'd said that night when you'd tied me to the wall," he said, sitting back on his heels.

"Yes," Eahlswith breathed. There was such hope in her eyes that he felt his own burn.

"Well, that was what I told you, that I was in love with you."

At the time he'd been less definite, but she didn't need to know that. She didn't need to be told of any doubts he'd once had, because now he was certain. He didn't *think* he was falling in love with her, he *was* in love with her. Would be for the rest of his life. He'd just told her as much. And even better, she returned his feelings.

"I suspected as much. Why did you speak in Norse for such an important declaration?"

"I didn't realize I was doing it. I don't always choose the language that comes out of my mouth."

"I envy you. It must be wonderful." She smiled. "Cwenthryth is learning Norse, with Steinar. Will you teach me also? And our child?"

"Anything you want, *ást mín*. My love," he specified when she tilted her head. "Our children will be like me, part Saxon, part Norse."

Children. The word sent a shot of delight up his spine. Yes. If he had his way, there would be many in the years to come, the family he'd always wanted.

Eahlswith sighed. "Sven. Please. Take me out of here."

She was back in his arms before she had time to blink, where she belonged. "Yes. I'll do better than take you out of here. I'll take you home."

22

They reached the village just after the sun had been swallowed by the horizon. The huts wrapped in their blankets of snow, the fields stretching as far as the eye could see, everything glowed blue in the rapidly fading light. Everything except the thinnest branches at the top of the trees, stark black against the purplish sky. Sven took in a deep inhale of crisp air scented with smoke and headed straight to his hut, Gulltoppr's hooves crunching the fresh layer of snow underneath.

When he closed the door behind him, he knew a familiar moment of panic. Eahlswith was here for now, but what of tomorrow? She was carrying his child and she'd said she loved him, but they had not exchanged any promises, not really talked of the future. Would she ask to leave in the morning? Worse, would she disappear during the night?

In spite of everything, he still felt that she could flee at any moment, like she had many times. They had already been there, in a place he thought safe, only to have to watch her walk away. What could he do to persuade her to stay?

Will you marry me, Alva?

The question was burning his lips but asking it might frighten her away. He knew all too well that he had to proceed with caution with her.

"Please say you will stay here with me, with our child. Please." He placed his forehead against hers, seized by sudden inspiration. "If you agree, I swear I will only ever call you Eahlswith, not Alva."

She chuckled, far from impressed by this promise. "It is no more than what you should have done from the moment I asked you to."

"I will look after our child."

"I know you will. You love children. It makes no doubt that you would look after your own."

Damnation, this was not going well. How could he prove to her that he wanted her?

"All right, then I... I promise I will never fuck you ever again!" he erupted.

She stilled. This she had definitely not seen coming. In truth, neither had he. Where had that come from? Would he even be able to hold on to that promise? Did he want to? No, and most decidedly no.

"This has to be the most ridiculous of all the promises you've ever made. Why would I ever agree to such terms?" she said before he could ask her to forget what he'd said.

"So you can see that I want you, not your body. You, not the pleasure I can get on my own or with others. You. Only you. Forever you."

"Listen, Sven, I know you want me. You said you loved me and I believe you, so I will stay with you." She threw him what he could only describe as a naughty look, one who set fire to his brain, his heart and his loins. "And I don't think I want a life in which you never fuck me. I don't think I would survive the frustration."

No. He wouldn't either. "So tell me, how can I convince you to make you stay this time? What do you want?"

"Marry me. Raise this child with me. Give me others, in time."

Relief almost brought him to his knees. She was not leaving. She would finally be his.

"I will marry you," he growled. "Tomorrow if you like."

"No. Tomorrow we'll go into town and tell Osbert about our wedding and this child I'm carrying. Then we'll go to my house to get the comb you gave me the other day. I cannot be parted from it." She smiled. "But there is one thing I'd like you to do before all that. Right now in fact."

"What is it?" Anything. He would do anything for her.

She lifted herself onto her toes and brought her lips to his ear. Then she said the most scandalous, arousing, delicious words he had ever heard in his life. "Fuck me, Heimdallr."

Need exploded in his skull and fire sparked through his cock. His Alva wanted him to fuck her? He would do that and more.

From the way he lifted her into his arms Eahlswith understood that her crude words had pushed Sven straight past all restraint. Tonight she would have the wild lover she'd had the first night in his hut, not the tender one she'd enjoyed in her house. Good. Because she was desperate for him and she wanted this lovemaking to be wild.

"Take your clothes off," he said, his voice reduced to a growl. "I fear if I do it, I'll only tear everything apart."

As tempting as that sounded, at the moment she had no other clothes, so she forced herself to be reasonable. "Very well. But you take yours off at the same time. I want you naked."

There was no need to tell him twice. Sven stood before her, in all his masculine glory before she had even disposed of her shift. There it was. The chiseled chest she had admired that first night in the summer. The arm ring on his right bicep that added mystery and allure to his already perfect body. The shaft jutting from its nest of gold curls. Oh, that shaft... so hard, so smooth, so ready for her.

Her mouth started to water.

"I want to taste you."

He said the words she'd meant to say before she could open her mouth.

Eahlswith knew he was a master at pleasuring her so she didn't find the will to refuse. Besides, there would be time to taste him later. She threw her shift to the floor and lay flat on her back, offering herself. In the next heartbeat Sven was over her, his mouth at her nipple, his hand at her core, ready to make her forget her own name.

"Yes, yes," she rasped. That was what she needed, what she had missed so much.

After one last flick of his tongue, he slowly started his descent down her stomach, teasing her navel and kissing her inner thighs as he settled himself in readiness.

Spreading her legs wide, he started to lick her with deadly intent, leaving no place untouched. Eahlswith's fingers buried themselves into his luscious hair. She didn't know if she was trying to stop him or urge him on. When he slid a finger past her folds and into the slippery wetness waiting for him, she knew the answer. She was too close already. She needed a respite if she didn't want to explode before they'd even begun.

"Don't!" she whimpered. "Please, stop, I want to come with you inside me. I want to feel you when I—"

"You will feel me, I swear. I'll make you come again later, when I'm deep inside you. Twice more if I can," he growled, resuming his wicked licks. His finger had not stopped teasing her for a moment. "But give me your pleasure first."

A moment later, she did. There was no choice. She could no

more have stopped the sensations building inside her from cresting than she could have stopped the tide coming in and the waves crashing ashore on the beach.

Her back bowed and she let out a keening noise that resembled nothing she had ever heard.

"Thank you, my love, that was perfection," Sven murmured into her ear. "Now, for that fucking you asked."

It was when he lifted her up to position her on her hands and knees that she remembered there was something she wanted to explore. Tonight seemed the perfect night for it, if she found the courage. As she felt him enter her slowly, savoring every glorious inch, she knew that with this man, she would be brave enough.

"Sven, there is something I would like to..."

"Anything. Just say the word."

He retreated before plunging in again. Eahlswith gasped. Forget courage, how would she find the strength to talk when so many heavenly sensations assaulted her body? She wanted to let Sven take her to dizzying heights of pleasure and not do a thing. But she also knew she would regret it if she didn't speak out now. There would never be a better moment. This was not a discussion she imagined having at the dinner table one night.

"You asked me once where I wanted you to take me. I had no idea what you meant at the time. Now I think I do," she rasped. "And I..."

"You're intrigued," he supplied when she faltered.

Yes. That was one way of putting it. "When you rubbed against me that night, it felt amazing, like nothing I'd ever felt. And I'm wondering if..." How could she be more explicit? Fortunately she didn't have to.

"Alva, you only have to ask."

Before she could even open her mouth, she felt his thumb

brush against the entrance offered to him by their scandalous position. He circled around it in time with his thrusts.

And it did feel amazing, just like she remembered. She let out a long, lust-filled moan that should, by rights, have embarrassed her. It only made her wilder. With this man, she could be scandalous, knowing he would be ten times more wicked.

"Is that good?" She moaned, giving him the answer he needed. "I know you can enjoy this possession," he purred in her ear, the very embodiment of temptation, "but I will need to prepare you first."

"How?" she managed to ask. Wasn't that what he was doing right now?

"I have chamomile oil in the hut. We can use that to make sure you're nice and slick for me."

Oh, she already was, she could tell from the ease with which he was sliding in and out of her that her body was ready for him. But, of course, they were talking about him entering a different place. This was all new to her but Sven seemed to know what was best so she was only too happy to let him decide what was needed.

"Yes."

After one last languorous thrust he withdrew and left the pallet. Eahlswith almost screamed. How dare he leave now, when her whole body was quivering with need? Before she could voice out loud her frustration, he had knelt behind her again and filled her in one effortless stroke. Ah. Yes, that was better. This was where he belonged. A moment later something cool and slippery slid over her puckered entrance. The oil. When Sven's thumb touched her again, it felt different than it had a moment ago. It was smoother, somehow and this time, the naughty finger slipped right in, pushing past the tight ring of muscles he'd only brushed before.

She inhaled sharply.

"Yes, just like that." Though his movements were slow, Sven sounded out of breath. She guessed arousal, not exhaustion, was responsible for it. "First you will take my finger, in and out, until I feel that you can take another. Then when I know you're ready, you'll come for me."

Oh, this didn't seem like it would take much effort on his part. She was already trembling, poised on the edge of something momentous.

He picked up the pace, added the promised second finger and the combined action of his rock hard shaft and his wicked caresses was enough to make her explode.

When she did erupt, and felt her muscles spasm around his fingers, she could not believe the intensity of the sensation. How much better it would feel with something bigger buried inside her?

"Sven," she whimpered, utterly undone. Had he not held her upright, she would have collapsed. But the unsatiable man had other ideas.

"Ready for me, my love? Your pleasure will ease my way further."

She could feel how wet she was from her release and understood that was what he'd meant when he'd said that she needed to come first.

"Yes, I'm ready." Only a moment ago she would have sworn she didn't have an ounce of energy left inside her but his question had her arousal level spike again in the blink of an eye. They were far from finished.

He withdrew, his shaft harder than ever, and started to rub at her most secret entrance in the way she remembered. Despite her eagerness, Eahlswith could not help but tense, an automatic response. He was big, much bigger than his two fingers and she wasn't sure how she could accommodate him.

"You need to relax and push out for me." He leaned over her, covering her with his big body and sliding a finger inside her still quivering sheath. "I will only go in as deep and as fast as you can take it," he promised, teasing her.

She did as he'd asked and all worry disappeared. He was so careful, so gentle. Soon he was moving in and out of her as easily as he had in her sheath. Her body was burning, encircling him in a ring of fire, and it was delicious.

"Now, Alva, I'm... You're too tight, it feels too good. Now!"

The gruff order, combined with the flick of his fingers on her core was all it took. She erupted, again, as promised.

With his member lodged deep inside her, the spasms of her release felt very different than usual. It was as if her whole lower body had seized. She heard what was probably a frightful curse in Norse and heat flooded her insides. One last cry escaped her lips. After that, she knew she would not have enough air left in her lungs to even moan.

They remained locked together while the beat of their hearts subsided and this time she knew she would be unable to move for a long, very long moment. She suspected even the formidable Norseman holding her would find it hard to stir.

Eyes closed, body numb, Eahlswith felt Sven withdraw from her and place her on to her side.

She opened her mouth to speak but something wet and soothing started to wipe at her thighs before a single sound could escape. Heart melting, she fell asleep.

SVEN WOKE up to an empty pallet. No! Not again. Eahlswith had promised to stay, they had made love last night, and agreed to get married. She couldn't be gone now, when he'd thought his world finally complete.

He bolted upright.

Before panic could overwhelm him, a movement from behind caught his eye. When he turned he saw the most beautiful woman in the world standing by the table, drinking a cup of ale. Eahlswith. His heartbeat settled back to a normal, sustainable rhythm. Thank the gods. She hadn't left. She was here. He could breathe again.

"I'm here," she soothed. His anguish would have shown on his face. "I'm sorry, I had to go out to see to my needs and... Well, I do not feel at my best in the mornings at the moment."

Of course. The babe. He sat up. "I'm so sorry."

"I'm not." She gave him a radiant smile that reassured him. "'Tis not pleasant, perhaps, but perfectly normal."

So brave, his Alva.

"It's cold, come back to bed," he suggested, lifting the furs for her. She was only wearing her shift and he could see two pert little nipples peering from under the fabric, two pert little nipples he longed to warm with his mouth. "Unless you don't feel well lying down?" he added, sobering right up. What was he thinking? She'd just admitted to being unsettled, he shouldn't be thinking of his pleasure right now, or even hers.

"No. I can come back to bed. I feel better now that I've eaten something."

Without further ado, she nestled in the furs by his side. He heard a chuckle, a delightful sound he wanted to hear every day of his life.

"Why are you laughing?" he asked, taking her chilled hands in his to warm them. Her feet were already imprisoned between his thighs. She wouldn't be cold for long.

"I was thinking that it didn't take you long to break your promise not to fuck me, Heimdallr," she whispered.

He snorted. Indeed it had not. "If you must know, I regretted the words as soon as I uttered them."

"Yes, apparently you did." She chuckled again. "Well, there is another of your promises I would like you to break. Can you... Do you think you could carry on calling me Alva?" She sounded unsure of his reaction.

"Why?" She had ranted against it so many times, he was surprised she would want him to use the name.

"In truth I've never liked my name, which sounds so much like Ealawynne. I like it even less now."

He felt her shiver against him and this time Sven knew it had nothing to do with cold. He started to nuzzle at her throat, offering comfort. He could not imagine what it would do to someone to know that their sister, their twin sister, had wanted them dead.

"I understand."

"Edwin gave me a special name too when we started to see one another. He called me Wren," she said somewhat shyly.

"Good name." Just as good as Alva. He smiled against the skin below her ear, one of his favorite spots on her body, so warm and smooth. "You are as soft and round and cute as the little bird." His hand came to rest on the curve of her hip. Yes. Soft and round.

Perfect.

Then he stilled, as he remembered. That day, when they had eaten snow, and she had inexplicably wanted to flee, he had just told her he had spotted a wren and the innocent statement had startled her.

"The wren," he said, sure of himself. She had not inexplicably wanted to flee. She had just been reminded of the man she had once loved, and felt she was betraying him just by being in the forest with another man, and enjoying herself. "That's why."

That she understood what he meant without any more details was an answer in itself.

"Yes. I think that's why I balked at you calling me Alva at first," she explained. "No one had given me a special name before Edwin and I hated that you were doing the same thing as he had. I hated how it made me feel. Special, cherished again. But now, I love it, precisely *because* it makes me feel special and cherished. So, will you please carry on calling me Alva?"

He kissed her tenderly, humbled that she should confide this with him. "I will do whatever you want me to." He did like the idea of having a special name for her as well, a name no one else was using, of making her feel special and cherished, because she was. "And you can keep on calling me Heimdallr. Or choose any other name. As long as you do call me."

"Always."

His hand landed on her stomach. He couldn't wait to see her bloom with the new life she was creating.

"I had an idea last night. If it's ok with you, I would like to place your father's carving on the cradle I intend to make for our child," he said, looking at her in the eye. "I think it would be fitting. But if you preferred to keep it as is, or even place it on the door frame of the hut, like it was in your house, then it's not—"

"No." She placed a hand over his cheek, eyes misting over with emotion. "Putting it on the cradle is the perfect idea. Thank you. It would mean a lot to me."

Sven took her hand and placed a kiss on her palm. "It would mean a lot to me too. My parents will be able to meet this babe. I wish yours had been as well. But at least we can tell Osbert." The old man was as close to a father as anyone could be.

She nodded, and a single tear escaped her eyes. "Yes, we can."

"Now. Are you ready to go into town or is there something you want first?"

Alva smiled. Her hand snaked along his chest in a trail of fire and landed on his shaft. He instantly went hard as stone. Praise be to the gods, he had finally found the woman of his dreams.

"There's something I want first," she whispered in his ear.

23

"Congratulations!"

From the way Osbert's eyes started to sparkle, Eahlswith could have sworn he was seeing her properly, like he had all those years ago, when she'd first arrived in town. A lump started to form in her throat at the memory.

"Thank you," Sven said, gifting the old man with one of his most stunning smiles.

"Call me a silly old fool, but I had hoped to see you fall for the strapping Norseman who did such a splendid job of repairing the roof," Osbert carried on, winking at her. "Why do you think I pretended not to be able to welcome him in my house that first night?"

The wretched man, plotting behind her back... But she could not be mad at him, not when he had welcomed the news so well. Her relief was so acute that she started sobbing. She had been so worried he would think she had forsaken his son and here he was, telling her he'd hoped to see her find love again. He'd even done what he could to bring her and Sven together. She felt humbled.

"Thank you. It means a lot to me. I didn't want you to think—"

"To think what?" Osbert interrupted sharply. "That you were wasting your life away? That you were too young to be on your own? That you deserved a chance at a family with a good man, like any other good woman? I did think all those things and I'm glad I won't have to worry over you any longer."

Eahlswith stared at him, dumbfounded. "You worried over me?" She would have thought it was the other way around.

"Of course I did! A woman with her life ahead of her cannot wallow in grief like you did. You're allowed to live a happy life, my dear." His voice wavered and his eyes clouded over once more. "And I know Edwin would agree with me."

Fresh tears burned her eyes because he was right. Edwin had been nothing if not generous and selfless. He would have wanted her happiness.

"Thank you," she murmured. "I think I needed to hear that."

As she was wiping at her eyes, Sven leaned in to speak into her ear. "Tell him what you told me the other day in the forest. Free yourself of the guilt you are carrying. Osbert is a good man. I trust him. He will understand, he will forgive you. I can leave you two alone if you prefer."

She grabbed his elbow before he could turn and disappear through the door. "No. Stay. Please."

She needed him if she really was to do this. With him she might find the strength to say the terrible words. He was right, she was about to become a wife, and a mother. It was time she told the truth and gave the old man at least the possibility to forgive her. If he couldn't find it in himself to do so then she would be no worse off. But if he did, with Sven's help and love, then she might be able to let go of some of the terrible guilt.

"Osbert, I'm so sorry. There is something I've never told you." She paused and swallowed hard. "That day, Edwin was on the road because of me. He wanted to go to my village to retrieve something precious for me, something I had told him about a few days earlier. I blame myself for his death. If I had not mentioned that carving, he would never have set off alone, he would never have been attacked."

For a long moment the old man stayed silent, as if weighing up what he'd been told. "Edwin loved you more than life itself. I'm not surprised he would have wanted to please you thus."

"No, but it cost him his life. I swear I never meant it to happen like that and I'm not sure I will ever be able to forgive myself. But perhaps you can help." Another sob escaped her lips. "Before I start on the new part of my life, I need to know that—"

"You don't need my forgiveness because I never held you responsible. You are *not* responsible for what happened, do you hear? Before going Edwin told me where he was going and why. I encouraged him, thinking it a lovely gesture." There was a long silence. "If you think you should carry the burden of his death then at least let me carry half of it. Or we could both put it down and try to live what is left of our lives as best as we can."

He'd known? Eahlswith was stunned. All this time Osbert had known that his son had been killed because of something he'd wanted to do for her and he had not once blamed her. He had loved her like a father, worried about her, the woman responsible for his loss.

She fell into the old man's arms, feeling both wretched and blessed. "I'm so sorry. I'm so, so sorry. I wish—"

"I know. Me too. But let me repeat. You are not to blame for what happened, any more than I am for not dissuading him from going. Now, enough of this, my dear. I'm afraid old men cannot stand to see young women cry," Osbert said gruffly, patting her on the shoulder before letting her go.

"Strapping Norsemen can't either, if you must know," Sven

replied, drawing her back into his arms. She melted against him, feeling lighter than she had in years, since Edwin's death.

Osbert chuckled. "I wouldn't have thought the two of us would have anything in common."

"No, but we do. We both want nothing more than Eahlswith's happiness."

"Your command of our language is remarkable, you know, for a Norseman."

"I know. But it is no wonder, since I've been speaking it all my life. I was born here and my mother is a Saxon."

"Is she now? But physically, you favor your father, I take it?"

Sven let out a sunny laugh. "So much so that I look exactly like he did at my age, or so I'm told."

Eahlswith listened to the exchange, gratitude swelling in her chest. The two men were giving her time to compose herself and she was pleased to see them getting on so well. Osbert would of course be invited to the wedding next week. But there was still something she needed to tell him.

"There is more," she said once she had herself under control. "I am expecting a child, to be born just after the summer."

Osbert stilled. He would understand from the revelation that she and Sven had started their relationship weeks ago. "My dear. This time I don't know what to say. Except that you will be a wonderful mother."

Sven's hold around her tightened. "She will. We'll bring the babe to you as soon as we can."

"I will hold you to that promise, young man."

A dazzling smile answered him. "Anyone who knows me knows that I always keep my promises."

After one last exchange of well wishes, Eahlswith and Sven exited the house. Outside the sun had pierced through the clouds, causing the thin layer of ice over the snow to glimmer like a thousand tiny diamonds. It was a spectacular sight, and would be even more beautiful in the village, away from the filth and the bustle of the narrow street. After five years living in a town, Eahlswith was ready to go back to the peaceful setting of a village.

"Let's go see the reeve, see what transpired with your sister and Richie's family," Sven declared once he'd tightened the girth on Gulltoppr's saddle. They had already gone to her house to get the white bone comb and the few possessions she wanted to take with her to his hut. "I just want to ensure she is making amends for her and Godstan's carelessness in some way."

"Yes." The boy might never regain the complete use of his leg. Ealawynne should pay for that. "While you were gone, the reeve and I agreed she should work for the family, who are chandlers, for three months, time for Richie's leg to heal. She will go from kitchen to kitchen collecting fat to make the candles. The backbreaking and dirty work should teach her some humility."

"Perfect." He smiled at her. "And when the three months are over, I will make sure he sends her back from whence she came, with an interdiction to come to town ever again on pain of far more severe punishment." The smile died on his lips. "It's only because she is your sister that I didn't make her pay for what she made you go through."

Eahlswith placed a soothing hand over his arm. She was grateful for his leniency, because, unlike Ealawynne, she wouldn't have been able to live with the death of her twin on her conscience. "I know, and I thank you for it. And in the end, nothing happened. You saved me, remember?"

"Come, my love." He gave her hand a squeeze." Let's go to the reeve. And then we can go home."

"Turn right, please."

Sven obeyed the request, though he had no idea why Eahlswith would want to veer off course now. After visiting the reeve, who had confirmed Ealawynne would indeed be working for the chandlers for the next three months, they had agreed to go straight back home.

She guided him toward a clearing that soon became familiar. When she jumped down from Gulltoppr and signaled that he should do the same, he'd already understood what she wanted to show him. Taking the hand she extended to him, he followed her to a young, particularly straight oak. On the trunk, recently carved, was a roundish shape complete with what looked like a beak on the left side and two spindly legs underneath. It was the carving she had done for Edwin the day she had confided in him, the day they had eaten snow together.

"A wren?" he guessed, giving the hand he was holding a squeeze.

"A wren," she confirmed, her voice barely above a breath. "Do you still have your dagger? I need to carve another symbol."

He reached into his boot and gave her the dagger that had allowed him to free himself and save her from certain death. It was fitting that it should be the tool that would leave a trace of their love in the heart of the forest.

"Please stay this time," Eahlswith said, a shy smile playing on her lips. "This is about you."

He watched as she started to etch the new symbol next to the little bird. One tiny nick at a time, she painstakingly created an image in the tree bark.

"I know it doesn't look like much but it's not exactly easy to do," she said once it was finished. She sounded dubious, and a little disappointed with her efforts. Sven wrapped an arm around her waist and drew her to his flank.

"It's an elf." He knew because he'd hoped that would be

what she would choose. And once you knew, you made sense of the admittedly crude drawing. "A female elf."

"Yes. But it—"

"But nothing. It's perfect." Certainly better than anything he could have done. He should definitely learn to be more creative.

"I love you, Alva. I have never loved anyone half as much as I love you in this instant and I thank you for wanting to declare your love to me to the world," he said, cradling her face in his palms.

"I love you too." She smiled and handed him the dagger back. "So now that the world knows, let's go tell your family."

"Osbert took the news into his stride, but I think the people here will be somewhat surprised to hear of my upcoming wedding," Sven said as they made their way back to Gulltoppr, who had found a patch of grass not covered in snow to nibble on.

That was putting it mildly. Everyone at the village, his own family included, thought marriage was the furthest thing from his mind. He would delight in showing them that it was what he'd wanted from the start. As to the news that he was to have a child within the year, he wasn't sure what they would make of it. What was certain was that he would strive to offer this baby a childhood as happy as his had been.

"Let's go see Steinar and Cwenthryth first," he decided, nudging Gulltoppr into a trot.

His brother and her best friend. It seemed appropriate that they should be the first to be told their news.

They found the whole family, all six of them, outside the hut, making the most of the sunny day to work in the garden. The two boys were sorting out root vegetables, selecting the ones that had best be eaten immediately from the ones that would keep. Steinar was digging a trench in which to put the vegetables that were to be buried for later use. Cwenthryth and Sanna were preparing the straw that would be used to cover them and little Liv was asleep, warm in her cot under a layer of furs. It was a perfect scene of contentment.

"Sven." His brother's greeting was matter of fact. Then he stilled and took another, closer look. His gaze fleeted to Eahlswith. "Sven?" he repeated, putting his shovel down. "Do you have something to tell us?"

"Yes, I suppose I do." He took Eahlswith's hand. "I am getting married to my very own Saxon beauty."

Cwenthryth let out a gasp and he was sure she would have thrown herself into her friend's arms if she had not already been holding Sanna on her lap.

"Oh, but that is wonderful news!" she cried out. "Does it mean that you're going to live here in the village next to us?"

"Yes. I missed you so much I'm delighted to be close to you. Besides, I think it's better for children to be raised away from towns, don't you?"

Eahlswith placed her hand over her stomach, smiling. Cwenthryth cried out again. "You're with child!"

This time even the boys paid attention.

"You mean that we are to have more baby cousins?" Rothgar, the youngest, asked, dropping a turnip into the pile to his left. Aged almost eleven, he fancied himself a man already. "Could we have a boy this time, at least?"

Sven laughed. Indeed, in the last few years the boys had welcomed three cousins, all girls, and two little sisters. "I'm sorry, I cannot guarantee this baby will be a boy. But I suppose if it's not we can always have another try."

Eahlswith blushed.

"Congratulations, brother. I'm happy for you." It was obvious Steinar was fighting a smile. Sven didn't let it bother him, he'd already known he would be met with incredulity when he announced his news. But people would soon see he was as reliable as the other men in the family.

"Will you please hold Sanna while Cwenthryth feeds Liv?" Steinar asked next, lifting his daughter up to him. Up until then her mother had kept an eye on her, but the baby had now woken up and needed to eat. "I don't want her to fall into the trench."

"No, that wouldn't be the best idea." The trench in question was almost as deep as she was tall and he could see the little girl's fascination with it.

As he took his niece in his arms, Sven felt a surge of pure joy course through him. Soon, he would get to hold his own child. What would his baby look like? Girl or boy, unlike Rothgar, he had no preference. All he wanted was a healthy child, if possible with eyes as dark as its mother's, just like Sanna's were. He smiled at the little girl, who was clapping her hands for no reason he could discern.

"Uncle Sen."

"Yes. Come with me, sweetheart. We're going to see your grandparents."

EPILOGUE

"Thank you. These are amazing."

With a smile Eahlswith took the four clay pots Eirik had brought as a moving in gift for her and Sven. All day well wishers had dropped by the new hut to deposit presents. The delicate pots were her favorite yet.

"Thank you, Eirik," she heard Sven say from behind her. "These will be put to good use when we tap open the cask of ale your uncle brought us earlier."

Eahlswith's heart almost stopped when she turned to face him. She was still not used to the fact that her husband liked to wander about bare-chested during the warmer months but she was certainly enjoying it.

Just as the two men started to talk about the foal Wolf had gifted little Emma, a woman with flaming red hair appeared at the corner of the forge. As soon as she spotted him, she walked over to Sven. She was accompanied by a girl of about ten summers and appeared unsure of where she was going—or rather, not certain where to find who she wanted to see.

Eahlswith's stomach dropped. Not another woman trying to lure Sven back into her bed, like Freydis had, back in the winter... Or perhaps it was even worse, perhaps the woman was here to introduce him to his daughter. He was certainly old and experienced enough to have fathered a child that age. Not now, not when their life was perfect and they were about to welcome their first child together!

As if sensing her agitation, he drew closer to her.

"Fret not, *ást mín*. It's not what you think. I've never even met her," he said quietly, placing a hand on her very swollen stomach. Cwenthryth had told her to expect the birth to happen within the month.

The woman stopped in front of their little group. She looked so nervous that Eahlswith's heart instantly went out to her. This woman would be no threat to anyone, much less to her.

"Good afternoon. Is one of you Wolf the Icelander's son?" Her accent was a lot stronger than that of the people of the village, as if she had lived abroad all her life.

"I am," Sven answered, taking a step forward. "I'm Sven, the youngest."

She relaxed, like someone finally reaching the end of a long journey. "I'm Freyja, Rune and Eowyn's daughter. You might have heard of my parents?"

"Rune and Eowyn?" Eahlswith watched as both men's eyes widened in surprise. Indeed the name seemed familiar to them.

Sven recovered first. "My father lives over there," he told her, gesturing toward the hut nestled in the shade of a majestic oak. "I'm sure he will be delighted to see you."

"I..." She seemed unsure of the welcome she would get.

Sensing her hesitation, Eirik nodded at her. "I'll take you there. I'm Eirik. My mother Frigyth was your mother's best friend when she lived here."

"Eirik, yes, I've heard all about Frigyth and Sigurd's family. I thank you." Freyja seemed relieved to meet someone whose name was familiar. "Come, Asta," she told the little girl, taking her by the hand. "We're almost there."

While the three of them made their way to Wolf's hut, Eahlswith turned to Sven. "You might not know her but you clearly have heard of her."

"Yes. Or at least, I've heard about Rune and Eowyn all my life. I wonder what she's doing here. Her family lives in Denmark." He shrugged. "Well. I'm sure we'll soon find out. Come," he said, taking her by the hand. "It's time we put Magnus' present to good use."

Eahlswith followed him back into the hut, a frown on her face. She didn't remember the blacksmith giving them anything today.

"Put these down, we won't be needing them."

More intrigued than ever, she placed the four pots on the table Sven had made earlier in the summer, while they waited for the hut to be ready and looked on, as he removed a piece of cloth hanging on the wall with a flourish. At about waist level was a hook embedded in the wall, just above the pallet they had piled high with a multitude of furs and blankets.

"Here. Magnus asked me the other day what I needed for the house. As I saw no use for a sword or another axe, I asked him to make this." His voice had gone impossibly husky.

"You didn't tell him w-what you intended to use it for, I h-hope?" she stammered.

Eahlswith would die of mortification if he had told his father's friend that he intended for his wife to tie him to the wall so she could have her way with him. Because she knew instinctively this was what the hook was for. Sven had alluded often enough to the fact that they needed to finish what they had started that day in the storeroom but she had imagined he would wait until after the baby was born for it.

Apparently, she'd been wrong and he had waited long enough.

"Of course, I didn't tell him. And to be honest, he didn't seem to find the request odd, as there are many ways a hook could be useful." He tilted his head, eyes ablaze with mischief, and reached out to the laces at his braies. "Anyway, forget about Magnus."

"I already have." Her whole body had caught on fire at the idea of what was to happen.

"Come, then, Alva. Heimdallr is ready to be ridden all the way to Himinbjǫrg."

Coming next
Eirik's Oath

ALSO BY VIRGINIE MARCONATO

Sons of the Wolf

Steinar's Gift

Torsten's Gamble

Sven's Promise

Eirik's Oath

The Welsh Rebels

A Husband for Esyllt

A Savior for Branwen

A Second Chance for Carys

A Rogue for Siân

A Lover for Lady Jane

A Scot for Bethan

The Noble Norsemen

Taming the Wolf

Soothing the Beast

Wooing the Devil

Baiting the Bear

Tempting the Saxon

Seducing the Warrior

Loving the Blacksmith

ABOUT THE AUTHOR

As far back as I remember, I have been attracted to the Middle Ages, to knights in shining armour and their ladies in spectacular dresses. Now I get to write about them, I feel like the luckiest woman in the world. Being French and married to a Brit makes each book I write extra special, as our countries share a long and sometimes painful past. But in the end, in life as well as in fiction, love conquers all!

I have published several medieval romances under my own name, including series, and also have a pen name, Judith Falcon, for spicier projects, still in historical romance.

Join my newsletter and check out my other books on virginiemarconato.com.

A small press bound by the belief that every voice matters.

Sign up for our newsletter to learn about new releases and more.
https://oliver-heberbooks.com/subscribe/

Follow us on social media:

- facebook.com/oliverheberbooks
- instagram.com/oliverheberbooks
- amazon.com/oliverheberbooks
- youtube.com/@OliverHeberBooksPublisher

www.ingramcontent.com/pod-product-compliance
Lightning Source LLC
LaVergne TN
LVHW041909070526
838199LV00051BA/2552